Bound to the Tyrant King

Bex Gil

Bound to the Tyrant King

Bex Gil

SERPENTS & DOVES

PUBLISHING

Copyright © 2024 by Bex Gil

All rights reserved.

No part of this publication may be reproduced, distributed, or transmitted in any form or by any means, including photocopying, recording, or other electronic or mechanical methods, without the prior written permission of the publisher, except as permitted by U.S. copyright law. For permission requests, contact bexgilauthor @gmail.com.

Without in any way limiting the author's [and publisher's] exclusive rights under copyright, any use of this publication to "train" generative artificial intelligence (AI) technologies to generate text is expressly prohibited.

Book Cover by Bex Gil

Illustrations by Bex Gil

1st edition 2024

A Note From the Author

Greetings!

First of all, thank you for taking the time to read *Bound to the Tyrant King*. This is a Korean Historical Romance based on the early Joseon dynasty after King Sejong the Great but before the Imjin Wars. Yi Seojun is a fictional king, as are the events that happen in this book. I was inspired by my love of Korean dramas and Korean history, as well as fascinated by the way factions influenced—and at times were more powerful than—the king and queen. Not everything is completely accurate, but I did my best to honor the history, language, and culture of Korea. There is some Korean vocabulary, but fear not, **there is a glossary in the back** (including some pictures). As always, I recommend readers to research for themselves and in this case, I highly encourage you to dive into historical kdramas such as *Under the Queen's Umbrella, The Crowned Clown,* and *The Red Sleeve.* If you'd like to keep it to books, I recommend pretty much everything from June Hur, especially *The Red Palace* and *A Crane Among Wolves.*

(I am not responsible for any kdrama addictions.)

To my friends.
Thank you.

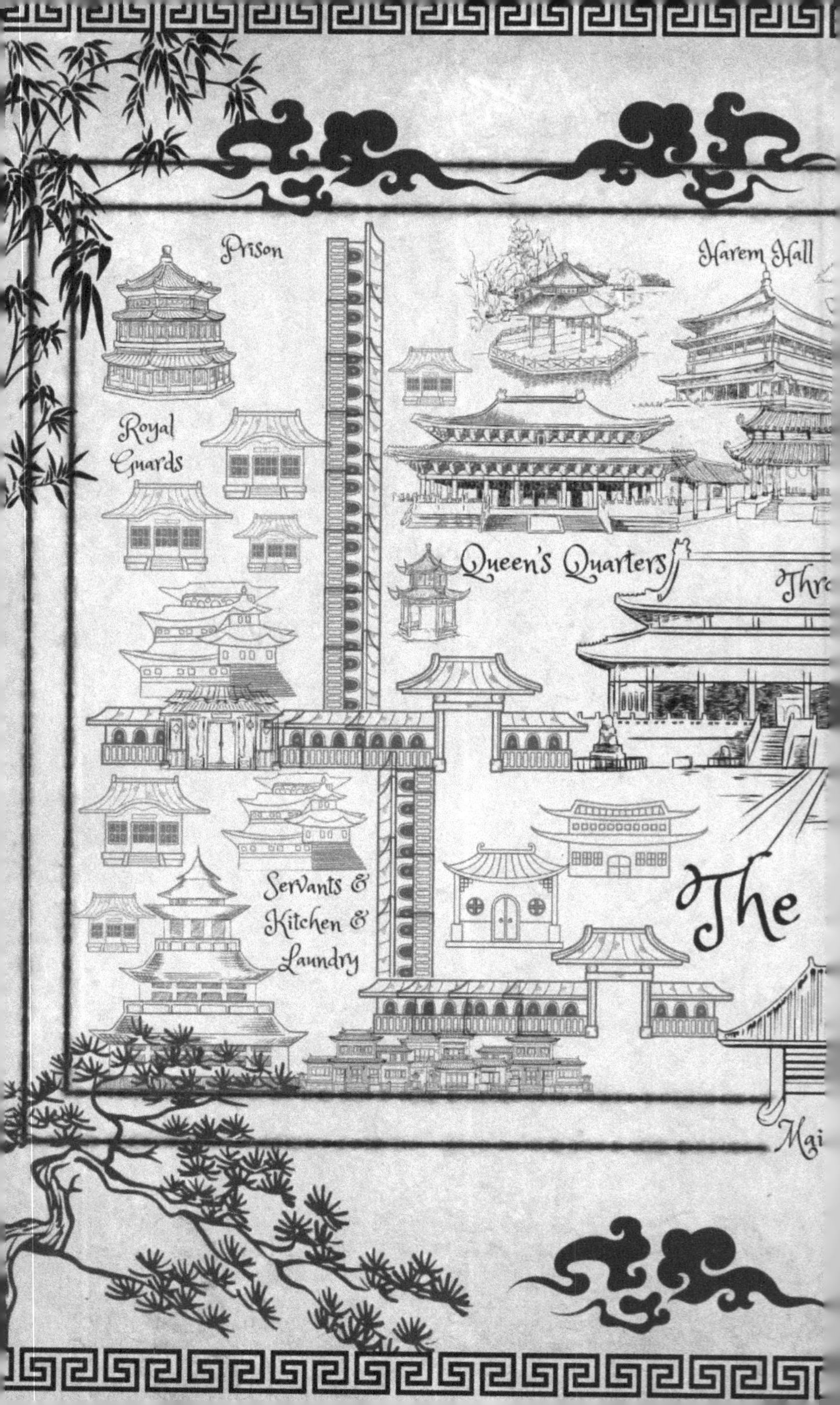

Prison
Harem Hall
Royal Guards
Queen's Quarters
Thro
Servants &
Kitchen &
Laundry
The
Mai

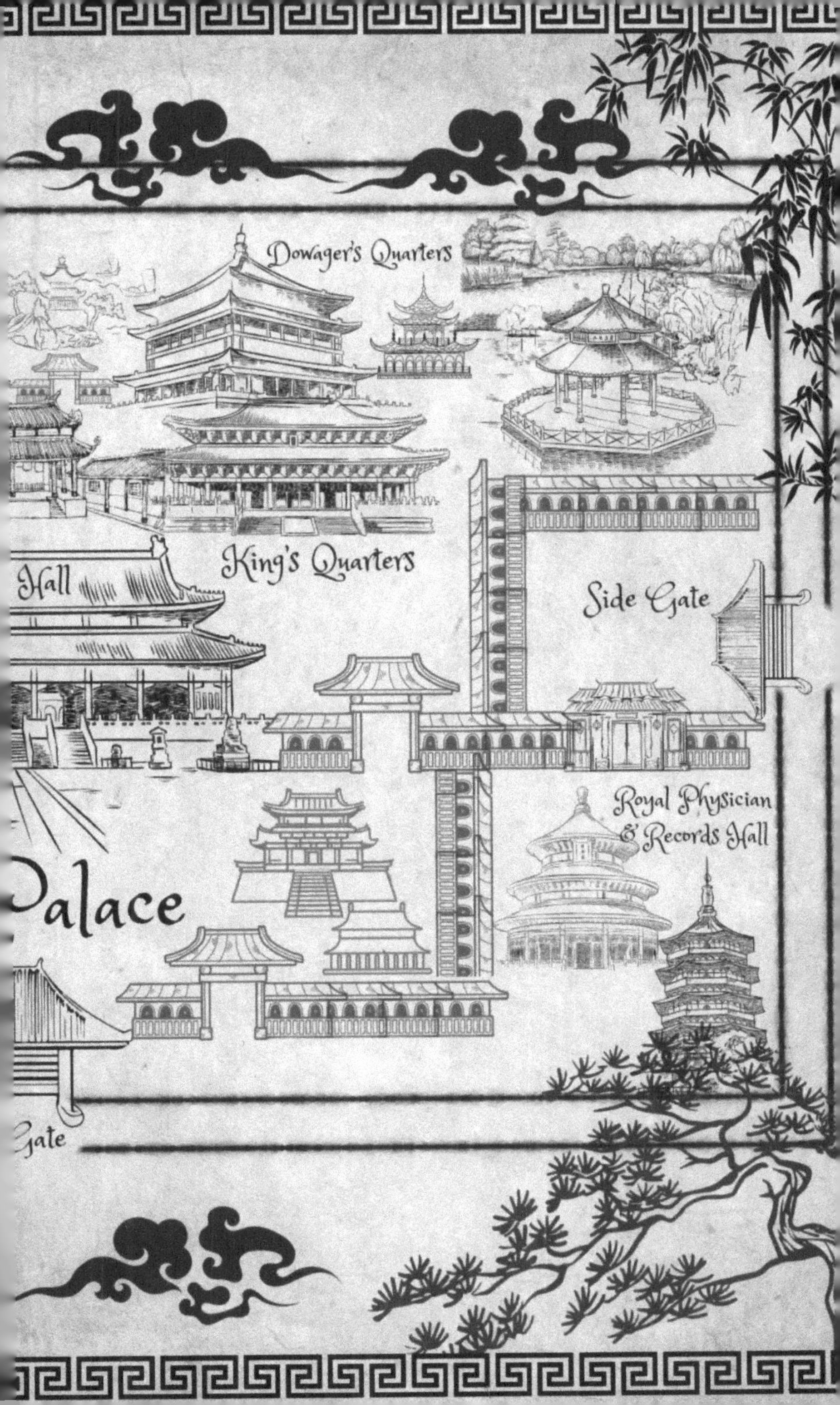

Dowager's Quarters
King's Quarters
Hall
Side Gate
Palace
Royal Physician & Records Hall
Gate

BexGilArt

Prologue

Seojun

CRIMSON BUBBLED FROM THE mouth of the body at my feet. I inhaled the smell of their fear and the metallic scent of the corpse, my nostrils flaring as I slowly spun. Bloody gurgling accompanied the sound of my footsteps as I walked back up to my dragon throne. It wasn't difficult to imagine what thoughts flitted through their minds—thoughts of terror and treachery.

When I whipped around, some of the blood from the blade splattered on my face. I sat and laid my sword across my knees with a smirk

The Chief State Councilor stood, keeping his posture hunched as he approached with scurrying feet like a bug, before bowing against the floor.

"Jeonha!" his voice strained, as if he actually cared about the death of the man that lay but a few steps away. "What reason was there to kill an official without an investigation by the Office of Inspector-General?" he questioned, his voice cracking in a dramatic display.

"I didn't realize the king was subject to his own ministers," I sneered, my lip curling.

"Such an unrighteous act will bring the wrath of the heavens down upon Joseon. The people are the ones who will suffer from the sins of the ruler," the Chief State Councilor wailed.

The Left and Right State Councilor joined him, each bowing with their heads against the ground. "Jeonha," they bellowed in tandem, a handful of other officials joining in.

My fingers tapped against the blunt side of my blade. Tilting my head, I inquired with a low tone that promised I was willing to add another corpse to the floor, "Are you aware of Minister Gil's crime, Chief State Councilor?"

The Chief State Councilor paused his trembling before slowly replying, "How could I know, Jeonha, what you have not shared with us?"

"Discerning whether one is a serpent or dove is quite difficult, with deadly consequences if one guesses wrong," I murmured, running a finger through the still wet blood. Louder so that all the officials could hear, I snarled, "Minister Gil colluded with the Ming Empire to assassinate me."

"Jeonha, such accusations should only be made with—"

Chief State Councilor Min broke his sentence off as a dagger landed an arms length away from his head. A letter that Minister Gil wrote to a Ming official wrapped around the hilt, both having been hidden in my sleeve until it found its new place near the Councilor's head.

He didn't move, his eyes frozen to the paper.

"I trust that my top official knows how to read a letter," I scoffed and gestured for him to unravel the parchment.

His hand stayed steady despite the shaking that had plagued him just moments ago. After unfurling the paper and exchanging glances with his fellow councilors, he immediately pressed his head to the floor.

"Forgive me, Jeonha, for I have spoken out of turn while the king was wise and quick to dispatch justice," he howled.

Turned out my ministers were such great readers that they didn't even need to look at the text to know the contents of the letter.

I grabbed the hilt of my sword and slammed its point into the wooden floor. "If anyone else would like to plead on behalf of the deceased minister, they may join him in his sentence."

Silence.

Only a sea of bowing bodies.

With a nod, I said, "Good." I glanced at where a Royal Investigator stood nearby. "Seungkwan, take some soldiers and arrest the men of the Gil family. Investigate if they were aware of their patriarch's plan."

"And if they confess?" Seungkwan asked, his posture as straight and stiff as the pillar he stood next to.

"Execute them."

Chapter 1

Bora

M ARRIAGE WAS SUPPOSED TO be a joyous event, a
union between a man and woman and their two families, but there was nothing to celebrate about going to what
could be my death.

"My B-Bora," my mother sobbed, her white garments shaking with her wails.

"Eomeonim, please don't cry. I will be alright. But you must
change out of mourning clothes before the king's servants come
to fetch me. If you are seen in them..." my voice trailed off.

If I spoke such a terrible thing aloud, the little calm I had infused into my tone would dissolve, only worsening my mother's
tears.

Scooting over on my knees, I wrapped my arms around her,
careful not to dislodge my large headpiece. My neck was already
sore from what felt like an entire black pagoda on my head, the
ornate gold pins and jewels making it even heavier. Taking care
to avoid that I didn't stab my mother with one of said pins, I
craned my neck as I squeezed her tightly.

Patting her back like she had on many occasions when I was child, I whispered, "Abeonim will make sure I am alright. The king cannot risk making an enemy of the Chief State Councilor and his faction."

"But all those horrible stories he has told us..." she whimpered, sniffles whispering from her nostrils.

"It will be alright. The king's temper must stop at women, right? And as queen, even the people would not stand for him hurting me," I murmured and stroked her hair, the false promises bitter on my tongue. Such a ruler would not care what his citizens thought of him. Leaning back, I smiled as wide as the blossoming tree in our courtyard. "I will be fine, Eomeonim. Really."

If I said it enough times, maybe I would believe it too. But I was about to step into a den of vipers with only my father and his position's power to keep me safe. With all that I had heard from him about the king, I wasn't sure if that was enough.

My lady's maid, Jinyoung, entered the room, the sound of her footsteps as silent as falling snow. "Lady Min, the palanquin is here," she murmured softly.

Jinyoung had always had a quiet voice and gentle temperament. I pursed my lips, imagining how hard life would be in the palace for such a kind woman. In a place where alliances were necessary even for the most lowly servant, how could someone as innocent as Jinyoung thrive? Nevertheless, I was grateful that my father was sending her with me. A friendly face would be much needed in such a vast and cold place. And since she would be attending the queen, perhaps the other servants would leave her alone.

Letting out a long breath, I squeezed my mother's hand and stood. "Are you packed, Jinyoung?" I asked, not even sure if the king would allow us to bring personal things into the palace.

"Don't worry about that, Mistress," Jinyoung replied. She turned to my mother and bent at the waist, one hand gesturing towards the door. "Madame, it is time to begin the first part of the ceremony."

"Jinyoung, please fetch my pink jeogori, the one with the yellow cuffs. Hopefully, the king's representative will simply find Eomeonim's fashion taste strange, but at least it will be harder to take offense just because of a white chima," I ordered while untying my mother's top.

Jinyoung scurried to my cabinet of clothing and pulled out a silk, peach colored jeogori. With hasty steps she brought it back to us, and together we helped my mother dress. The fabric consumed my mother, her arms resembling flapping wings, but it would have to do.

"This should be enough to avoid father's and the representative's displeasure, although no woman in the capital will be looking to the Mins for fashion inspiration." I chuckled.

"We must be going, Madame," Jinyoung said shrilly, her eyes darting to the door and her feet shifting like an uneasy deer.

My mother nodded, stood, and wiped her face. "Let's walk together," she said, taking my hand.

"Abeonim would not be pleased with the breach in protocol," I argued with a soft shake of my head.

"Well, he can be mad, then. I don't know when I will get to see my daughter again, so I am going to soak up all the time I have left before..." Her voice trailed off, both of us not desiring to speak such terrible predictions aloud.

Besides, those horrifying outcomes were not a guarantee. If I was kind and didn't cause any trouble, nothing bad would happen to me. Perhaps the king would be enamored with me and treat me well... or maybe a dragon would fly into our home and take me away. Both were equally improbable.

We walked arm in arm through the hall towards the main room of our estate, Jinyoung trailing a respectable distance behind us.

At the entrance, I paused. "Eomeonim, please enter first."

She sniffled once more but acquiesced, and Jinyoung opened the door for her to step through. I waited a few breaths before entering, my footsteps heavy as I approached my father and mother. Another man was present, garbed in rich red robes. He must have been the representative of the king, coming to fetch me to the palace. I bowed in greeting before turning to my parents.

My father held a small cup of wine, the bittersweet scent wafting into my nostrils. I was never fond of the drink, and only a few sips would make me drowsy. But it was a ritual, so I held my hands out as the rite demanded, praying my legs would be steady after consuming the potent liquid.

"Obey your husband, and bring honor to your family," my father said, handing me the wine.

"Remember to be polite and generous, Bora, and everything will be alright," my mother added, her voice cracking as her eyes watered once more.

Don't cry, I mouthed as subtlety as I could manage, glancing at the king's representative and praying he would only see a mother's cry of joy and not treacherous tears.

"I will do as you have taught me," I replied loudly, forcing my lips to curl upwards despite my shaking voice.

The lump in my throat remained clogged for now, but it felt like it might soon explode and release all the emotions I was trying desperately to shove down. Pressing the cup to my lips, I sipped the liquid down, hoping it would take the lump with it on its way. Jinyoung received the cup from my hands, and we all turned to face the king's proxy. He waved a servant forward, a honking goose furiously flapping its wings in the man's hands. My father called for a servant to take the bird.

"Lady Min Bora enters the palace as the Queen Consort," the proxy stated in a booming voice.

I was Queen of Joseon now.

Except, the ceremony was far from over, the long, public parade to the palace, the private first meal, and finally, the wedding night in which I would—

I cut the thought off. *One step at a time.*

It should have felt wonderful, the dream of many eligible noble women, but it felt like I was walking out of my home and into a cage. Nightmares and dreams were all about perspective, and to a fawn, a wolf was no fantasy.

As I turned my back on my parents, my mother blubbered, "Forgive me, Mama, for not teaching you more."

My shoulders stiffened, my heart aching. Even my own mother could not call my name anymore. How I hated hearing her address me as her superior, as her queen. She bathed me, rubbed my head when sickness overtook me, and laughed as we painted together. A set of stairs had been erected between us, a barrier between subject and ruler. My chest tightening, I walked out and into the dusk light.

In the courtyard stood many members of the Min clan, including Samchon Gyumin, who worked in the Ministry of Rites, his mouse-like wife hunched next to him. Even my Imo Jiwon, who had married into the Oh family, had come for this momentous occasion. Ryu Woobin, a close family friend, and his elder brother Ryu Wooseok—the Right State Councillor—were also there. My smile faltered at the absence of Woobin's son Hanbin, as I had expected my friend to send me off with blessings. Even though we had not seen each other for over a year, as I'd been busy with preparing to be queen, and he was occupied with learning from his father and uncle, I'd expected him to be here on such an important day. Perhaps his preparation for his Kwago exams to enter the Royal Academy prevented him from being present. What a marriage did for a woman, the Kwago exams did for a man.

The proxy led me through our mansion, passing the trees I had climbed in with my brothers and sister, and the pond I had listened to stories by. Memories flashed in my mind, as if they were about to disappear forever. In some sense it was true, since Lady Min Bora was no more. When we exited the large, arching doors of our estate, I nearly gasped at the sight of the long line of servants, guards, officials, and horses.

I swallowed. *Back straight and feet moving. You can do this.*

He brought me to the second palanquin in the procession before heading to his own, gold and red tassels dangling off the top while curtains draped from maroon painted wood, leaving only the front open in order to funnel attention to the person seated in it. Four canopies jutted out from each side, the litter seemingly designed to take up as much space as possible. From each corner, a pole stretched longer than any man was tall.

I clambered into the palanquin, the wood groaned in warning, urging me to turn back, but I couldn't. I didn't choose this. There was no other option, only going forward to meet my fate.

My eyes darted to the men stationed five at a pole. Gulping, I hoped they were deceptively strong with oxen muscles hidden under their dark blue sleeves. The headpiece on my head forced me to swivel my head like a snake, lest the giant thing tumble off and cause an even bigger humiliation to my family and I.

The curtains whispered as they fell back into place, the cushions of the palanquin cupping my backside. So this was what the wealth of a king could afford. The Min family had the second largest estate in the capital, second only to the Yun clan, and we lacked for nothing. Still, the gama that myself and other noble women used was much smaller and completely covered—a box carried by only four to eight servants.

I pushed aside the drape to my left, putting on my brightest smile that conveyed confidence I did not possess, and waved to my mother, who held back my siblings. At the sight of Iseul bouncing next to Minho, and Jinho wiping fake tears, I felt the smile turn genuine. My mother scolded them, sending them scurrying back inside, Jinho pushing Minho's chair. As my mother turned around and joined the line of people in the procession, she waved back, her eyes red and puffy.

The palanquin lifted into the air, my hands bracing against the wooden sides.

Deep breaths.

I would have preferred to walk, but it would be improper and a great insult to the king. I could not give him a reason to depose me—or have me executed. Placing a palm over my heart, I begged it to settle, my stomach twisting enough to knead dough.

Through the curtain fabric, I could make out the blurred figures of the crowd, their shouts ringing in the air as they waved and hollered, pressing in on each other like my siblings and I did when our cook made hwa-jeon. Just the thought of the honey coated fried cake made my mouth water, but as soon as my stomach joined in on the imagining, bile began to rise in my throat. Maybe food wasn't such a good idea right now.

I had only seen the king once, and it was from quite a distance. When I tried to picture kind eyes and a soft face, cold, serpentine irises formed instead, venomous fangs revealed in a malicious smile. My skin prickled, and a chill creeped down my spine. My father had always regaled tales of a tyrant, and I had to prepare for that. A viper should best be treated as one, and I needed to watch my step if I wanted to survive.

When I turned around to try to look at my parents, the motion caused the palanquin to lean, grunts emanating from the carriers. I gave up and turned back around. My full frame on top of the weight of the palanquin was a lot for them to bear, and if they dropped me on my wedding day, the humiliation would crush me. Something so inauspicious could give the king a reason to kill me right away.

The strings that held my headpiece on suddenly became itchy and suffocating, and I pulled at the knot in a feeble attempt to loosen it.

The palanquin lurched forward, and I tried not to sway, forcing a stiffness into my limbs lest I topple out of the large window.

Thump. Thump. Thump.

Each jolting step the men took brought me closer and closer to my fate.

Eventually, we came to a stop, and I let out a long breath.

"Please step out, Mama," a deep voice called out.

Using all the poise I possessed, I climbed out of the palanquin, my neck feeling like it would snap in half like a twig under the weight of the headpiece as I watched my steps. After I successfully exited without falling on my face, I glanced back to see my parents a few stairs down, my mother's eyes still glistening in the light of the setting sun while my father's face remained blank—devoid of both worry and joy. Was he sad to see me married off? I couldn't tell what thoughts occupied his mind.

Jinyoung, who had been with them when we had left our home, had disappeared. I supposed she wasn't allowed to enter the palace this way and would need to enter either after the procession had ended or through another entrance. It didn't make sense why my own maid could not accompany me, but many of the palace rules were just as incomprehensible.

"The Queen Consort enters the palace," the eunuch who had spoken before bellowed.

The looming entrance towered over me, like a wide open mouth of a predator ready to consume its prey. I glanced around, looking for the king, but I could not find him. At this point in the ceremony, he was supposed to come and replace his representative.

"This way, Mama," said a servant who appeared from nowhere, and I nearly jumped. Her age was difficult to discern, her face smooth and her black hair pulled back into a bun.

Glancing once more at my mother and father, who were waiting on the steps—where they would stay, as the next part of the ceremony was not for the public—I almost broke out into tears. I bit my lip to distract myself.

No tears. No worrying Eomeonim.

I followed the maid, the wooden gates groaning shut.

We came to the king's quarters, stopping just outside where two tables, food, and wine were all prepared. I searched once more for the king, but he was still absent. My hands gripped my silk chima as I clenched my teeth. He obviously intended to humiliate and disrespect me, and subsequently my family. All previous thoughts of the king being enamored with me, or at least not as bad as my father spoke of, flew away.

"Please sit, Mama," the maid murmured with a bow.

"Where is the king?" I questioned in a mild tone I hoped veiled my displeasure.

"He will be joining you for the final part of the ceremony," she replied, her hand still pointed in the direction of the table on the west side of the courtyard, even though this ritual normally took place *indoors*.

But apparently, the king only cared about the final part of the ceremony...when we would have to consummate our marriage.

I huffed and sat, the representative taking the seat on the eastern side of the courtyard.

"The couple will drink," a eunuch called out, and both the proxy and I reached for our cups, taking a sip of wine.

"Next, the couple will share a meal together," the eunuch announced.

A rainbow of foods sprawled before me, and although I usually would have been excited over such delicacies, each bite tasted bland and dry. I chewed as though I was eating raw bamboo. After what seemed about half an hour, we were finished.

"The couple will enter the chamber and consummate their nuptials," the eunuch announced, and I eyed the representative as he stood.

Certainly the king didn't intend to have his proxy do that for him too? The very idea of it caused me to nearly expel the meal I'd just consumed. If we did not consummate our marriage, then I was not officially queen—the ceremony incomplete. If the proxy entered the chamber, would that make me an adulteress? Was he going to use that as some excuse to kill me?

I released a breath when the man walked the opposite direction of the king's room, and I got to my feet. My hanbok felt like it was stuffed with bags of rice, dragging me, urging me not to enter. But a thin thread that pulled me forward.

A small, brown shrike flitted above my head. A shame it was not the size of a phoenix, not large enough to take me away from this palace and outfly my dark destiny.

Alas, there was no escaping my marriage to the tyrant king.

Chapter 2

Bora

MY WEDDING HANBOK WAS red, and that was for the best, as it would match the blood that would pour when my husband killed me. Scarlet silks draped from the rafters and curled around the pillars of the king's quarters, and crimson rose petals sprinkled the floor. Candles lined the path from the sliding screen door to the bed of blankets I sat on, as if escorting death right to me. At least the warmth of the ondol heating the floor kept the chills away.

Footsteps echoed down the hall, my heart beating in tandem as my impending doom approached. My stomach began to turn, and my sweat soaked hands wrung together. I was going to die tonight, a fact as sure as the sun rising. A shame I wouldn't get to see it rise again.

I closed my eyes and prayed that it would be over quickly. Perhaps a slice to the throat or maybe a lethal poison? So long as he didn't draw it out with great agony, I could face it.

The footsteps stopped and so did my heart. A towering silhouette appeared through the thatched cloth door, and I inhaled sharply. Now that I faced death, each breath felt so very precious, and I was reluctant to cease them.

Roiling indignation replaced my resignation. This wasn't fair. But what could I do?

My eyes scanned the room for anything I could defend myself with.

Wait.

No.

If I harmed the king in my escape, then I would be executed for treason. The entire Min clan could be killed for such a thing.

Besides, where could I run to? My father provided no haven, since this marriage was a royal edict that none could evade, so I couldn't return home lest I implicate my family. Running out and into the woods to find a secluded village was out of the question. I had grown up learning etiquette and embroidery and possessed no knowledge of how to live on my own. Fighting and hiding would both end with my family being executed.

The screen door slid open to reveal the king dressed in black and gold robes, his raven hair cascading down his back. Why was death so handsome? Maybe it was a blessing so that the last thing my eyes laid upon before I departed this world was one of beauty—cruel beauty.

My sweaty palms gripped my chima in attempts to hide the shaking that wracked my body. As he approached, head tilted and eyes peering at me like a wolf prepared to devour a fawn, my breath lodged in my chest, cries for help wedged in my throat.

What did it feel like to be stabbed? Did it burn? I heard from the soldiers who became guards at our family estate that some men went into shock when wounded and felt nothing.

Please don't let it hurt too much, I prayed to the heavens, begging for one final mercy.

The wide sleeves of his robe flapped like an elegant crane, his strides steady and sure in his approach, but I couldn't help but wonder if a knife hid in the vast wings of fabric. I swallowed and forced myself to inhale, my fingers turning pale as they crumpled my chima into clumps. I gathered what little bravery I had to meet his eyes.

If I had to die, I might as well face it with courage—even if it was a façade.

I forced a smile on my face, albeit a faint and feeble one.

He came to a stop before me, towering above my seated position. Was this how a bug felt before being crushed? Slowly dropping to one knee, he brought his hand up, and my smile faltered as I prepared to feel cold fingers wrap around my neck and squeeze the life out of me. But instead of choking me, his hand brushed against my skin with a whisper, his finger caressing my cheek more like his long lost lover instead of the daughter of the court official he loathed.

When he leaned forward, his onyx hair fell to the sides, creating a curtain around our faces. He smelt of citrus and incense. Squeezing my fists, I steeled myself to meet his gaze. My eyes traveled from his sharp collarbones, up his neck to his hard and rounded jaw, to his full lips, past his flat nose, and finally, to his chestnut eyes. The corner of his mouth curled up, our stares clashed, and my breath hitched.

Why was the tyrant so handsome? It seemed rather unfair of the heavens to give someone with so much power such good looks as well. He wasn't even a kind king.

My father had regaled many a horrifying tale of the king's wrath and whim. Court meetings were like dancing on the sharp end of a blade, the ministers always wary of the volatile ruler. The king was malevolent and fickle, following whatever desire and killing all who displeased him. One specific occasion came to mind. My father could not recall the details of the king's proposal, only that the minister who opposed it was hauled off to the dungeons. No one saw him alive again. No investigation by the Office of Justice or Inspector-General, no opportunity to defend himself against accusations, just death.

It appeared that there would be dungeons in my near future too.

His whisper slithered and coiled around my ears, sending shivers down my spine. "I wonder what's hiding beneath your clothes," he growled softly, his words tinged with a threat.

I gasped and clutched the top of my dangui, trembling fingers pinning the fabric to my chest, my smile wilting and falling from my face. I knew to some extent what was expected of me on my wedding night, but I had always hoped it would be with someone I loved instead of a monster with a throne. I suddenly missed the large headpiece and voluptuous ceremonial robes that the maids had taken off once I entered, wishing to hide underneath it like a turtle shell.

Faster than a diving crane, the king pried my hands away and ripped my dangui off, the crisp air kissing my shoulders. A yelp escaped my lips, and I slammed my eyes shut, wishing I could ignore what was about to happen. His hands unwrapped my chima, the fabric pooling around me in a ghostly whisper. Dread dug its claws into my stomach, nausea roiling inside me. A hand crept along my legs, fingers exploring the sides of my thighs while another crawled along my ribs. My body stiffened and prepared for pain.

Nothing.

The hands disappeared.

My undergarments were still on, and I peeked open an eye to see the king sitting to the right of the bed, an omok board on the table in front of him, white and black orbs locked in a battle. I opened my other eye and cocked my head.

The king glanced at me and made a noise somewhere between a sigh and a laugh. "I was checking for weapons," he said, twisting to peer at me. His eyes bore into me as if he could see into my very soul.

I shuddered.

"But if you would like to engage in another activity, I am happy to oblige," he drawled, a sultry smirk slicing his mouth in a cruel crescent.

I shook my head, but the motion caused one of the pins to dislodge from my hair, which had been piled behind my head. The golden pin clattered to the floor, my hair unknotting itself and falling down my back.

The king's eyes flashed for a moment with some emotion I couldn't decipher. Whatever it was, it was nothing good for me.

He turned back to the omok board and murmured, "A shame."

What was? Me? Because I was the daughter of his most adversarial minister? Or because I hadn't been eager to sleep with him? I twisted a lock of hair around my fingers, a habit my mother had tried unsuccessfully to scold me out of.

The king reached into a wooden bowl and pinched a black omok piece between his thumb and forefinger. His eyes burned into the square block with engraved, crossing lines as if he studied something far more serious, like a military formation. Having played with my father as a child, I knew the game intimately, but it had been many years since he'd made time for a match. A tightness in my chest formed, but I didn't know if it was from fear or longing.

The threat of death hung over me like a blade hovering by a string. The thread could snap at any moment. My shoulders stiffened, the hair raising on the back of my neck. I switched from strangling my hair to choking my hands, my stomach twisting and tumbling.

For a brief moment, I worried that perhaps the problem lay with my looks. Did he not desire me due to my appearance? For a year before my marriage to the king, I'd undergone a multitude of beauty treatments. Perhaps it was my shape then? My face was round as the moon, but that was a desirable trait, so perhaps it was the rest of my body? Although the hanbok puffed up like a cloud and made seeing a woman's shape difficult, one could guess from the thickness of my arms that the rest of my body matched in plumpness.

Once again, a slow growing fire replaced the shivering fear that seeped deep into me. He didn't want me? As if he was all that special? Well, I supposed he was, actually. He was king of Joseon and one of the most handsome men I had ever seen. Not that I had seen a lot, especially up close, as the increasingly strict codes of conduct kept an invisible wall between men and women that didn't afford me the opportunity to do so very often.

A deep chill bloomed inside me, my mind screaming, *danger, danger.*

Glancing towards the sliding doors, I considered making one desperate run for it. Maybe my family and I could make it to Ming and start a new life there. Minho spoke multiple languages, including that of the great empire to the northwest.

My thoughts must have been too obvious, for the king spoke with a frigid calm, "You will only leave this palace with my permission or in a coffin."

The cold consumed my entire body. I tore my eyes from the exit, staring down at my round and full fingers. I didn't want to die.

The silence felt like an eternity, my emotions swinging back and forth between anger and anxiety. The candles were almost down to their wicks, their light waning and wax coating the floor. I sighed and glanced once more to where the king sat, still fixated on the board.

If he wanted to ignore me, then I could do the same to him. The day's events wore me out, and sleep was a wonderful remedy for worries. Tomorrow brought a new day. I yanked all the remaining pins from my hair and laid down on the bed, my back thankful for the reprieve. After turning onto my side, I stared at the wall where a painting of mountains and cranes draped. The birds were far more fortunate than I, able to come and go as they pleased. Despite being queen, I related more to a bird in a cage.

As my eyelids grew heavy and sleep demanded to make itself known and displace my nerves, I closed my eyes. Just as I was about to drift into the sanctuary of slumber, I felt a presence lay next to me.

Perhaps I was already dreaming.

Chapter 3
Bora

COLD HAD LONG SETTLED into the place next to me. Thankfully, my underlayers still covered my body. I bolted upright, my hands scrambling to check that all my limbs were still attached to my body. For good measure, I pinched myself.

"Ouch!" I exclaimed.

Not a dream. Not dead.

I was alive.

I exhaled, my shoulders relaxing and my stomach settling. The door to the bedroom slid open, and I yanked my knees to my chest, my body squishing together. Oh, to be a turtle that could hide in its shell, or better yet, a bird that could fly freely. But the cruel face of the king didn't greet me, and instead, a willowy woman, perhaps around my age, with her hair braided back, came forward, holding a folded set of garments in her arms. She wore a dark emerald hue—a court lady, then. My eyebrows drew together as it dawned on me that she must be my new attendant

"Where is Jinyoung? My father said he would send her to be my lady," I asked, frowning.

The woman bowed. "The king has ordered that I am to serve you, Mama."

No, that wasn't the plan. My father was supposed to send Jinyoung to the palace with me. She had taken care of me for the past several years. I curled my hands into fists. The king must not want me to have anyone from my father's house around me. Was he so cruel as to deny me the comforts of familiarity?

Forcing myself to calm and release my clenched fists, I stood and adjusted my underlayer chima.

"Very well," I mumbled. "Thank you for serving me then."

The lady approached with her chin tucked, although her swift strides and straight shoulders made her meek show seem suspect as she set the folded garments on the bed. I lifted my arms, and with deft fingers, she slipped on a golden silk top and black chima, gold dragons—a symbol only designated for the royal family—embroidered on the shoulders.

She guided me to a seat with a bronze mirror on a small table, and I asked, "What is your name?"

"Haeji, Mama," she replied, her face blank while she gathered my hair behind my head.

She pulled out a golden dragon pin, the sharp end whispering past my neck. I sucked in a shallow breath, thinking that she might be an assassin sent by the king. But the pin never pierced me, and she fastened my hair with gentle tugs. Of course the king would never send an assassin when he could do it himself, or perhaps he planned to stage an accident so that he could feign innocence. Nothing would garner the common folks' sympathy more than a mourning widower. My grumbling stomach interrupted my thoughts of how I would die.

Haeji folded her hands in front of her and asked, "Would you like to have breakfast?"

I nodded and stood, forgoing any cosmetics. Aside from special occasions, a virtuous woman allowed her natural beauty to shine—one of the many morals that had been instilled in me since childhood. Most noble women in Joseon, along with queens and royal concubines, tended to instead favor hair decorations. I recalled seeing paintings of previous royal concubines with more jewels than actual hair. Would the king take on concubines? Knowing what I did about him, I assumed he possessed plans to fill Harem Hall with women.

Haeji led the way and slid open the door, and I stepped over the threshold. The hanbok of the queen was more voluptuous than the ones I had worn as the daughter of a minister, and I prayed I wouldn't trip and make a fool of myself.

I had visited the palace only a few times, the most recent being a year ago when I had received the royal edict decreeing my marriage to the king. Since I was unfamiliar with the layout, I gestured for Haeji to lead the way. The palace was one giant rectangle surrounded by a mountainous wall with two entrances: the main gate and the side gate. Inside, everything was arranged in six rectangles, all interconnected by hallways so that one didn't need to take a step outdoors once inside the palace. Lucky for me, the stairs leading to the throne hall were on the southern facing side, and the Queen's Quarters, where I would be staying from now on, were on the northeastern side next to the king's rooms from which we had just left, so I wouldn't need to climb them on a daily basis. Although, my mother would probably suggest that I make a habit of walking up and down the stairs to slim my naturally full figure.

But I was perfectly content with how I looked, and as we made our way to my rooms, I started imagining what would be served for breakfast. Kimchi-jeon was my favorite. Did royals eat it? My mouth watered, my stomach thundering in anticipation.

My brows furrowed and pinched together as I noticed that we had turned right and were heading to the northeastern-most point of the palace. I could have sworn we had passed the turn to the Queen's Quarters. Was I supposed to eat somewhere else? Back at home, we had all eaten together, but I'd heard that the king and queen ate in their rooms.

"Haeji, where are we going?" I asked, scolding myself for allowing my voice to shake.

She didn't look back. "The king instructed me to bring you to see something first."

What could he wish for me to see? No matter how hard I tried to conjure what was so urgent it needed to be seen before breakfast, nothing came to mind. The king's thoughts were not that of a normal person, and I was better off giving up on trying to predict them.

As we passed under tiled roofs and wooden pillars, I gaped at the vastness of the palace. The Min Mansion felt so small in comparison. However, the birds flying in the cool spring sky were the same birds that lived near my home, and their melodies lulled my nerves into tranquility.

We stopped in front of a door guarded by two armed men who were donned in red and black garments with wide brimmed black gats, a white feather protruding from the center and hanging down the back.

"Mama," the two guards said in tandem, bending at the waist.

After they rose, they pulled open the wooden doors and revealed a faintly lit corridor, the lanterns fighting to provide light in the dark hall. Haeji stepped inside, holding out her hand for me to take as I followed. A strange smell assaulted my nostrils, and my hand instinctively covered my mouth and nose. I glanced at Haeji, but she offered no information before she began walking into the darkness.

We descended a flight of stairs, a metallic scent slithered through the air, and cries of pain echoed in the stone chamber. Turning the corner, cells came into view, but at the end of the rows of bars, a woman stood tied to a post with her arms splayed like a crane. Scarlet stains dotted her white undergarments—a pair of billowing baji and a wrapped top. Her damp raven hair hung loosely around her face, and her skin had turned an unnatural shade of white.

When we got a little closer, a gasp escaped my lips. Jinyoung peered up at me with dull eyes as we approached. I ran the last of the distance, my hands darting to cup her sweat covered cheeks.

"Oh, Jinyoung," I whispered, my voice cracking, pain piercing my heart.

"Mistress..." she rasped, a drop of sweat falling down her temple.

"She is the queen now. You should address her properly," a low voice boomed from behind me.

I jerked my head to see the king reclining on a chair as if it were a throne, two crimson-clad guards behind him. He had a knife in one hand, his finger dancing on the tip as he observed me with a dark gaze. His hair piled atop his head, hidden under his mountainous black ikseongwan—a headpiece that dwarfed the samo my father and other officials wore. Scarlet robes with golden dragons on his chest and shoulders billowed from his body—all the better to mask the blood.

A chill crawled down my spine. He was the epitome of all the stories of the tyrant that my father had told. Even last night could not compare to the cold biting my bones now. Was I brought here to join Jinyoung in this cruel display of power? We had done nothing wrong.

I gritted my teeth, gathering the courage to confront him.

"What is the meaning of this? This is the lady my father sent to care for me. She has served the Min family for years," I said with all the scorn I could muster, or more accurately, all that I dared to use towards the king.

I almost expected him to use the knife in his hand to slice my throat as he stood to his feet with the calculated slowness of a stalking predator. He stepped towards me, and I flinched, forcing myself not to flee as my instincts were demanding. He came so close that our noses were almost touching. I held my breath. His flaming eyes bore into mine. The sharp and cold end of the knife nestled against my neck.

"Then you were aware that your father sent her?" he asked in a threatening tone.

"Yes, of course. She is my lady," I whispered, afraid that if I talked too loudly the blade would puncture my skin.

Don't swallow. Don't move.

My legs were beginning to shake.

A flash of what almost appeared to be disappointment appeared across his face, but it so swiftly switched to a cold ire, that I thought I'd imagined it. He leaned back, and I exhaled when the knife left my neck.

He dropped his weapon-holding hand to his side. "Haeji, take the queen to her chambers," he ordered without a hint of emotion, his voice as empty as my stomach, which I was grateful for, since I would have vomited anything I had eaten.

I opened my mouth to protest, but Jinyoung interrupted, "I'll be fine, Mama. Please go."

I gritted my teeth and allowed Haeji to grab my elbow and gently drag me forward. As we walked back towards the stairs, I glanced back at Jinyoung one more time. The king held his blade near her face, and the fear written on her features was easy to see even from a distance. I ripped my gaze away, my legs threatening to give out.

Screams bade us farewell as we ascended the stairs.

Chapter 4
Seojun

I STARED AT THE queen's retreating chima, the flash of black and gold disappearing around a corner. It was a good thing that I asked Haeji to bring her here. She should know what awaited those who betrayed their king.

My lip curled of its own accord as the maid—Jinyoung—wailed and screeched.

The woman hanging from the posts hadn't screamed at first, only gritting her teeth and veiling her eyes in a cold aloofness. There was no hatred, no personal vendetta that had spurred her actions. She was simply the servant to her master, bound to carry out his will even if it meant forfeiting her life. But once the queen came into view, the maid began to whimper like a poor puppy.

Perhaps the queen wasn't aware of her assassin guising as an ordinary servant. Why else would the woman act so pitiful in front of her mistress?

"Minje, make sure she doesn't pass out until she has divulged all her secrets," I ordered, tossing the dagger to him.

He caught it in his palm and brought it to Jinyoung, the sharp edge licking her sweat slicked skin.

"Jeonha, we must be careful with our interrogation tactics. The ministers could accuse us of coercing a confession," Inspector Kim from the Office of Inspector-General protested.

"This woman attempted to kill the king last night! She deserves worse," Minje snapped, slashing a small cut across Jinyoung's arm, eliciting a hiss of pain. "Who ordered you to do this?" he demanded, pressing the weapon to her neck.

Silence.

"See, Inspector Kim, this is why you should let the Royal Investigators handle this. Assassins don't squeal like the cowardly ministers you interrogate," Minje said with a pointed glare.

The Inspector didn't reply, simply crossing his arms and stepping back against the wall.

"Official Moon," I began to the man hunched over the small desk in the corner. "Make sure not to get any blood on the papers this time. The Office of Records complained about the previous ones."

"Yes, Jeonha. My apologies," the man mumbled barely loud enough to hear.

"Why don't we get another man from the Office of Censors? Or better yet, someone actually from the Office of Records?" Dongbin whispered, leaning down to avoid Official Moon from hearing.

"You know they tend to be weak in the stomach for these types of things. Besides, he may talk like a mouse, but he has the courage of a tiger," I replied quietly, gazing at the man as he scribbled down everything that was being said and done.

The records gave me hope that even if everyone hated me while I was alive, they would look back and see what I had done—*why* I had done it. I would be loathed in this life, but if the heavens were gracious, I would be loved after my death. First, I had to make sure I lived long enough to accomplish all that I had planned.

Forcing myself to focus, I shook my head, staring at Jinyoung once more. The servant from the Min Clan looked the same as she had last night when she had attempted to assassinate me, except for the blood and screaming, of course. She had been much more quiet when she tried to slit my throat on my wedding night.

I sighed, rotating my neck and stretching my shoulders.

Relief washed over me that it wasn't Bora who'd tried to murder me. Not yet, at least. She seemed sweet, but poison could be sweet too. Just because she hadn't tried to kill me yet, didn't mean she wouldn't in the future.

"Do you think the queen was aware of what happened?" I pondered aloud.

Jinyoung rasped, her chest heaving from the laborious and painful interrogation, "My mistress knew nothing. I acted alone."

"Liar," I huffed, my eyes narrowing.

Dongbin offered, "Haeji will be able to discern if the queen was a part of the plan or ignorant of it. The truth will be found out, so do not worry, Jeonha."

I thrummed my fingers against the arm of my chair. "By the way, Minje, have there been any messages from Gweonho?"

"No, Jeonha. Our best little spy has been silent," my guard replied, dipping a cloth in a bowl of vinegar and bringing it to one of the open cuts on Jinyoung's flesh.

The maid hissed, biting her tongue to endure the pain.

Unlike the Min estate, the Oh family was much easier to infiltrate.

All of the information that my men had gathered on Bora regaled a young woman who loved sweets and animals and always seemed to be smiling. During the year between our betrothal and wedding, she had rarely been allowed outside her family estate, and thus intel was scarce from then on. Every servant we had tried to bribe at the Min Mansion had ended up dead or disappeared. Whether Bora had been learning palace etiquette and expectations of the queen or learning far more nefarious skills, I could not be sure.

Bora's face, soft and squishy with beautiful, crescent moon eyes and plump looking lips flooded my mind. I'd been so disappointed to think of her as complicit in the attempt on my life. Despite what she may have heard from her venomous father, I did not relish fear—only justice—and making people afraid of me served as a tool to meet that end. When I had searched her for weapons, the way her eyes closed, the way she was afraid of me, made my chest tighten, made me hesitate.

Hesitation was dangerous.

Once I'd stripped her down to her undergarments, I'd been tempted to keep going, a warmth spreading over my body as my desires overtook logic. But I wouldn't force her, and since she had no weapons, there was no reason to touch her. Instead, I turned away and sat at my omok board. It always helped me think, a realm in which I possessed control, all the pieces visible. There were rules in the game, unlike in life. Some people played by a moral code, while others would burn everything around them until they were the only ones left.

As much as the idea that all people should be treated as innocent and good individuals infatuated me, the fact of the matter was, some people were wolves, and if you tried to pet a wolf the same as a common dog, you'd get yourself killed. Naivete would not be the death of me, not like my father.

Another scream shattered my thoughts and brought me back to the present. Jinyoung's sweat-soaked clothing clung to her frame, and had she not been tied to the post, she would have collapsed, her legs limp beneath her. She would not see relief until she relented and confessed. I needed her to testify against Councilor Min, to admit that he'd ordered her to kill me.

That round face and cherry lips floated in my vision, but I shook the image away. As much as I wanted her to not be culpable, the most likely outcome was Bora dying along with her father and his schemes. I had a hard time believing that she was ignorant of his deeds.

"Dongbin," I said softer than I intended, my thoughts still lingering on Bora in her red silks.

"Jeonha," the stocky guard replied, his posture as rigid as the wall he stood in front of.

"Ask Haeji to investigate if the queen was aware of Jinyoung's assassination attempt."

That question demanded an answer, one that my life depended on, and if she colluded with her father...her life depended upon it as well.

The daughter of my enemy was dangerous, no matter how lovely and kind she appeared to be.

Chapter 5

Bora

AN APPETITE ELUDED ME, my stomach twisting and nauseous as the image of Jinyoung's sweat-slick skin and scarlet stains on her white garments refused to leave my mind. The pepper paste of the bibimbap had the same color as her blood. I shivered and shoved away the bowl.

"You should eat, Mama," Haeji insisted, pushing the bowl back towards me. "You have to attend court today."

My head whipped towards her as I gasped, "What? Why?"

Haeji grabbed the metal chopsticks and silver spoon and held them out towards me. "It is not my place to question the king's commands."

The words she left unsaid were clear: it was also not my place to question or disobey.

I ripped the utensils from her outstretched hands and scooped a spoonful of rice and vegetables into my mouth. I would need a full stomach to put up with the king and his antics. My disgust developed into irritation while my mind worked hard trying to think of a way to help Jinyoung, but I was powerless, as most women in Joseon were. The only hope I had required me to seek my father's help to free her. Surely the highest ranking man, second only to the king, would be able to help a simple maid. And what father would deny such a request from his daughter?

Due to my thoughts being consumed with Jinyoung, I didn't even get to savor my food, my hand moving between my mouth and the bowl without thinking. When had she last eaten? When would she be set free? Could I send her some medicine to help with her injuries? By the time I focused on the present, the dish stared back at me, empty.

Haeji nodded in satisfaction. My heart skipped a beat as I considered the possibility that the food had been poisoned, and Haeji was congratulating herself on a job well done. However, that made no sense if the king had requested my presence in court today. Paranoia dug its claws into me like a falcon's talons. Perhaps the stress of not knowing when I would be assassinated would kill me all on its own.

No.

I would not give this mad king the satisfaction, and I would survive out of spite if nothing else. My hand slammed the spoon against the table with a rattle, the shaking and sudden noise causing Haeji to flinch. She stared at me with wide eyes and raised brows before she wiped away the shocked expression and replaced it with stoicism.

"If you are finished, we should make our way to the throne room, Mama," Haeji said, standing to her feet as another servant came and cleared away the empty dishes.

The way she veiled a command as a suggestion amazed me; it was almost admirable.

Following suit, I got to my feet and fluffed my chima. I cleared my throat and inhaled, steeling myself for whatever schemes or public shaming the king wished to impose upon me. I really had no idea what to expect, and despite having only been in the palace for a day, the suspicion and speculation exhausted me. Living on edge was daunting, and all I yearned for was home, of my mother's well intended scolding and my brothers' stories of their scholarly studies. I missed my room with the pink curtains and the blush-colored cherry blossoms outside my windows.

Throughout my life, I'd learned social etiquette, music, and embroidery, but no one prepared me for surviving life in the palace with a ruthless ruler. Even in the year before my marriage, I had to memorize all the ministries, important officials, and special palace rules, but there was never a section detailing how to deal with a deranged king. My father told us many stories of the king's wicked deeds, including confiscating a minister's entire food storage just because he dared to disagree. Although my father had failed to equip me with the power, connections, or skills to defend myself, the knowledge that he would always protect me comforted my nerves.

I chewed my lip as I walked, my lady trailing behind me as we exited my chambers.

Gaping, I halted at the sight in front of me. Haeji nearly bumped into my back from the abrupt stop. A group of six women waited outside my quarters, all clad in jade-colored hanbok. More court ladies? Wasn't Haeji enough? Back home, we had a plethora of servants, but I had only one personally assigned to me.

"Who are all these women?" I asked, trying to keep the shock from my voice.

Steady voice and straight shoulders, I reminded myself.

Haeji stepped up beside me, head bowed. "These are your attendants, Mama. It is typical for a queen to have a multitude of ladies present to care for your needs."

I closed my eyes and exhaled slowly. My head ached from all the change that had been wrought upon my life like a summer monsoon. After opening my eyes, I continued walking, the group of women following me like baby ducks. My embroidered silk and leather shoes—much more flamboyant than the ones permitted for nobles—were nearly silent on the paved walkways as we made our way to the court hall.

It was only my second time in the courtroom. I gritted my teeth and entered, my ladies stopping outside the entryway with bowed heads, only Haeji accompanying me inside. The ministers were already gathered, clad in a mixture of dark red and blue robes and black caps that always reminded me of a butterfly with its two wings protruding from the sides. There were also a few feathered-gat-wearing generals standing near the front on the left. My eyes were drawn of their own accord towards my father, twin cranes embroidered on the chest of his burgundy garment, delineating his high rank.

"Mama," the courtiers cried out in unison as they bowed.

The hem of my chima brushed against the carpet that led all the way to the golden dragon throne where the king sat, his red robes surprisingly clean despite where he had been earlier that morning. He sat tall and still, his face reminiscent of a stoic statue. His cold, calculating eyes followed me as I approached. When I reached the steps, he stood, and I couldn't help but flinch at the unexpected movement. He held out his hand towards me, and I stared at it. A stone settled in my stomach, his fingers reminiscent of a venomous snake ready to strike. My body froze in place, unable to move despite the sea of eyes bearing into my back.

His voice came out in a low whisper, as frigid as his expression. "My queen, if you don't mind, we are waiting for you to begin." His eyes drew a line between me and his palm.

Bowing my head, I took his hand, surprised by the warmth of his touch as he guided me to sit next to him. It was not common for queens to be present for court, and I glanced at the king from the corner of my vision, wondering what purpose he had planned for my presence. He caught me staring, and my face flushed as I darted my gaze away. I peered down at my father, who stared at us with blank eyes. He must have perfected an empty expression over the years, a necessary defense against the volatile ruler.

It was not out of the realm of possibility for the king to have demanded my attendance just so he could kill my father in front of me, but since my father was the Chief State Councilor, even the most tyrannical ruler could not escape the fury of the common folk and the retribution of the ministers. That fact calmed my worries and settled my somersaulting stomach.

As I sat, the ocean of ministers bent low at their waists, their collective voices echoing in the hall. "Jeonha."

The king waved his hand in the air with an attitude of nonchalance, his face looking almost bored or even peeved at presiding over the court meeting.

"Rise," he ordered, and the ministers all lifted their heads, their mouths obscured by the ivory ceremonial scepters they held in their fists.

One of the few aspects of politics I was familiar with was factions. There were always two, sometimes more. But how could one tell who was with which faction when everyone was dressed in their court attire and arranged in the hall according to rank? Some officials spared glances at one another, but were they subtle threats or secret acknowledgments? The only ones I knew for certain were not a part of my father's side were the military leaders. He'd cursed many generals on drunken nights.

One of the blue-clad ministers with a single crane on his chest stepped into the center of the aisle from my left side and addressed the king.

"Jeonha, a fire raged in Gangwon-do that destroyed many crop storages, and the people have requested aid."

Those gathered made poor attempts to veil their grumblings while they critiqued the king, assuming that their scepter-obscured mouths, as well as the sheer amount of men, would keep them anonymous and unable to be found out.

"The king must have angered the heavens."

"He has brought the ire of the divine down upon us."

Many held the belief that natural disasters were the fault of the ruler, and as I peered at the king from my seat next to him, I grunted quietly in agreement. How could the heavens not be outraged at such a terrible tyrant? But it was still bold of them to say such things in front of the scowling man next to me.

The minister who brought the subject before the king spoke again. "Jeonha, please acquire the needed food from the other provinces to provide relief for the people of Gangwon-do."

Such a suggestion would sow strife amongst the provincial governors, who were not present in court yet had people representing them in their stead. The men on both sides broke out into mumbling disagreements.

"It is not Jeolla-do's responsibility to bail out the people of Gangwon-do."

"Only the neighboring provinces should have their storages raided. There is no need for the capital's supplies to be taken."

"If we do not aid them, we will all suffer from the lower crop production this winter."

"My storage will remain unaffected."

"That's because you own too much land in Gyeongsang-do."

I chewed my lip, unsure why so many officials were reluctant to aid the victims of the fire. Weren't we all one people? I saw my father step forward, and relief washed over me, a small smile forming on my lips. My father would handle the matter, and the citizens of Gangwon-do would soon have their much needed supplies.

"Perhaps the king should visit the province to appease the heavens and the people," my father suggested with sparkling eyes.

I waited for the second half of his proposition, in which he would petition for the rest of Joseon to support their hurting member, but it never came. My fingers tangled together, and my brows bunched inwards.

"Are you opposing Minister Choi's request?" the king asked with a hint of bitterness, his lip curling ever so slightly.

"If there was a fire, then it is the wrath of heaven—a clear sign of displeasure," my father said, his sneer thinly veiled, yet he did not dare to speak of *who* might have incurred it.

The king laughed at the men before him, the sound jarring as an earthquake. "How exciting, how humorous, that the nobles before me complain about the troubles of the people under their care. But I find such things rather irritating, so how about I just take half of your storages for myself? Then you can be on the same ground as the commoners you oversee."

My mouth dropped open at the audacious order, and the shock and anger was written clearly on the ministers' faces, the displeasure palpable as if the fire that had raged in Gangwon-do was present in the very courtroom. My father's eyes burned into the king, his nostrils flared, and the grip on his scepter tightened, his knuckles turning white.

The king's word was law, and the men could do nothing but bow and move onto the next issue.

Talks of the Ming Empire consumed the rest of the time, the morning having given way to midday when the king finally called the court meeting over. Grumbling officials stomped out, while a few remained behind, giving smiles and bows to the king.

I spotted my father conversing with his fellow State Councilor near the entrance and stood.

The king struck his hand out like a snake, his fingers slithering around my wrist with a tight grip. "Where are you going?" he demanded through narrowed eyes.

I tried to pull my wrist free to no avail. "To see my father," I grumbled, my arm as taut as a rope between us.

The king yanked me down towards him, our faces almost colliding. I inhaled a sharp breath, my eyes wide and visible in the reflection of his own. I squirmed under his burning gaze, as helpless as a trapped fawn. With his other hand, the king traced his fingers along my neck, a tickling sensation much like a feather whispering along my skin.

"I don't take kindly to scheming in my own palace," the king hissed.

My eyes darted around his face, trying to escape his freezing gaze. "I–I don't understand," I muttered, my heart beating faster than a rabbit's.

"Just know this, I may not always win, but I never lose," he growled before letting me go, the jarring release causing me to stumble backwards.

Right as I was about to fall back down the dais steps, the king bolted to his feet, his arm curling around me and pulling me into him. He surprised me, his skin not cold to the touch but rather warm. Heat crawled along my neck and cheeks as our breaths mixed together. We stood there in silence for what felt like an eternity, time pausing and everyone else ceasing to exist. At last, I opened my mouth to speak, but before the words could come out, the king released me and stepped back.

He smoothed his red robes and cleared his throat. "Come see me after you are done speaking with your father," he commanded, the coldness in his voice having thawed ever so slightly.

Then, with a swoosh of his silk garments, he turned and disappeared down the carpeted walkway and out of the court-room, guards and eunuchs trailing behind him like a pack of wolves.

What did he mean about schemes? He was the one always concocting some cleverly cruel way to show his power. I stood motionless for a few seconds before shaking my head. Attempting to decipher the king's intentions was too arduous a task and felt more like an unending labyrinth that I didn't care to wander through. I walked down the dais steps towards the looming entrance of the hall, the pillars lining the room like domineering guards.

As the ministers trickled out in trios, I maneuvered through the sea of men until I came upon my father, his brows and lips heavy with frustration. I assumed that after the court meeting, he would be in a foul mood, especially with the involuntary forfeiture of our family supplies, but I figured he wouldn't be so upset that he would refuse to discuss Jinyoung with me. I was his own blood after all. My hand brushed against his elbow, my fingers pinching the fabric of his robes and pulling down with a gentle tug.

The scowl melted from his face, and I smiled as our eyes met.

"Abeonim, it is so nice to see you. It has only been a day, but it feels like years have passed. I fear that I will age quicker than you inside the palace," I joked, hoping it would help lighten his mood.

He did not return my smile. Inclining his head, he corrected, "Please, Mama, it is inappropriate to refer to me in that way."

My smile faltered. "I understand, Chief State Councilor," I mumbled, my shoulders drooping.

"What can I do for you, Mama?" he asked. With a wave of his hand, his fellow officials bowed, muttered farewells, and left.

I took another step towards him, careful to keep my voice low. "The king arrested Jinyoung and had her detained in the dungeon. Oh, Abeonim, it was a horrible sight. Poor Jinyoung was covered in cuts, and her skin looked like a ghost's. I'm not sure why he did that, but we need to free her. You know how gentle she is. I don't know how long she can endure."

My father patted my shoulder while taking a step back. "I'm afraid there is nothing I can do."

My mouth gaped, and my voice raised to a pitch that was unbecoming of a queen. "But–but she is my lady. We can't just abandon her," I stuttered shrilly, reaching for his hand.

He avoided my grip, instead adjusting his garments and replying in a stern tone, "She is only a servant, and it is her duty to live—and die—for the Min family."

I took a step back, my brows contorting in confusion. "But—"

My father cut me off like a blade demanding silence. "I will hear no more of the matter, Bora."

Wrapping my arms around myself, I bit my lip to keep from crying.

My shoulders hunched, and I nodded, mumbling, "Alright."

He huffed and turned back towards the ministers who waited several steps away, glancing back once more to say, "Your mother misses you. Come home for a visit sometime in the next few days." And then he left.

Although it was not according to custom for me to be the one to visit my family's home—protocol dictating that they should come to me in the palace—I didn't mind. My lips bloomed into a grin, my concern for Jinyoung momentarily displaced. I also missed my mother, and perhaps that was a subtle way of my father expressing that he missed me, too. I spun on my heel and headed back to my chambers, my feet a little lighter.

My father didn't really intend to leave Jinyoung in the dungeon. He was just slyly saying that we could not discuss the matter in the palace. When I went to visit home, he was going to help devise a plan to free her.

Haeji and the other ladies followed behind me like a silent shadow, but I didn't mind having them, as it felt nice not to be alone in the palace. If the king wanted to kill or imprison me, he would have done so by now. The ladies may be spies, but they weren't assassins. I hoped that given time, they would even come to genuinely like me. Kindness could melt even the coldest of hearts.

Chapter 6

Bora

A SHOUT OF SURPRISE burst from my mouth when I entered my chambers, the unexpected presence of the king causing my innards to tremble. Why was he here? Had he somehow gotten word of my conversation with my father and was now infuriated that I was trying to free my maid? Would he use it as grounds to execute me for treason? Sweat began to form on my skin despite the cool spring weather, and my knees felt weak as I walked towards him.

He glanced up at me from where he sat on my bed, his sharp eyes narrowed like a snake. His voice dropped low with displeasure. "I told you to come to my quarters after you were done," he said, his tone chilling my bones.

I'd forgotten his instructions, but the tension in my shoulders relaxed a little knowing that he was ignorant of the details about my conversation.

"My apologies," I mumbled, my gaze descending to the floor.

"How is Chief Councilor Min?" he asked without a drop of sincerity, a venom coating my family's name.

I paused my approach, my feet freezing to the floor and my heart suspending in my chest. My mind swung in a pendulum between speaking some sort of appeasing platitude and betraying my true thoughts, specifically concerning the injustice of Jinyoung's incarceration.

Inhaling, I gathered what little courage I possessed. "He is troubled about the unlawful detainment of his servant sent for me."

As soon as the words left my mouth, so did my bravery. My courage wilted like a flower, the king a scorching sun as he stood and stalked forward. My legs threatened to give out from under me, but thankfully they didn't collapse and instead moved me backwards. They retreated until they collided with a wooden pillar.

The king's breath slithered across my skin, his eyes filled with a poisonous glare, his arms caging me in, hovering beside my head. "How could you plead for the life of an assassin?"

My whole body stilled, and my eyes widened. "What?"

Jinyoung? An assassin? It was a ludicrous accusation. Jinyoung once cried because she accidentally spilled one of my paints, and she jumped every time a breeze banged a branch into my window. It was impossible.

His suspicion and bitterness washed away, replaced for a few seconds with what I thought was confusion and surprise. Then there was nothing, only the cold, natural state his face favored.

His jaw unclenched, and he pulled back, my breath returning to me.

"Never mind. Don't bring her up again," he ordered in a gruff voice, his gaze peeling away from mine as if I was something unpleasant to look at.

"But—"

The king whipped his hand up, cutting me off. "Enough." He looked past me towards the entrance and hollered, "Haeji, prepare the queen for a trip into the city."

"Yes, Jeonha," she said from the hallway, her reply melting my frozen feet.

I turned my head back and forth between them. "The city? Why?"

The king strode past me, his silk robe hissing. "You'll see soon enough," he grunted before exiting my chambers.

Haeji received a pile of green garments from another servant and slid the door closed. The clothes in her arms were that of one of the palace ladies. I opened my mouth to protest before clamping my lips shut. Opposition offered me nothing. The king had given an order, and as his wife and subject, I was bound to obey.

While Haeji untied my chima and dangui, slipping them off with a gentle tug, I sighed. My life felt so pointless. All I wanted was to live in peace, and if I had been able to pursue any position, I would have been a cook.

I closed my eyes while Haeji dressed me and dreamed of a restaurant in the crowded capital city. It would be two stories with cascading curtains and the best musicians, beautiful music accompanying the most delicious food and paintings that I had created hanging on the walls. I would serve spicy noodles and juicy pork trotters along with an array of fermented cabbage and radish with marinated lotus root and black beans.

My mouth began to water, and I flung open my eyes, hoping that exiting my dream would prevent the saliva from spilling out.

After tying off my top, Haeji stepped back with her head bowed. "Mama, I know you are disappointed with not having the servant from your family's house, but I will do my best to serve and please you."

I mulled over my words for a few moments before replying, "It's not your fault. It's just..." I sighed. "It would be nice to have a friend, to have someone familiar. I miss my family, and all this is still so new to me," I explained, waving my hands around.

"The king has reasons for detaining her," Haeji said with a bit of hesitance, as if she wasn't sure if she should continue to speak. Although I had not known her for long, I thought hesitation was foreign to Haeji. What did she mean? The only reasons for the king to have Jinyoung in the dungeon were either some show of power or because he wanted to leave me isolated in the palace. Her being an assassin was an excuse for his cruel tricks. I wouldn't buy his lies so easily.

Bottling my thoughts, I simply replied with a smile that didn't reach my eyes, my lips folding on themselves in my poor attempt. "I am sure he does."

Haeji tilted her head ever so slightly, and my skin began to itch as she studied me. Luckily her analysis didn't last long.

"Let's depart, Mama," she said and gestured towards the exit.

I swallowed and strode towards the door, doing my best to feign confidence. Perhaps I could pretend I was someone powerful, but such a sentiment dissipated as soon as I came out of my chambers. The king towered outside the door like a pagoda, his shadow casting itself outside the threshold. Even in his new outfit—one of the Royal Guard's uniforms—he was resplendent. My shoulders shrank as I stepped out. I was a fool to think faking power was anything even remotely close as actually possessing it.

Time seemed to stop when in the presence of the king, as if life held its breath. No guard, eunuch, or court lady dared move without his permission. With a single word, he could have someone killed or saved. With a single order, he could start a war or end one. With a single command, I could be in a grave.

The words from our wedding night would not fade from my memory, creeping chills crawling along my skin at the thought of it.

You will only leave this palace with my permission or in a coffin.

At last, the king moved, and we all trailed after him. He blended in with the other guards and I with the court-ladies. Why did a king need to sneak out of his own palace? As we headed west, I realized we were leaving through the side gate of the palace.

The birds chirping from the tiled and tapered roof of the buildings felt like friends, cheering me on as we passed by them.

Watch over me please, and if the king is leading me outside to kill me, guide people to my body, I whispered my thoughts to the little songbirds.

We arrived at a box carriage, the king dismissed the ladies and eunuchs with a wave of his hand, and even Haeji bowed and left, only a couple guards remaining. My legs began to tremble.

Palanquins were always used in the city by royals and nobles, and carriages were only for longer journeys. We were not going to the city, then. He had lied.

"Problem?" the king asked, raising one brow.

"N-no," I stammered and forced my feet to move and climbed the two steps up into the carriage.

The king entered after me, the seat far too cramped, although perhaps his intimidating presence consumed more of the space than his body did. I still preferred this to the palanquin I rode yesterday.

"Dongbin," the king hollered through the brocade curtain that covered the entrance.

A pair of hands jutted through, holding two pairs of clothes that looked to be made of burlap, or some equally rough fabric. I leaned away, my gaze darting between the king and the clothes.

He reached forward and took the garments from Dongbin, and as he sat back, he tossed a pair of tan baji and a blue jeogori at me.

"Change into these," he ordered, his voice booming and devouring the remaining space in the carriage.

More changing? What was the purpose of this? Was he finally going to kill me and hoping to hide my body or disguise it so that people thought I was just some poor commoner killed by a bandit?

My mouth hung open, and he glared at me from the corner of his eyes.

"You have your undergarments on. It's not like I haven't seen those before," he commented with a huff, his fingers already tugging at his cheollik that matched Dongbin's, the fabric slithering off his body.

My hands immediately whipped to my face, covering my eyes as my face flushed. He may have stripped me down to my undergarments on our wedding night, but I had not seen any part of him that anyone else wasn't privy to. My face and neck warmed, my fingers a curtain between me and my embarrassment.

Rustling and bumping against the wooden sides of the carriage sounded beside me.

After a few minutes, the king said in a condescending tone, "I'm done. You can uncover your eyes."

I slowly peeled my fingers from my face, my eyes peeking open one at a time. Even in rags, the king was gorgeous. He jutted his chin out towards me, the burlap clothes still in my lap.

My hands worked at the ribbon of fabric that held my jeogori together. I had not dressed myself in so long, and my fingers were incompetent and slow, feebly fumbling at the knot.

The king guided my shoulders with an unexpected gentleness, his voice softer than before. "Allow me."

Once more my face reddened. How many women had he slept with that he was so accustomed to untying tops? Then again, the law allowed for kings—and nobles—to have concubines, and knowing his disposition, he would even be willing to have mistresses without ever appointing them the title of concubines.

How wretched.

The heat vanished from my face, and my arms stiffened as air brushed against my skin where the jeogori fell open. Without looking at the king, I slipped off the court lady uniform as quickly as possible and replaced it with the commoner's clothes. My skin protested against the rough fabric, and my hands kept adjusting the garments.

The king cocked a brow, a slight smirk curling the corner of his lips. I turned away, brushing the smaller curtain of the window.

Birds were fluttering to and fro outside, and as I listened to them sing, I whispered, "Thank you for following me. It is nice to have friends I can trust."

I felt the king's freezing eyes burn into my back, but I paid him no heed, focusing on my feathered friends, who despite their ability to go wherever they wished, kept by my side.

Chapter 7

Bora

WE WALKED DOWN DIRTY alleyways that no noble had ever traversed, the long carriage ride taking us to the outskirts of the capital where buildings blended with the forest. The coarse commoner's clothing that the king and I were garbed in would help us blend in, although I wasn't sure why the king would want that. Aside from two guards clad in similar simple garments, we were alone.

But why would he take all this effort to disguise ourselves? Despite my previous worries, he couldn't just kill me and leave my body behind even if I was dressed like a poor commoner. I had already married the king and entered the palace, so people would notice my sudden absence and demand answers. I chewed my lip, contemplating the purpose of this strange outing.

As we made our way further into the shack littered streets, I glanced into the haggard and hollow homes, the skeletal structures made of wood scraps, sticks, and mud, some of the doors nothing more than a rectangle of straw woven together. Guilt gnawed at me, my chest tightening as I considered how many people in Joseon lived this way while the noble class was able to live in such luxury. My family was a clan of powerful officials with men occupying positions in a multitude of ministries, and I had never known hunger nor cold.

But my father did not oversee the local government of the capital city, so it wasn't his malice or neglect that created such slums. At least, that was what I told myself lest the shame eat me all the way to my bones.

The constant looming shadow of my potential death drained me. If he planned to do it, he might as well do it now.

I scratched my itching arm and whimpered, "If you're going to—"

"Samchon Taeho!" a gaggle of children squealed as they charged us like a flash flood during monsoon season.

Dirt covered arms reached towards the king, and his eyes twinkled, his lips curling into a smile.

And it didn't look menacing.

He was...happy?

He kneeled to the ground and spread open his arms, which were quickly filled with tiny bodies. He chuckled, and the sound reminded me of chimes. It was nothing how I imagined it would be, not the dark and sinister sound I expected.

"How is everyone?" he asked, his eyes scanning their faces.

I felt a pang of jealousy hit my chest. My father hadn't shown me such affectionate attention in a long time. The last time he inquired of my health was right before he informed me I would be wed to the king.

"We are good but hungry," one small girl with matted hair said with a squeak.

The king nodded and waved one of the guards forward. I glanced towards him, and the guard untied a pouch from his belt and handed it to the king, the coins clinking together. He opened the pouch and plucked out a coin before plopping it into the girl's hand, repeating the action with all the children until each one held a shining copper. Their faces grew brighter than the metal and their eyes just as round in excitement.

"Thank you, Samchon Taeho!" the children shouted in unison.

This time a scrawny boy spoke. "Who is she?" he asked with inquisitive, wide eyes.

The king twisted his torso and looked up at me, the corner of his mouth twitching up. "This is my wife, and you can call her Imo Soyeon."

My head whipped towards him. I wasn't sure why, but my heart skipped a beat at hearing him refer to me as his wife. I felt my face flush, and I coughed in an attempt to chase away the blush. The smallest of all the children, a chubby girl perhaps no more than three, reached out and gripped the bottom of my baji. A smile bloomed on my face, and I bent down and picked her up. Without warning, the little girl kissed my cheek.

I brushed the dust covered hair out of her face. "Hello, children. It is a pleasure to meet you."

A few of them giggled while others glared with a wariness that held sad stories. One child even hid behind the king, clutching his clothes in small fists. I gaped at the king, who had another two leaning against each leg, both with big grins on their faces. If they knew who he really was, that the hands they were holding on to with their tiny fingers were actually blood-covered, they would run screaming in terror.

"Imo," one of the boys, perhaps no more than twelve, poked my arm, his eyes peering up at me with a spark of curiosity.

"Yes," I replied, readjusting the little girl in my arms and positioning her against my hip.

"Would you like to play with me?" he asked with a faint smile and tilt of his head.

Glancing at the king, I raised my brows. He nodded and gestured towards the boy before returning to chatting with the group of children. I thought I heard one of them beg for a ride on his back.

"Sorry, sweetie, but I need to set you down to play with..." I turned to the boy.

"Minhyeok," he replied, grinning.

"And what's your name?" I asked the little girl as I set her back on the ground.

"We call her Daeun. She doesn't talk, though," Minhyeok provided while he began drawing lines in the sand.

I licked my thumb and wiped a smudge of soil from her forehead. "Daeun is a very pretty name," I gushed and poked her softly in her tummy, eliciting a giggle.

Minhyeok pulled at my sleeve, bringing my attention to the lines he had drawn.

"Three in a row wins," he explained and drew an *x* in one of the nine squares.

It seemed like a simpler version of omok. Certainly three in a row was easier than five. I grabbed a nearby twig and drew a circle in the dirt.

He beat me in two more turns.

I scratched my head. "Well, that was fast," I said, chuckling.

"Again?" Minhyeok asked, rolling back and forth on his feet.

"Sure," I agreed, determined to win.

"You can go first this time," he offered and took a step back.

I drew an *x* in the middle. The strategy didn't differ much from omok, with there being an advantage to going first, and I wasn't about to be beat by a child twice.

At least this time we filled all the squares by the time he beat me.

My brows pinched together as I twirled a strand of hair that had freed itself from my braid, my pin left behind in the carriage.

"One more?" I suggested.

We wiped the shapes from the dirt and began again.

Drawing the the winning circle, I shouted, "I win!" I dropped the stick and danced around the lines. "I won! I won!"

Minhyeok and Daeun started laughing, igniting the rest of the children who had been watching into a chorus of giggles.

Clapping caught my attention, and I spun around to see the king smiling and slapping his hands together.

"Not too bad for a novice," he offered with a smirk and a dip of his head.

I tossed my braid over my shoulder and planted my hands on my hip. "Well, I think it is time for Samchon Taeho to play. Who wants to ride on Samchon's back?" I asked mischievously.

The children flooded the king with hands waving in the air and shouts of "me, me".

He glared at me, a cold blooming in my blood. Had I gone too far? How foolish I was for forgetting *who* he was.

But then his expression turned unserious, shaking his head as he smiled and groaned, "Alright. Let's start with Daeun."

Satisfied with my mutiny, I went to a nearby log and sat.

The king jogged to and fro, a child on his back at all times, bouncing up and down. Every time he set one down, another took their place, each with wide eyes, puffed lips, and hands clasped together as they begged for a turn. The king gave in to each one, crouching down for them as they climbed onto his back and wrapped their arms around his neck.

Eventually, he grew tired and broke the disappointing news, "Your Samchon is too old. I need to rest."

He collapsed dramatically on the log next to me. A chorus of complaints arose, but after they were certain they couldn't beg their way into more rides, they gave up and began playing amongst themselves.

While some of the children ran around and others fought each other with sticks, shouts and laughter echoed in the trees, the king watching them with a wide grin on his face. He looked like what I imagined was a proud father, an expression that my siblings and I had rarely seen.

Daeun waddled to where we sat and crawled up onto my lap, nestling her head against my chest. I wrapped my arms around her, and she curled a small hand around my forefinger.

"Where are their parents?" I asked, my eyes wandering around the clearing where not an adult stood in sight except for a few elderly women who were peeling garlic at the end of the row of houses.

"Dead or working. A few old widows down the street help watch them during the day, but there is only so much they can do. The children have more energy than them," he replied and picked up a stick, doodling in the dirt. "All the older children are working too. Minhyeok will have to start next year."

"Oh..."

I didn't know what else to say. Looking down to where Daeun's eyes were closed, head tucked into me, a lump formed in my throat.

"I want to help them," I whispered so softly I was surprised the king heard it.

He shook his head and scoffed.

"What?" I questioned quietly, afraid to wake the sleeping child on my lap.

The king replied, his voice strained in sorrow while he lifted the stick up. "Joseon is like this branch. Rigid and limited in what it can become." He snapped it in half and began peeling the bark off, gathering the strips into a small pile. After he stripped the wood naked, he started twisting the bark and weaving them together. "I want to make it something new," he murmured in a wistful tone.

After a few knots, he handed me his creation—a norigae. The bark had been crafted into the shape of a diamond, although far more crude than its normal thread counterpart.

I had been rather isolated growing up, only visiting other nobles and ministers and sticking to the merchant district of the capital. For all my life, I thought that Joseon was fine because there was opportunity for advancement through the scholar exams or the military. My father and his colleagues were supposed to ensure it, along with the king. If the problem didn't lie with the king...

Well, there were factions in the court, albeit small compared to the major two: the king's and my father's. The other ones must be the cause then. He was not the warmest of parents, but he was not evil. If he knew about this poor village full of hungry children on the outskirts of the capital, he would do something to help them.

Liar, I chided myself.

I didn't want my father to be a cruel man—a corrupt official—but he had made up lies about the king, or at least deceived us by omitting certain facts, twisting the story so we, so *I*, would fear and hate him. Such as the court meetings. Although the method was unorthodox, the king did help the victims of the fire in Gangwon-do.

The man sitting in commoner's clothing next to me, shoulder heavy with the concerns of his citizens, was no tyrant.

No.

Maybe he was just putting on a big show, an act to turn me against my father. Jinyoung was still in prison after all, and I had seen the red lines left by the whip, the blood from the blade's cuts. I wished to return to playing with Minhyeok. It was a far more simple game.

Chapter 8

Bora

A s we waded through the crumbling shacks and thatch work alleyways back towards the carriage that had brought us here, I studied the sharp face of the king. In the light of the afternoon, the sunrays kissed his skin, making it shimmer and soften. Without his dragon embroidered robes and black, mountainous ikseongwan crowning his head, he lost much of his intimidation, appearing more like a common man. Although even in the coarse clothes, he was handsome, and no amount of dirt or dingy garments could mask his attractive features.

When he caught me staring, I whipped my head forward, my cheeks and ears warming. I chewed my lip, my mind filling with images of the king with those children, unconcerned for their status or the dirt coating their hands and faces. He had embraced them as if they were his own, knew them each by name. I doubted my father was aware of the king's excursions to the poor district. My mind worked harder than a desperate farmer, digging for an answer as to what his true nature was.

His voice broke through my thoughts, and I flinched, nearly tripping over a rock.

He gripped my elbow, his breath hot against my skin as he asked, "Are you alright?"

I jerked upright, my face reddening. "Y-yes," I stuttered.

An unexpected disappointment settled in my stomach when he released my arm, the area where his fingers had been now cold.

You're too naïve, Bora. A snake steals heat; it doesn't provide it, I scolded myself.

Desperate to change the subject, I mused, "I hope those children can advance their station when they're older. Minhyeok was rather smart for his age. I'm sure he could pass the Kwago with ease."

"The Kwago," the king said with a scornful laugh, "is a joke. It doesn't matter if it is available for anyone to take it if they cannot afford the time or materials to prepare for it. In name only, it is a civil exam open to all. It is no more than a farce of equal opportunity, and people like your *father* are the ones who ensure that the commoners are too poor to pass it. It is a cycle of nobles and nepotism and a disgrace to the kingdom."

My skin flushed with fury, and I opened my mouth to spit back a retort. But no words came out, my mind comprehending what he'd said. It made sense, his sentiments, and although I was reluctant to believe him, there was no reason not to. My head pounded like a drum from trying to discern what was true and what was a lie.

"I wanted to build a public library, but the faction that your father leads opposed the plan," he explained with bitterness, as if he had eaten something sour.

"Well, maybe he just worried that the taxes to fund the building would be too much for the people," I retorted, the words spilling out in a desperation to defend my father's honor.

He wasn't that bad, not like the king implied.

"I had even offered to fund it with my personal money," he scoffed and kicked a stray pebble that had wandered into his path.

I didn't reply because I didn't know what to say. There was no way to spin that to make my father look good. Perhaps some caveat existed, something that the king omitted from the story. Yes, that must be it. His words were half-truths, an attempt to make me loathe my own father.

At last we came to the carriage, but the king paused outside.

"Go ahead and change first," he instructed without looking at me, crossing his arms as he turned to talk with one of the guards—Dongbin, if I recalled correctly.

Nodding, I climbed up and pushed back the curtain. I stripped and changed clothes as quickly as I could in the cramped space. This was not what I had expected when becoming queen.

"Alright, I'm done," I shouted softly.

Silence.

With a sigh, I crept forward, calling out once more as I stuck my head out, "I'm d—"

My words were cut off as my head collided with the king's, both of us hissing in pain. I fell back against the side of the carriage as the king came inside, rubbing his forehead.

"Sorry," I mumbled and pressed my palm to the sore spot on my face.

"There was nothing to be sorry about," he grumbled in reply, wincing as he touched the red area above his brows.

We settled into the cushioned seats, and the carriage began to move, jostling roughly back and forth on the rougher roads of the poorer area.

I curled my hair around my fingers, contemplating the day's events. I wasn't sure how to reconcile the two versions of the king that I had seen. The same man who had tortured my maid was the same one who knew the street children by name. Was it all fake? Some grand scheme to get me to trust him? But what did he need my trust for? Did he want to use me to get to my father?

I glanced at him from the corner of my eye, hoping he wouldn't notice my staring. Perhaps the king was still a snake, just not the venomous kind.

Chapter 9

Seojun

BORA STARED AT ME, although I did my best not to let on that I noticed. My lips twitched as I tried not to let a smile fully form. Turning my head away, I let myself grin for a few seconds before swallowing it.

She was one of the wolves, no matter how innocent she appeared on the outside. Perhaps she was a better performer than her father, able to put up a pretense of pity for the poor children. I scolded myself, remembering that trust was earned and not inherent. And even then, who knew what kind of game Bora and her father were playing, how long she was willing to wait before she pounced.

Haeji had yet to inform me on whether or not the queen was aware of the assassination attempt. The answer to my inquiry scared me more than it should have for a woman I barely knew, for someone I shouldn't care about, for the daughter of my enemy. I urged the walls around my heart to build to new heights.

I cleared my throat, fighting the intoxicating scent of blossoms that drifted from her, luring me *to* her.

"It probably goes without saying, but just in case," I said, pausing to glance at her face shining in the light that peeked through the curtains of the carriage, "you must keep our outing a secret." For extra precaution, I added, "Especially from your father."

A test.

If she informed her father, I would know where her loyalty lay.

Her brows furrowed, and she frowned. For a moment, I thought she would protest, or at least question why, but she just agreed.

"Alright." Her voice came out soft, tinged with what I could only assume was confusion.

It was only natural for a daughter to trust her father. The sudden urge to reach up and caress her cheek, to banish the frown from her face, grew inside me until my body was forced to act. My hand rose, but before I got near her, she wiped away the expression and replaced it with a smile.

My hand fell to my lap.

Did she always smile even when she wasn't happy?

What made her happy?

Just because her father was my enemy, didn't mean she had to be. Bora had accepted those children so easily, despite the class systems that plagued Joseon. She did not shy from the dirt and grime or their peppering questions. Her father, despite all his dedication to appearing as a generous man, would never deign to touch low class children, not even if all the kingdom was watching. Perhaps the only thing the two shared was their blood, and with each day, imagining spilling hers grew increasingly unpleasant.

Maybe it would be fine to be friendly with her. Maybe she would even come to trust me, to see that whatever lies her father had poisoned her with about me were false.

Was I really willing to risk my life, to put myself in jeopardy all on a bet that Bora was genuine and kind?

The smooth, black omok stone sat in my palm, an anchor to keep me steady amidst the tumultuous waves of palace life. My ears pricked at the sound of someone approaching, always attuned to whatever noise was nearby. The habit formed out of necessity. The lesson had long been learned, with whispering threats hiding in every alcove, around every corner, and in every food and drink.

I lowered my hand to place the piece.

Four in a row—on the cusp of victory.

From the corner of my eye, I saw Haeji enter, and I pivoted in my seat and leaned forward.

"Well? What did you find out?" I asked, my voice rising to the rafters.

Haeji kept her face blank as she bowed and greeted, "Jeon-ha."

Leaping to my feet, I gently tugged her up. "No need for formalities. Get to the point."

She unbent her back and nodded, her fingertips tapping one at a time as she rattled, "The queen likes kimchi-jeon and lotus root along with anything sweet, pink peonies, feeding the birds and fish in the courtyard, painting, and listening to stories."

I nodded along, securing each fact in my mind. With all this, Bora would see that I was not the bad one—her father was. She could be convinced to see the truth. I waved my hand in the air. "Good. And her dislikes?"

Haeji switched hands, counting once more on her other fingers. "She is afraid of heights, hates embroidery, doesn't eat shellfish, and..." her voice trailed off, her gaze running from me.

"What is it, Haeji?"

"Jeonha. She doesn't like you, Jeonha," she murmured with reluctance, almost as if she was sorry and could change Bora's opinion of me.

My chest deflated and my head drooped. "And was she aware of the maid's assassination attempt?"

Haeji shook her head. "I cannot confirm that yet. Forgive me for my ineptitude, but I need some more time. She cares for the maid, but I think that is just the queen's personality."

Maybe she really was ignorant of her father's ways.

"Get me some wood and a carving knife," I ordered, each word rising in pitch as it tumbled from my mouth.

I was wonderful at deception, had kept up a farce to ensure my safety as well as the security of Joseon, but a tiny gnawing worry in the back of mind thought that I was deceiving myself. Despite her family origin, something about her was alluring, and I was tempted more each day to ignore the warning that rang in my head. The desire to trust the daughter of my enemy, to believe the best of her, was foolish for a man and deadly for a king.

Just one chance, I vowed.

If Bora failed my test and informed her father of our trip to the village or if she tried to harm me, then I would crush the hope in my heart without mercy.

If Bora chose her father, then I would kill her.

As Haeji left, Dongbin's eyes lingered on the fading figure of the court lady.

"What do you think of the queen?" I asked, trying to keep my voice as casual as I could.

Dongbin looked at me at last, Haeji having disappeared entirely from view. "Well, I am not sure how many noble women in Joseon would have been fine with a low class child wearing rags nestling onto their lap."

He handed me an oblong ceramic, and I took it, unplugging the stopper.

"People will do a lot of things they normally wouldn't if they are afraid saying no leads to death or punishment," I retorted dryly, plopping my daily pill into my mouth.

My face contorted from the bitter taste. Despite taking it for over a decade, my tongue could not grow accustomed to it.

Dongbin shrugged. "That's true. I am sure the queen fears you, but the look in her eyes as she cradled Daeun was not that of someone scared, but of a deep compassion."

"Do you think she will try to kill me?" I pondered, disappointment blooming at just the thought of it.

"I cannot be sure, Jeonha. Only time will tell if her loyalty to blood is greater than her honor."

"Indeed."

Silence grew between us, but just as I thought our conversation ended, Dongbin added, "I do pray that for both your sakes, she is not like her father. It would be quite nice to have a king and queen in love."

"Love," I burst into a chuckle. "I think your head is too high in the clouds."

"Not my head but my heart, Jeonha," he replied, smiling.

I had a feeling he was imagining a certain court lady. But I also prayed for the same, that the queen and I could at least be cordial with each other, that we would not be enemies. Her father would work hard to ensure the opposite, but I was quite accustomed to thwarting his plans.

Chapter 10

Bora

I T WAS ONE OF the rare moments that Haeji was not attached to me like a shadow, and I would not let the opportunity go to waste. I had wanted to visit Jinyoung in the dungeons, still set on seeing her free. Somehow. Until I figured that out, I wanted her to know she was not forgotten about, at least by me.

I stacked the fried rice cakes coated in honey next to slices of persimmon, a smile dusting my lips as I pictured Jinyoung eating them, a bulb forming in her cheeks as we laughed and ate just like we did back home. I had very few true friends, as many of the fellow noble girls who'd approached me growing up were pawns of their fathers, vying for any ties to the Chief State Councilor. Of course, I had been naïve back then, had thought they were interested in me and not my family's prestige.

Genuine friendship was hard to come by, and I could count on my fingers the amount of people whom I called real friends. And now Jinyoung was in a cell, likely because she was *my* lady. A warm goo spread in my palm, and I opened it to reveal a smashed persimmon slice. The vermillion pulp plopped onto the table, narrowly avoiding the basket I had painstakingly packed and repacked.

I reached for a nearby cloth and wiped the sticky juice and fruit chunks from my hand before anyone noticed. Wincing at the remnants of the persimmon, I sighed. What a waste of delicious food. I collected the pulp into a mound and wrapped it in the cloth, making sure no juice was left behind on the table.

Setting the cloth aside, I closed the wooden box with its square lid and turned to exit. A figure stood in the doorway, having entered silently without me noticing.

Defeat dragged my shoulders down.

Haeji inquired, "Where are you going, Mama?"

Despite already knowing what she would say, I replied, "To see Jinyoung."

Haeji's eyes started tracing invisible lines on the floor in an uncharacteristic sign of discomfort.

I cocked my brow. "What is it?"

"The king decreed Jinyoung's execution this morning," Haeji mumbled softly.

The box collided with the floor, rice cakes and persimmon scattering like mice. All I heard was a ringing in my ears.

Jinyoung dead?

For what?

A petty power squabble?

Because the king was just in a foul mood?

The skittish maid was no assassin. At best, she was killed over a misunderstanding, and at worst, she was collateral damage in the fight between the king and my family.

My legs started moving before my mind did, my feet squashing Jinyoung's food as I stormed out, my shoulder brushing past Haeji while she scurried out of my way. Without even a second of consideration of what I was doing, my vision red and my blood boiling, I found myself outside the king's chambers.

Haeji's feet fluttered behind me, racing to catch up without breaking palace etiquette and running. Yet apparently I was not worthy of such manners, for she dared to pull on my sleeve.

"Please," she said, voice full of warning and worry, "Mama, you cannot just enter the king's chambers."

Yanking my arm from her grip, I glared at her with the wrath of the scalding summer sun. No one ever listened to me. No one ever included me in decisions. I had no desire to be a piece in someone's hand, being passed back and forth between two entities who cared not for me nor anyone else.

The sliding door tore open, and I stormed into the king's chambers.

Gone were the red silks and flower petals, but everything else was the same. I stalked forward, swiveling my head until I found the king.

He sat hunched over the omok board, a white stone pinched in his fingers.

My courage flew from my chest, along with my breath, when the king spun his head and looked up at me through his cold eyes. Then Jinyoung came to mind, how when she would braid my hair she would pretend she'd made a mistake and braid it again just because she knew I liked the way it felt, or how she used to sneak me leftovers late in the evening so I could avoid being scolded by my mother.

I unfroze, my anger returning.

My hand rose of its own accord. The sound of the slap crackled like thunder. The red of his face reminded me of the marks on Jinyoung's skin after they'd tied her to the post and tortured her.

A gasp echoed behind me as Haeji processed what I had just done.

I couldn't say I regretted slapping the king.

But perhaps that would change.

The king stood, not quickly with outrage, nor did he break into yelling, and instead he arose slowly, like a snake unwinding to its full height. He looked down at me through narrow slits, and I half expected a forked tongue to dart from his mouth.

Courage truly abandoned me this time. Chills crept along my skin.

I opened my mouth to say something, anything, to ensure I kept my head on my shoulders, but only a feeble squeak came out.

The king reached his hand out, and I winced as his finger gripped my chin.

"To what do I owe the pleasure of my queen seeking me out like this?" he asked with a tone that completely contradicted the warm words. It was low and as frigid as the freezing winters of the north, making my stomach tighten and my body shiver.

Words eluded me as I stared into his dark irises. I could see my reflection in them, my eyes almost as round and wide as my full face.

"I...I..."

Haeji fell to the floor at our feet, her head bowed until her forehead pressed against the wood. "Jeonha, I beg you. Please spare the queen. It is my fault for informing her about Jinyoung. Mama is simply upset at the death of her friend and maid," Haeji said with a shrill tone, her words tumbling out in an attempt to outrun the king's wrath.

Was she crying? Haeji was as emotionless as a log. Why was she pretending to care about what happened to me? Was she just using this to win my trust so she could better spy on me and relay information to the king?

I supposed the notion of spies and who I could trust didn't matter if I died here.

The king took a step closer, his presence consuming the very air as I struggled to breathe. Yes, this was the king my father spoke of, the ruler of rage and wrath who made even his most loyal people shake and shudder.

"Jeonha, the maid was only a friend," she rambled.

"*Friend?*" he asked incredulously.

Haeji nodded, daring to glance up. "Yes. *Friend.* Just a rare connection between servant and master."

Their eyes were locked, and it felt like some sort of secret communication passed between them.

"You should be careful who you choose to attach yourself with, Bora. If you associate with spiders, you are going to get caught in their web," he murmured in a cold warning, releasing his grip on my chin.

I clenched my teeth together to keep the words from spitting from my mouth. My father would protect me; he would always do whatever it took to save me. I repeated those words over and over, begging my body to calm down.

The king's eyes dug into me, his claws ripping my mind apart and baring my thoughts. "Are you thinking about how your father will always rescue you? What about Jinyoung?"

How did he...

"What do you mean?" I squeaked out, my legs trembling beneath my chima.

Wisdom dictated that I stop speaking and beg for forgiveness, but that wasn't fair. I didn't do anything wrong. The king had killed my maid for no reason, or at least not a good one.

"I mean—" He stepped closer like a prowling tiger, and I shuffled back, clutching my hands to my chest until I felt the wall behind me.

With a finger in my face, he scolded, "You should reassess where your loyalty lies. Your father is a great game player, but he has no qualms about discarding his pieces."

Was he implying that if he imprisoned me like Jinyoung, my father would do nothing? That he wouldn't help me?

Forcing myself to meet his steel cold stare, I answered confidently, knowing that my father would not allow me to fall to such a fate, "I am his daughter, of course—"

"Jinyoung was someone's daughter too, and he had no problem using her and then throwing her away. Don't delude yourself that he won't be willing to do the same to you."

My father was cold sometimes and had always been strict with his children, but he loved us. Familial fealty was a sacred bond. This must be what my father meant when he said the king manipulated people. The king was trying to turn me against my father. An argument died on my lips as his frigid gaze bore into me, his jaw clenched. I would rather be alive than right, so I held in my retort.

After a few seconds, his finger disappeared from my face, and I remembered to breathe. I took a step back, my hand going to the left side of my chest to calm my rapidly beating heart. The king rolled his shoulders.

He wasn't going to hit me, was he?

But he didn't harm me, simply waved his hand in the air and said with an unexpected quietness, "Take the queen to say her farewells. Then make sure she rests in her chambers."

"Yes, Jeonha," Haeji stood, her back still bent at the waist in reverence.

Was that code for "kill me"?

I flicked the thought away.

Of course not.

If the king wanted to kill me, he would have done it just a few moments ago. I had certainly given him enough reason too, the five red stripes on his cheek a testament to my treachery.

Rubbing my arms while we walked, I was still not completely convinced that they had no intention to execute me as we wound our way through the palace. Haeji led me back to the dungeons, and dread dug in my stomach.

From the dark and dim corridors to the musty stench permeating the air, this place whispered death. We wove through the halls of cells, and I waited for them to swing open and swallow me. But no one and nothing touched me. Haeji brought me down a different path than last time—when Jinyoung had been alive.

My chest folded in on itself, tightening and crushing my heart. I forced myself to take a breath, and Haeji opened the wooden door of a brick square room.

A body lay on a table in the center, a white cloth draped over the top. Its outline bore the shape of a woman. The smallest rays of light from outside broke through a barred rectangular window on one wall. A lump formed in my throat as I walked to the table. When I pulled back the sheet, my vision blurred, rivers running down my cheeks.

There were no stab wounds, no marks around her neck to indicate a hanging, only the shallow but certainly painful marks from the whip and knife. Her lips were purple though. She must have been executed by poisoning.

I was about to ask Haeji to give us some privacy, but thought better of it. After the stunt I had just pulled, it was not likely my shadow would ever leave my side again. But there were worse things than being watched, than being in a cage, and that was being dead.

Making my way to the head of the table, I gently tugged her hair from underneath her, the long river of black cascading like a waterfall. My hands began to part her damp locks into three sections, wrapping them one at a time over one another.

"The king of the ocean became sick one day," I sniffled and repeated the story Jinyoung had shared with me many times. I continued twisting her hair, mumbling the next part, "The healer said the Ocean King needed the liver of a rabbit to get well. So the Ocean King ordered a sea turtle to go to the land and find him a rabbit."

Haeji had stepped closer, but I paid no heed. This was nothing worthy of spying on, only a simple story to send off my friend.

"The turtle found the rabbit, but of course, if he revealed his true intentions, the rabbit would not go with him. So the turtle deceived the poor creature, regaling the wonders of the ocean, the magnificence of the Ocean Kingdom, of the Sea Dragons—who had no taste for rabbits—and shining palaces where they resided. But the rabbit asked, 'How can I breathe? And I cannot swim.' The turtle told him that the Ocean King had granted his blessing for the turtle to choose one special guest, and that blessing would allow the creature to breathe underwater. As for swimming, the rabbit could hold onto the shell of the turtle. The rabbit agreed, and they both went down to the palace of the Ocean King."

I paused to wipe my nose. "But it was then that the truth was revealed. The Ocean King was a Sea Dragon, and he intended to eat the rabbit's liver. The rabbit cleverly came up with a plan and quickly said, 'I will give you my liver, Great Dragon King. It is an honor to sacrifice myself to such a great being, but I left it on the land. You see, a rabbit's liver is too valuable to travel with, so I leave it in the forest. If the turtle escorts me back, I will bring you my liver.' The Dragon King allowed the turtle to take him back to the land, but a rabbit is much faster on land than a turtle. The rabbit ran off, keeping his liver and his life." I tucked the last lock of hair into place.

"Thank you," I croaked, sniffling as I forced out the words, "for taking such good care of me."

I bent over and tore the corner of the sheet off and fastened the end of the braid with it. Leaning down, I pressed my lips to her cold skin.

"Rest well," I whispered.

Wiping my tears, we left the room, Haeji whispering something, most likely not realizing I could hear. The words felt like a monsoon, crashing into me and flooding me with mixed emotions. I forced myself to keep walking, to not allow her to catch on that I had heard.

Her words stuck in my mind like fish jerky in my teeth. I couldn't get them out no matter how hard I tried to pry them.

Every footstep felt light and heavy at the same time as we walked back to my chambers.

"Jinyoung tried to kill the king, but he still let her die such an easy death. And the queen can't even see who the Dragon King really is."

Those words began to unravel a knot, but I wasn't sure what waited on the other end of the thread.

Chapter 11

Bora

THE MIN ESTATE HAD felt enormous and as vast as a royal residence when I was a child, but with each year I grew, the grounds grew smaller and the walls grew taller. After the age of sixteen, my parents allowed me outside only for festivals and ceremonies and always with a chaperone. After entering the palace, even though my station was greater than the rest of the women in Joseon, the rules were the same. A gaggle of servants stood outside my family's house, the palanquin the same as the one used on my wedding day. I was surprised that Haeji had agreed to stay with the others, but gratitude filled me, a bit of the tension leaving my shoulders.

Home.

It was my first time visiting since marrying the king, and as my eyes soaked in the familiar arched entrance and the wall with tiled tops, my heart ached. Jinyoung would not be in my room, waiting with a sweet treat. Before the tears could form, I inhaled the scent of cherry blossoms wafting into my nostrils. Flowers were always good for the soul.

The wooden gates groaned apart to reveal my father with his arms open wide, a grin wider than the walls that surrounded our villa plastered on his face.

I nearly ran through the entrance, the Min servants closing the doors shut behind, shielding us from the palace servants on the other side.

"My dearest daughter," he bellowed and wrapped his arms around me.

For a moment, I froze. He hadn't hugged me since...since... I couldn't recall actually, but perhaps my absence had made him miss me. I melted into his embrace and curled my arms around his torso. He smelled of cinnamon and ash.

"I can't imagine how difficult it must be to endure being married to that vile man, but don't worry. Your father has a plan," he said with a conspiratorial lilt.

"Actually, it's been rather uneventful, even pleasant at times," I mumbled, shifting my feet as my father released me.

I didn't mention Jinyoung nor my outing with the king. Which, in reality, only comprised a small fraction of my time in the palace. Most of my days were spent in leisure, feeding the fish in the teal ponds of my courtyard, listening to musicians or painting the cranes that flew above the palace and the cherry blossoms that bloomed. Thus it wasn't untruthful of me to say things had been uneventful.

The desire to ask my father about Jinyoung, and more specifically what she had done to end up dead, pestered me like a bug bite, but no matter how much I wished to relieve my itching curiosity, the words were lodged deep down. Had she really been an assassin? And was that why my father had shown no desire to see her free, lest he further implicate himself?

The soft arms that had just embraced me turned stiff, and his hands reached out and dug into my shoulders. "No, you mustn't allow him to manipulate you. He is clever and conniving. You cannot trust his sweet words or faux kindness. Only pain and betrayal lies beneath the façade."

My eyes fell to the ground as he removed his hands, and I muttered, "Yes, Abeonim."

"Good," he said, and his shoulders relaxed. "I need you to gain his trust, and then you need to put this in his tea." He pulled out a tiny ceramic jar, removing the cover to reveal a white powder. "Careful not to inhale any of it," he warned.

My eyes widened, and I jerked my head up. "Is that—"

"Now, now. No need to bother with the specifics," he chided with a grin that didn't quite reach his eyes.

I noticed for the first time the lack of wrinkles by his eyes. Had my father ever truly smiled?

"Just put this into some tea, or better yet, some wine. Your father will take care of the rest."

My arms felt heavy at my side, and I couldn't get myself to meet his eyes. His hand darted out and yanked up my own. He shoved the ceramic into my palm and curled my fingers around it.

"I trust you to make your father proud, Bora," he said with equal parts pride and a threat.

No, not a threat. My father would never harm me, or anyone else. Staring down at the jar, I told myself that it was a harmless drug, maybe even medicine to help calm the king's temperament. I didn't know if such a concoction existed, but it was easier to imagine than the fact that my father wanted to hurt the king. Besides, even if it was something fatal, that man had ordered Jinyoung's death. I nodded at last, and my father stroked my hair.

"Good girl," he said before turning and walking back into the main building.

With my head lowered, I followed him inside, the smooth ceramic burning in my grasp like a hot coal. I tucked it inside a pocket I had secretly sewed into my waistband—originally intended for sneaking some personal items from my room back into the palace. There was a comb Minho had carved for me and a pin Jinho had bought for my last birthday that I wanted, but it appeared I would not be able to take them today. A sickening weight pulled on my stomach.

I forced a smile, because though it was fake, it made me happier, even if it was just a fraction so. A morsel of joy was better than none. Perhaps if I smiled enough, the strange feeling in my stomach would disappear.

When I stepped into the main hall of our home, a pair of arms embraced me.

"Bora!" my eldest brother, Jinho, exclaimed as he squeezed the breath out of me.

"Orabeoni, you're going to really miss me if I die from lack of air," I coughed out.

Jinho released me and offered an apologetic, lopsided smile. "Sorry," he said, scratching his neck.

My second brother, only a couple years older than myself, wheeled himself forward. "Forgive me for not bowing to the queen," Minho said with a mischievous twinkle in his eyes.

I laughed and bent down to hug him. "I am feeling magnanimous today, so I will let you off this once," I said, my lips tugging upward into a grin.

Despite his legs being taken in a terrible accident several years ago, Minho had adjusted as well as one could, finding joy in carving figurines and making model cities out of small pieces of wood. Honestly, the loss of his legs likely hurt less than the cold indifference from our father, who ignored his son ever since—a disgrace to the Min family, as my father had put it, after the doctor confirmed my brother would never walk again.

A gasp of excitement sounded from behind me, and I turned to see my mother and sister entering. My younger sister, Iseul, took a few running leaps towards me, her braid bouncing against her back, but she stopped herself suddenly. She inhaled, placed her hands together in front of her and adjusted her posture, pushing her shoulders back before she took steady steps forward.

I glanced towards my brothers, my eyes asking, *What's wrong with Iseul?*

They both shrugged and shook their heads, trying to hold in their laughs as our youngest sibling strived to walk elegantly.

Iseul stopped in front of me and bowed at her waist. "Mama, thank you for gracing us with your presence," she stated in a deep reverence.

I could hear my brothers snickering, the dam holding back their amusement quickly weakening and on the verge of collapsing. I bit my lip to keep my own laughter inside as Iseul slowly straightened.

"Look who is all grown up," I said affectionately, tucking a stray strand of hair behind her ear.

Iseul smiled, her plump cheeks squishing her eyes. "How did I do?" she asked, her voice hopeful.

"You were the epitome of a poised young woman," I replied, but those words were the final crack in my brother's dam, laughter flooding around us.

All grace left Iseul as she stuck her tongue out at Jinho and Minho, the former leaning on the latter's wheeled chair to brace himself, the cackling shaking his body. Iseul flung herself towards Jinho, who then swung his body behind Minho, using him as a shield to hide from the wrath of the thirteen-year-old girl.

While the two went in circles around a helpless Minho, I turned to face my mother. The last time I had seen her was the day of my wedding, her eyes nearly as red as my wedding hanbok. She had cried often for the entire year of my engagement, pleading with my father to find a way out of the marriage, fearing that she would lose me to the violent king. Obviously, my father had been unsuccessful in avoiding the union.

Gray hair kissed my mother's temple, small wrinkles lining her eyes and lips, and the light of the afternoon sun outlined her in a golden halo. Her eyes traced every inch of me, likely looking for any injuries, but I was fine. The only thing that hurt was my aching heart.

I didn't realize how much I missed my family until now, missed Jinho cracking jokes and coming up with the most outrageous stories about our father's fellow ministers who visited, Iseul imitating what I did—trying to act more mature than her age—and Minho, who would lie and say he was the one to take an extra helping of dessert instead of me. Meanwhile, I was always the one to listen to their complaints and mediate our sibling squabbles. In each other, we had found the affection that our father withheld from us.

And my mother... I missed her scolding and forehead kisses. My mother and I moved at the same time, closing the distance between us in no time at all. We threw ourselves into each other's arms.

She sniffled as she spoke, her voice trembling, full of both joy and fear, "Oh, Bora, I worried the next time I'd see you would be..." She covered her mouth, unwilling to speak the thought.

Because the king was selfish, cruel, and cunning. My father had said as such. My mother believed that. *I* believed that.

Jinyoung's cloth covered body laying on the table, *that* was the true nature of the king.

My eyes were drawn to where my father sat at the end of the main hall, his gaze glued to an omok board, his brows pinched together in cold calculation. The ceramic in my pouch felt like a thousand stones.

Haeji's strange words from that day floated away like a leaf in the breeze, already forgotten and replaced with new ones.

I trust you to make your father proud, Bora.

Determination to make my father smile displaced my discomfort. After I completed this task, maybe he would even play a game of omok with me.

Chapter 12

Bora

SLEEP ELUDED ME FROM the tiny poison powder tucked under my pillow, for fear that Haeji would go snooping and find it. It felt like a hot ember or a pebble in my shoe. I could not ignore it, could not ignore my father's command. Tossing and turning, my mind toiled to figure out how I was going to get it into the king's drink. Sneaking into the kitchens was out of the question, as my body was not exactly prone to silent sneaking, nor would I be able to slip the falcon eyes of Haeji or whoever else was tasked with watching me. Every day, no matter where I went, the court ladies and guards trailed after me.

Even as the sun yawned, yellow fingers of light greeting me through the curtains, I had yet to conjure a concrete plan. My fingers tangled with my tresses, time slowly running out like sand through my hands. There was no way I would be able to hide the poison from Haeji for more than a day, and I already felt the burning gaze of invisible eyes boring into me.

I bolted upright, an idea forming in my mind. I tossed the blankets off and slipped my feet into my silk shoes, heading to a cabinet that held some wedding gifts. I pulled out a box full of floral tea. It would perfectly mask the sweet fragrance that had permeated from the poison.

The sound of the door sliding open caused my heart to skip a beat, my stomach twisting. I placed the ceramic jar in the box and slammed it shut. When Haeji entered, I did my best to smile and to act as I normally did. However, my eyes kept glancing at my pillow. Had some of it spilled out last night? Would Haeji find it and then drag me to dungeons? Maybe my family would see me next in a coffin, fulfilling the king's words and my mother's worries.

No.

My father would keep anything bad from happening to me. I was his precious daughter, and he had promised to take care of everything.

Make him proud.

As Haeji turned to give my worn clothes to one of the maids, I slid the box open and tucked the jar into my hidden pouch. I had moved as swiftly as I could, but my heart was beating as rapidly as a rabbit, certain that Haeji had seen me. If she had, she gave no indication.

I exhaled and smiled. "Haeji, I would like to invite the king to have tea with me."

Her face remained emotionless, except that her gaze narrowed just a hair, a flash of something I could not decipher flickering in her dark irises. It was so small and so brief that I thought I had imagined it, or perhaps a bit of dust or sunlight had gotten into her eyes.

She bowed. "As you wish, Mama. Would you like to send a message or invite him personally?"

With my hair braided and pinned behind my head, I could not twist it, so instead I chewed my lip. I didn't think I had the courage to personally invite the king to drink poison.

"A-A message will do," I stammered.

Don't be nervous. Don't be nervous.

Haeji inclined her head and turned to speak to one of the maids, who scurried out the door.

While the maid went to fetch the king, I tried to convince myself everything was fine. No one had noticed. I could do this.

I stood, smoothing the pink silk of my chima and dangui. "Please have someone fetch some hot water in a teapot, as well as some snacks," I ordered with a voice that didn't sound even a little authoritative.

At least it didn't crack or quiver and reveal my nerves.

My hopes that Haeji would be the one to go and bring me what I asked were quickly smashed when she delegated the task to another maid. It had been a bit naïve in the first place as Haeji was always present. I wondered if she even slept here at night and only pretended to enter my chambers each morning.

Resigning to having my hovering hen with me, I exited my chambers and headed to the pavilion. Cherry blossoms surrounded the elevated structure, one end nestled by the edge of a large pond. Hopefully, the aroma of the flowers would add another layer to hide the presence of the powder in the tea.

One of the multitude of maids that were allotted to my service brought the teapot, a string of steam coiling from its spout.

She placed the ceramic cups and pot on the table, and I looked up at her and asked, "What is your name?"

The woman, who had defined cheekbones and a jaw as sharp as a crane's wings, froze for a moment, her face flushing. Was she scared of me? Certainly not. Then was it my father she feared? He wouldn't hurt anyone without reason though, so as long as she was kind and loyal, what did she have to fear?

That only left the king. The servants must not be used to being shown consideration and care, and who knew what terror they lived in every single day under that man and his violent ways. She could easily be the next Jinyoung.

I reached out and patted her arm, but instead of being comforted by the gesture, she flinched, her eyes widening.

I yanked my hand back. "I'm sorry," I mumbled, turning my face away.

Haeji leaned next to my ear and whispered, "She cannot speak, Mama. Please forgive her silence."

My lips parted as my head whipped towards the woman who had stepped back, her head bowed and cheeks red.

"What is her name?" I whispered back to Haeji.

"Sunhee, Mama," she replied.

Before I could ask why she was mute, the sound of a group of people approaching grabbed my attention. I twisted to see the king striding towards me with a trail of eunuchs and guards.

Suddenly my blood turned cold, the warmth draining from my body, all strength disappearing from my legs.

I moved to stand, but the king waved his hand and said, "No need. Please remain seated."

I sighed in relief. If I'd had to stand, I would have likely collapsed immediately, my legs like limp noodles. What if someone saw me put the powder in the tea? Would one of the nearby guards stab me with his sword? Would the king kill me slowly, relishing my screams? Oh, how I wished I could hurl the ceramic into the pond in front of me, but it was too late to turn back now.

Make him proud.

The king sat, tossing his golden sleeves out of his way. He spread his legs wide, his posture relaxed despite how close our knees were to touching. He had no clue what I had in my possession.

"How was your trip home?" he asked, his voice tinged with the tiniest bit of disdain, as if the very thought of the Mins disgusted him.

I scooted forward, trying to ensure that the table would obscure my hands from the view of those around us.

As I withdrew the ceramic from my pouch, I replied, "It was lovely. I missed seeing my family."

"You see your father often around the palace," he muttered coldly.

I pulled the lid off of the jar. "Yes, but not my mother or siblings."

His stares pierced deep into me. Did he know?

No. Of course not. There was no way he was aware of the powder in my palm.

"Are you close with each other?" he asked with what almost sounded like longing.

"Yes. Of course, siblings have their silly squabbles, but we love each other," I said affectionately, my tone warming as I pictured them all.

"It must be nice," he said, almost too soft for me to hear.

He looked almost pitiful, a shadow shading his face, his shoulders hunching.

He is clever and conniving. My father's words rang in my ears.

Yes. This was an act. He was trying to manipulate me like my father said.

Smiling, I reached for the teapot, wishing the sleeves of my dangui were as vast as the sleeves of the king's robes. It would have been helpful to have some extra cover. Instead, I pulled the pot and cup towards me, doing my best to obscure it from his view as well as the servants all standing behind us. I trusted that the pond that sprawled in front of us would not spill my secret.

I poured the brown tea into the cup, letting the powder snow down into the liquid. After I finished, I tucked the jar back up my sleeve and placed the steaming in front of the king.

He nodded his head in thanks, but he did not reach out to drink it right away.

My stomach knotted like a norigae, my courage fraying like the tassels that dangled from the string ornament. Sweat dripped down my back. My eyes refused to budge from the small ceramic cup filled with camellia tea. The white powder had disappeared entirely, well dissolved by the warm liquid. My fingers curled into my chima.

At last, the king reached out and grasped the cup, time seeming to slow as he brought it to his lips.

I shouldn't stare so intently at him, or it would become too obvious. But would looking away not arouse more suspicion?

Deep breaths, Bora, I encouraged myself.

My father's face flashed through my mind, and I could almost feel his arms embracing me and hear his compliments, telling me how happy he was to have me as a daughter. But then that image was replaced with the king, his sharp eyes and pink lips, of him carrying bouncing children on his back.

I could not fail my father for such foolish facades. All of it was an act.

But then soil-crusted, tiny fingers floated in my vision, a gaggle of children squealing like high pitched chimes while the king laughed richly as he chased them around. Their beaming faces when he handed them each a coin, a small circle that held a month's worth of food for them, was engraved in my memory.

He knew their names. He knew each face. No one could put on such an elaborate performance. Who would look after Minhyeok and Daeun? What would happen to the village children if the king was replaced? There were only a few living members of the Yi clan, and there was no guarantee the next would be kinder. He had said that many were orphans. I could not take him away from them.

My father was not as bad as the king made him out to be, but he could be fallible. And he was certainly *wrong* this time.

Breaking through my memories, my father's smile disappeared, replaced with a frown and flaming eyes.

I had never disobeyed him in my entire life.

The king parted his lips to drink.

"Jeonha, no!" I shouted, darting forward and knocking the cup to the ground, the ceramic shattering, and the tea seeping into the wooden floor of the pavilion.

I fell back into my seat, my chest heaving and my eyes heavy and unable to meet his own. I scolded myself for how conspicuous I had been. Everyone would be suspicious. There was no excuse that was believable for why I shouted and batted the cup away from him. I couldn't even feign innocence, for how would I know to stop him from drinking a poison if I wasn't responsible for it being in his drink in the first place?

In my head, I apologized to my mother. Hopefully, the king would keep my body intact and allow me a proper burial. I closed my eyes and clutched my chima, preparing to feel the pain of the guard's blade.

"Why'd you stop me from drinking the poison?" he asked, his words steady and soft like a calm spring breeze.

My eyes flung open, and my head jerked up.

"You knew?" I gasped.

How did he know? Why was he going to drink it? Was this a test?

He leaned forward and reached out a hand, and I flinched. What was he going to do to me? He paused for a breath before continuing, his finger brushing my cheek and moving a stray strand of hair out of my face.

"It would be an honor to drink your poison," he whispered, his voice lilting in a playful manner.

I inhaled sharply, my eyes staring into his, wondering why he would say such a thing. Was he playing with his prey, lulling me into a sense of security before killing me? The king had every reason to be suspicious of me due to my father, and now he had every reason to end my life. I had almost killed the king, and death was the only punishment befitting such a crime.

He leaned back, my face cold where his hand had just been. "Besides," he said, "I know it was your father's doing."

Was he going to kill my father? My whole family?

I moved towards him, my knees colliding with the table and shaking its contents with a rattle. I ignored the biting pain.

"Please, don't kill him," I pleaded, tears welling into my eyes.

The king cocked a brow, a flash of what I thought was anger blazing through his eyes. "For you, I will let him off this once."

I sighed with relief, my shoulders relaxing. "Thank you," I whispered with a sniffle.

Pleading for my father's life had come so naturally, but for the first time, I doubted if he would do the same for me.

Chapter 13

Seojun

POISON WAS ONE OF the ministers' favorite methods, and the most expensive ones were nearly unidentifiable. Fortunately for me, I had begun poisoning myself since my adolescence, gradually building up a tolerance to many of them. Of course, that meant my body was weak during that time, and thus my skill with weapons was limited. I had done my best to make up for it in training once I became king along with surrounding myself with skilled guards like Dongbin and Minje.

Blades were not the Mins' specialty anyways.

When Bora had invited me to have tea with her, excitement and cynicism warred inside me. Was she showing me her loyalty or was she trying to gain my trust in order to take me down? A naïve part of me prayed for the former, and I couldn't help but smile as I made my way to the queen's section of the palace.

All joy had drained when I caught sight of a speck of white powder perched on Bora's finger, my suspicions confirmed by the strangely sweet aroma that wafted from the warm drink.

As much as I wanted to dismiss it, or blame someone else, that little white dot shattered my heart. Haeji would judge me for having allowed Bora into it at all. There was a reason I only talked about the queen to Dongbin, as he was a sappy romantic compared to the cynical court lady.

My mind filed through all the poisons, and between the color of the powder and the sweet, floral scent—different from the camellia tea that attempted to mask it—I figured it was most likely Phoenix's Crown, an aroma that reminded me of my father.

Luckily for me, and unluckily for Councilor Min, I took pills every morning that neutralized most poisons, including this one. Most others I'd become immune to by now, and as for the rest... Well, if a poison I couldn't cure existed, then I supposed it was heaven's will that I die.

A small part of me still wanted to believe in Bora, so I'd decided to give her one last chance to prove her loyalty. I would even accept her disloyalty to me, so long as she forfeited her fealty to her father—becoming some neutral party in our power struggle.

She didn't need to love me; she just needed to not want me dead.

That would be enough.

So I picked up the cup, my heartbeat slowing and time crawling through mud as I lifted the drink to my lips, my arm heavy as if my sleeve were laden with stones. Every breath stabbed my chest, the closing distance increasing the pressure in my heart. Why didn't she stop me? Was she really going to let me drink it? Even after all these weeks in the palace, she still wanted me dead?

The fact that Bora had stopped me and had not gone through with her father's bidding was proof enough that my belief in her was well founded. Hope bloomed brighter in my chest. A breath rushed from my lungs, my lips curling into a faint smile, while the shards of the cup laying shattered on the floor. The relief was not from the avoidance of the poison, but from the fact that she had stopped me, chosen me.

Although I knew her father had put her up to this, knew she was not cruel, I hadn't known if she could defy him.

But she had.

"Please don't kill him," she pleaded with water in her eyes, her voice breaking as she begged.

She still had the audacity to plead for her father's life? I held in my desire to punch the pillar of the pavilion. How could she not comprehend the gravity of attempting to kill the king?

Haeji would have one more reason to scold me, because whether it was the way her voice broke or the tears in her eyes, the words slipped from my mouth.

"For you, I will let him off this once."

Her shoulders slumped, and she exhaled, her normal color returning to her face. She raised a hand to wipe her eye, but before she could make contact with her skin, I lurched forward. I yanked her hand towards me, her eyes widening to full moons.

"What are you doing?" she gasped, attempting to tug her arm away.

I tightened my grip but not enough to hurt her.

Leaning forward until her fingertip was a breath from my lips, I warned, "Careful. I can let your father off for hurting me, but not for hurting you."

Her brow bunched in confusion, another question poised on her lips, but before she could say anything, I licked the top of her finger where the white speck had been.

A shout of surprise escaped her lips. She yanked her hand away and clutched it to her chest.

"J-J-Jeonha," she stuttered, red blooming on her cheeks.

Her eyes were darting everywhere like a bee, everywhere except me.

Shaking my head with a slight smile, I leaned back and pointed to her hand that she still tucked to her chest. "Before you accept any powders, perfumes, or other probable poisons, I recommend asking what they are and how their toxin spreads. Phoenix's Crown can be deadly when inhaled or ingested." I paused, wiggling my finger in the air before gesturing to my eye. "Or absorbed by sensitive areas."

Her face drained of color as she realized what I meant. I wondered if she recalled the words I had spoken concerning Jinyoung, and more importantly, her. Her father had no qualms about using his daughter, hence the strong insistence I marry her in the first place.

I had loathed the idea of marrying the daughter of the Chief State Councilor and had done my best to find a way of avoiding it. For once, I was glad I had failed to foil his plan.

With one leg sat atop the wide seat of my dragon throne, my arm hanging loosely over my knee, I steeled my face into a cold apathy. There could be no weakness in front of wolves.

Councilor Min obscured his mouth with his ceremonial scepter, his back bent in a show of respect, but his reverence was as shallow as a puddle of piss. I didn't deign to look at him, instead digging at some imaginary soil under my fingernails. I allowed the silence to hang in the air until the ministers' feet shuffled and whispers creeped between them.

Let them squirm. Let their minds struggle to predict what I was thinking.

At last, when the silence began to get to me, I waved my hand for the Chief State Councilor to rise.

"Speak," I said nonchalantly, as if I was bored, as if I couldn't bother with being king that day. These performances were annoying but necessary. I just needed a little more time, a little more power, and then I could finally pull the weeds from my court.

The words that left his mouth felt like a punch to the stomach, the air rushing from my lungs as my chest and fists tightened.

"Jeonha, myself and many of my fellow officials have a petition pertaining to the security of Joseon. Please accept this proposal

for the marriage of my eldest daughter, Min Bora, to the king of Joseon."

Ignoring the blood rushing and roaring in my ears, I forced myself to breathe, to relax my white knuckles.

My laughter echoed in the hall like a gong—hard, slow, and drawn out.

"I thought I had made myself clear concerning my marriage, that I was discussing with Minister Song about a union with one of his daughters," I replied, working hard to maintain a confident calm to my voice.

The Song family was new to the noble class, having obtained it through the current patriarch's father through merit and passing a series of Kwago. They had few alliances due to their lack of long-standing prestige that many of the other families looked down upon. They had yet to join a faction, and thus would be loyal to me without being powerful enough to attempt to control me or my court.

A sly smirk peeked from behind Councilor Min's scepter, and he twisted and called out, "Minister Song, please tell the king what you told me."

My blood turned cold, all the warmth having been sucked out of the room. Minister Song shuffled out from the back row of officials, his skin pallid and slick with sweat, his eyes darting from the floor, to Councilor Min, and to me. He came to a stop just a few steps behind the Chief State Councilor and bowed. He trembled like tree branches in a breeze.

Whatever plans I had prepared had apparently already unraveled.

Minister Song confirmed my fears as he spoke in a quivering voice, "J-Jeonha, I am a-afraid that I c-c-cannot offer my d-daughter for marriage."

"And why is that?" I asked, my words as tapered and sharp as a blade.

Minister Song collapsed to his knees and pressed his forehead to the floor, his long, cobalt sleeves pooling around his head. "Forgive me, Jeonha! My daughter has brought great shame to our family and has not kept her chastity. She is unfit to marry the king."

My eyes were pinned on the Chief State Councilor while Minister Song spoke. The subtle twitching of his lips confirmed who was responsible for the Song daughter's sudden loss of her chastity, effectively disqualifying her from becoming queen. A wolf was indifferent to the pain of its prey. Such a man cared not for the fact that he had ruined her life, and she would have a hard time finding a husband in Joseon. If her father favored her, perhaps she would not be cast out, would be allowed to stay with her family and under their care. In the event that that wasn't the case, I made a note to ask Dongbin to help her. Minje would need to find the man Councilor Min had hired for the assault. It would be the only justice the Song daughter could receive until I was able to convict the councilor and his co-conspirators.

For now, I needed to find a way to evade the petition, to refuse the proposed marriage between myself and the Min daughter.

Perhaps not.

Maybe having a hostage would benefit me.

Or maybe it would be the end of me, allowing the wolf's cub into my chambers.

Chapter 14

Bora

During the night, I had nightmares of being hauled off to the dungeons in chains for attempting to poison the king, but during the day, I dreamed of his hand holding mine, his words playing over and over again in my head: *"I can let your father off for hurting me, but not for hurting you."*

What did that mean? Well of course, I knew what it meant, but I didn't understand *why*.

My ponderings were interrupted when all of sudden, Dongbin—who had accompanied us to the village and was present for my poor poisoning attempt yesterday—appeared, the broad-shouldered and wide-faced guard striding towards the pavilion Haeji and I were sitting under. Upon seeing him, Haeji arose and the two stood out of earshot, mumbling low, their sounds indecipherable. I cocked a brow, wondering what they were whispering about.

After a few more breaths, they broke apart.

Haeji bowed and said with a monotone voice, "Apologies, Mama, but I have some matters to attend to. Dongbin will watch over you and attend to you while I am away."

I nodded. It didn't matter if I asked where she was going as she wouldn't answer, and if I asked her not to go, she wouldn't obey. Seeing as Dongbin was the one to come, it was most likely the king had called for her.

Was there something between them? Kings often had affairs with palace ladies, and most kings had a multitude of concubines. The thought of the king taking on a harem made my stomach turn. I shook my head to banish such thoughts. Whether the king took more women was not my choice, not something I had control over. Harems were a dangerous place, though. Haeji seemed nice, even if she was a spy. If she did become a concubine, I would make sure she received good treatment. Maybe she would even help me keep the other concubines from fighting with each other.

But then thoughts of the king's hand holding mine once more entered my mind. I chewed my lip, and my brows furrowed.

"Dongbin," I mumbled softly, slowly gathering the courage to ask my question.

"Yes, Mama," the guard replied.

What was I doing asking one of the king's most trusted guards? But I wanted answers and had few options to cure my curiosity.

"What do you think of the king? How does he treat you?" I inquired, rubbing my thumb along the smooth wood of the paintbrush in my hand.

"The king is..." he paused, mulling over his words as if he were chewing a tough piece of meat. "His methods are unconventional but clever, and he always treats me with respect despite the fact I am his subject. He asks how my family is, how I'm feeling. But he also isn't afraid to use me for..." He glanced at me before slowly stating, "uncouth but necessary tasks. He cares for the commoners, as you saw yourself."

It was to be expected that the king's loyal guard would speak only well of his master, but he was right. I had seen for my own eyes his kindness towards the low-class children, and he had spared me despite my poisoning attempt. This was not the mad and violent ruler that my father had told us about at dinners.

The king was perhaps not so vile as my father had said, but what did that make my father?

A liar?

The poison would have made him a murderer, and I had almost become one myself.

Haeji had returned rather quickly, and the conversation between Dongbin and myself was cut short. After moving to my chambers, we sat, and she brushed my hair. I could make out the murky shape of her in the bronze mirror. Who was she before coming to the palace? Why was she so loyal to the king? Although absolute fealty was demanded for any servant to their master and any subject to their ruler, it had not prevented many a coup before.

"Haeji, tell me about yourself. Even if it is just a lie," I muttered with a long breath, my finger twisting a lock of hair.

She paused her brushing. "Mama—"

"I already know you report to the king. But I would still like us to get along, even if it is a farce." I may not be able to change my circumstances, but I could make the best of them.

Clearing her throat as she hurried to resume her combing, Haeji started slowly, "I was the daughter of a kitchen worker at one of the restaurants in the capital."

"And your father?" I asked, rubbing strands of hair between my fingers.

"Dead. I killed him."

The hair fell from my fingers. In the bronze mirror, I could see my own shocked face, and that Haeji's eyes were trained on that expression. I rushed to clamp my mouth shut and smooth my features.

"He raped my mother, so when I grew old enough, I hunted him down and dispensed my own justice," she murmured in a low voice, her brush strokes surprisingly light despite the heavy words that she spoke.

This was no lie. A subtle pain glowed in her eyes at the recollection—an anguish and anger dulled but still present despite time passing by. I turned around and squeezed her hand.

She swallowed, saying nothing, but she didn't retreat from my touch.

"Didn't the officials at the Ministry of Justice help? Couldn't your mother report what happened to them?"

Haeji removed her hand from mine, her voice hardening. "Reporting a crime is easy, getting someone to believe you is difficult. Maybe it is not so in the noble class, but for the rest of us, justice does not come so easy. You need to have money or connections to someone important. If you have neither, then revenge waits for the afterlife or those willing to take it in this one."

I slowly turned around, shame burning my skin. "Oh. I didn't realize."

She continued her story. "The king found me in the dungeons back when he was still the Crown Prince. He said it was a shame for someone with my aptitude for finding people and dispatching them to just die. Although I needed to work on the 'not getting caught' part." Her voice filled with a warmth, her tone softer than before as she explained, "I am certain he came to know the circumstances of the case, and took pity on my plight, on the plight of many women in Joseon. He gave me the choice, be executed, exiled, or..." A faint smile tugged at her lips as she recalled, "I could join him and help fight such injustices, even if our methods were at times unorthodox."

What did that mean? It sounded like the king didn't mind sacrificing people for his goals, didn't blink at a little collateral damage. Still... What he had done for Haeji was noble. He collected another factor in his favor. The children and Haeji showed that he was capable of kindness, but Jinyoung showed he was equally capable of evil. It was impossible that Haeji was unaware of my servant's situation. How could she be okay with it? And the court officials that had been killed or exiled, were they not dispatched simply for displeasing the king?

My head was starting to ache. There was a missing piece somewhere, or if I was being honest, hidden and repressed. They said Jinyoung was an assassin—although my father may not admit it—and he had also given me poison to kill the king. I had even told the tale of "The Rabbit Liver" to Jinyoung, one that she had often retold to me...

Who the Dragon King truly was, was slowly being revealed despite my best efforts to ignore it.

"Thank you for sharing, Haeji. I am sorry for your loss," I murmured, staring down at my hands.

"It was a long time ago," she replied quietly.

Raising onto my knees, I scooted around and embraced her, her body stiff in my arms. "Still. I am sorry."

When I pulled away, a faint wetness glistened her eyes, her nose turning red. "Please excuse me, Mama," she rasped and leapt to her feet, shuffling quickly out of the room.

I didn't need an attendant to go to sleep anyways. After resting my head against the pillow, sleep claimed me, but it wasn't a restful night.

The grid of the omok board stared up at me, a white stone pinched between my fingers. Across from me sat the king, who was placing a black piece, creating a cross with three stones in each line. No matter what I did, he would win in two turns.

As his stone met the board with a click, he did not smirk despite his looming victory, and instead his lip puffed out, a tear sliding down his cheek. "Bora," he rasped, his voice straining—broken. "Why did you have to kill me?"

"I didn't! I stopped you from drinking the tea!"

He lifted his head, a trickle of blood slithering out of his nostril. I dropped the omok piece in my hand, the stone clattering to the floor.

"Can't you see that your father is a threat to Joseon? Can't you see—"

The king couldn't finish his sentence, the figure of my father replacing him. While the king's face had been filled with sorrow, my father's was shadowed and sinister, a sneer slicing his lips as he placed the winning piece on the board. "You did well, Bora. Fealty to your family is a virtue."

No. No. No.

What my father was doing was not virtuous. The king was not the tyrant he told us he was. Jinyoung, no matter my affection for her, intended to assassinate the king by order of my father.

He was a liar. He was a killer.

"*I will not play your game anymore,*" I cried out, knocking the bowl of omok stones off the table, the sound of their clatter echoing around us.

My father lurched over the table and clamped his hand around my throat. I jerked away but could not free myself of his grip. My fingers clawed at his hand, drawing red lines on his skin, but still he did not release me.

"*If you will not do what I say, then you are not my daughter,*" he snarled.

"Let it be so," I croaked.

Then everything went dark.

Chapter 15

Bora

THE NIGHTMARE HAD NOT yet faded from my memory by the time I woke up, and a deep discomfort remained in my heart. The rainy season was still a good way off, the monsoons favoring the later summer months, but today the skies were dark and heavy, a wetness to the air that matched my melancholy mood. Nightmares had been plaguing me almost as much as guilt had.

Unfilial daughter. Murderer. Traitor.

A flurry of shameful thoughts raged in my head.

I had lied to myself that day when I visited home, had deceived myself into believing that my father was not the greedy minister that the king made him out to be. What was I supposed to do now?

Without realizing it, my feet had carried me to the threshold of my hallway, the skies beginning to sprinkle.

One step. Two steps.

My skin became wet, my hair growing heavy with water. But instead of turning around, I lumbered forward.

"Mama, please go inside," Haeji urged.

But the rain was a friend who joined my weeping, who disguised it so it was a private affair between the two of us.

Haeji rushed to cover me with a bamboo umbrella, but I moved away, scorning the shelter.

"You will get sick if you get wet," she wailed with worry-soaked words.

Why did she care? Spies weren't supposed to be concerned for the wellbeing of their targets.

"Leave me be," I croaked.

But as the raindrops and my tears mixed together and my face pointed to the ash, swollen skies, I allowed myself to grieve at the cracking vase of my world. There was little opportunity to be alone with my sorrow, but in that moment, the heavens lamented with me. An onlooker would see only the wet face of one in the rain, not the deep sobs of a broken woman.

She took another step toward me, the umbrella outstretched. "Mama—"

"Haeji, that is a command!" I snapped between sobs.

At last she relented, watching from under the canopy of the parasol with pursed lips.

Collapsing to my knees, my emotions spilled over with my tears. I missed Jinyoung. I missed my siblings. I missed not having to worry about dying.

I never wanted this marriage.

This was all too much for me.

Why did I have to choose sides? Why couldn't they just get along? No matter what I did, I couldn't win. I lost my friend, and soon I was bound to lose more—my family, my honor, or even my life. Who was deceiving me was too difficult to discern. What did my father gain from lying to me?

I wasn't prepared for all this.

My breaths grew more rapid as my thoughts ran wild. Tears dripped from my eyes faster than the raindrops fell from the sky.

All of a sudden, the pelting rain waned, and I peered up into a wing of crimson fabric draping over me.

The king didn't deign to meet my eyes as he commented casually, "You will get ill."

"Why do you care?" I asked, whimpering.

Shouldn't he celebrate my demise?

No.

Those were the sentiments planted by my father.

The king had been merciful to me on multiple occasions. He had even saved me from the poison. Why did I still think badly of him? Why did I desire so strongly to hold onto the hope that my father was not a monstrous minister and a terrible parent?

The vase shattered completely, my heart breaking into a thousand pieces.

But perhaps there was still hope for my father, perhaps I could convince him to cease his grappling for more power. Maybe there was a way to repair things, to put the pieces back together.

I peered up at the king, water droplets clinging to my eyelashes. "What are you doing here, Jeonha?"

"Am I not allowed to visit my queen?"

"Well, you had no desire to see me on our own wedding day," I pointed out, sniffling.

He turned, lifting his other arm to shield me while the rain showered his own head. "I am sorry about that. It was unfair of me to disrespect you like that."

My eyes widened at his words.

The king was actually apologizing?

"Please return to your rooms. Your father will not be pleased if you become sick," he added.

A laugh burst from my lips, the king's brows lifting at the unexpected sound.

"I wasn't aware you were concerned with what my father thought."

"I'm not."

"Be honest, please. Do you want to kill me?"

"No," he responded immediately, as if he didn't even need to think about it.

Was he lying? Why had I asked if I wasn't willing to believe his answer?

Since I had started this game, I might as well keep going. "Do you want my father dead?"

He paused before answering this time, hesitation drawn on his features. "Yes."

His eyes studied my face, waiting, perhaps, for shock or anger. But I had none to give. The two were locked in a battle, but maybe I could be the key to finally ending it.

"Thank you for telling me the truth," I said, slowly standing to my feet, the king gently helping to pull me up.

As we walked back, the king held his sleeve over my head all the way to the entrance of the hall.

I rested my chin on my palm, staring blankly at the omok board, black and white stones checkering the wooden square, but neither close to obtaining victory. I sighed, my mind wandering. It seemed like the king had two sides to him, but I couldn't discern which was the true one. What was a façade and what was genuine?

A voice broke me from my thoughts.

"There is someone who is asking to see you, Mama," Haeji said as she leaned to look at my face.

"I'm not in the mood to see anyone right now," I grumbled.

"Not even if I brought kimchi-jeon?" a voice deep and rich like honey rang from behind me.

"You cannot enter without the queen's permission!" Haeji scolded and charged at the owner of the voice.

As I turned, my eyes widened, and a smile bloomed on my lips.

"Haeji, stop. It's fine," I exclaimed, leaping to my feet.

In the year and half since I had seen him, his voice had grown deeper and his body thinner, no longer the chubby boy from our childhood. But Ryu Hanbin's almond-shaped amber eyes and black hair that never liked to stay in a neat pile on his head—a few strands always escaping the confines of his hairpiece—were the exact same.

A green robe with a single crane on the chest hung over his body.

"You passed the Kwago!" I shouted, the grin still plastered on my face.

Hanbin returned the smile, his eyes squishing into crescents. "Yes. It was my second time, but I always told you I would pass no matter how many times I had to take them."

I closed the distance between us and grabbed the hand that was empty, his other occupied with a cloth full of what I assumed were kimchi-jeon, the slightly sour smell drifting to my nose. As soon as our hands met, a spark flashed in Hanbin's eyes. He must've been so happy at passing the Kwago.

"Thank you, Bora," he whispered, his voice coming out strained.

Did he have a sore throat? Perhaps he had been studying too hard that he had neglected his health. He was always a passionate person who pushed himself to extremes. Even as a child, he had often hurt himself by trying to climb trees the highest or skip a stone across the pond the farthest. His competitive nature drove him past his limits, and it reminded me of another man I knew.

"It is improper to address the queen in such an intimate manner," Haeji scolded from behind us.

My cheeks flushed, and I dropped his hand, a shadow casting over Hanbin's face. Why did she have to ruin our reunion? Although I had been unable to meet Hanbin alone once we became of age, we still met often when our families gathered. The Ryus and Mins were closely tied by marriage, one person from each generation always marrying into the other family.

Hanbin shook the shadow from his face and held up the cloth containing food. He untied the top to reveal the savory pancakes, the green onions the only spot of color amongst the orange circle.

"You remembered," I gasped and reached for them, my cheeks hurting from my wide grin.

He yanked them back out of my reach, a smirk sprawling on his lips. "Just because you are queen now, you think you get to take what you like for free?"

I crossed my arms over my chest and rolled my eyes, but no one would be fooled into thinking I was annoyed due to the smile on my face. Oh, how I missed my friend. Since Jinyoung was gone, I was alone. Although I had Haeji, it was nice to have someone who knew me as Bora and not the queen, who cared about me instead of suspecting me.

"Then how about this," I suggested slyly. "Let's play omok. If I win, I get *all* the pancakes for myself."

"And if I win?" he asked, his gaze fixated on my own and his voice filled with an eagerness whose source I couldn't quite identify.

"Then I will grant you a wish," I said, shrugging.

Hanbin took a step closer, but I remained in place, unwilling to forfeit any space to him. I could be just as competitive when I wanted to. I stared back at him, refusing to look away first.

"A queen must honor her word," he spoke with a sudden seriousness.

I nodded, cocking my brow at his unexpected earnest expression and tone. "Of course."

At last he stepped back and gestured towards the pavilion where I had been sitting and where the omok board lay waiting. I pivoted on my heel and strode towards the low-lying table and cushions. I flung my layered chima, and they fluttered as I sat. Hanbin sat across from me, both of us doing our best to ignore the disapproving look on Haeji's face, her lips turned down in a frown and her brows pinned together.

We cleared the board, the omok pieces clinking into the ceramic bowls like rain against a roof. One bowl lay on each side of the board, and Hanbin gestured to the one containing the black stones.

"Ladies first," he said with a honey coated tone, slick and sweet.

I shook my head but couldn't help but smile. I didn't think I had been so happy since entering the palace, and I wished that our match would never end, that this breath of peace, this moment of joy, wouldn't end.

Plucking a black stone from the ceramic, I placed it in the middle of the board. Hanbin reached and grabbed his white piece, setting it a few lines away from my own. I cocked a brow and looked up at him, as it was not his usual strategy. In the past, he always followed me, his pieces directly next to mine like a shadow I couldn't escape.

"What?" he asked, having noticed my curious stare.

"You've changed how you play," I commented as I created the beginnings of an *L* shape.

With a shrug and smirk, he replied, "A lot has changed since we last met, but we will always share our childhood memories."

He was creating a cross, setting himself up in a strategy that I felt like I had seen recently but could not recall when or where.

I sighed, placing a black piece at the end of another line in order to block his row before it made it to five. "That was definitely a simpler time, and I can't believe it has already been a year since we last saw each other."

"Too long," Hanbin mumbled so quietly that I almost didn't catch it.

A sadness clung to his face, but he replaced it with his normal jovial expression. He was always so outgoing and positive, and it seemed like that part of him hadn't changed.

"How is life in the palace?" he inquired, placing a white piece on the board, encircling my own.

I pinched my black piece in between my fingers until they became pale. "It's been...fine."

"How does the king treat you?" Concern painted his eyes, and his brows dragged down.

I glanced at Haeji before muttering a reply, "Fine."

Hanbin's lips pursed into a hard line, and he reached out and placed his hand atop mine, covering the omok pieces beneath us. His skin was warm and comforting, and his touch sent me back to a simpler time.

He glared at Haeji from the corner of his eyes as he leaned forward and whispered, "If he ever hurts you, let me know."

My other hand reached over and patted his, and I offered a faint smile. "He would never harm me."

Indeed the king hadn't harmed me, but I was still not confident that it was not his way of manipulating me in order to use me as a weapon against my father. A headache began to form again as I tried to reconcile all the things I experienced over the past two months with the beliefs I had held since I was young.

"Does he love you?" Hanbin asked, his expression sadder and his voice even more so.

Was he pitying my situation?

"No. Of that I am certain. But I do not think love is something often shared between kings and queens. He treats me well, and that is all that matters."

"The Bora I knew would have dreamed of love," he replied with a bit of a bite.

"Aren't you thinking of Iseul?" I threw back with a laugh.

He shook his head, leaning over the table as he reminisced, "Don't you remember when you were about seven? You vowed to marry me if I climbed the peach tree to bring you fruit. You even gave me the pit of the peach as a promise."

I scratched behind my ear, glancing at where Haeji stood, hoping she didn't hear what Hanbin had said. "I-I don't recall that."

"I could never forget," he whispered.

"I don't think—"

"I win," Hanbin interrupted triumphantly, a crescent grin beaming from his lips.

I had been so lost in conversation that I had let him win in so few moves. I sighed but smiled. "Alright, what do you want?"

He made a show of contemplation, rubbing his chin as he scrunched his brows. "Hmm..." Hanbin leaned across the board, a faint scent of cinnamon and ash wafting from his clothes. "Accompany me at the Lotus Lantern Festival," he murmured so softly that only I could hear.

Glancing at Haeji from the corner of my eye, I could see her straining to hear Hanbin's words.

"You know that is impossible. If I go at all, it will be with the king," I whispered back.

"Then just break away to light a lantern with me. It will only take a few minutes," he replied, his tone almost sounding like he was begging, his eyes sparkling with hope that I would accept.

"I'll try, but that's all I can promise," I murmured.

He leaned back, his smile even wider as he gave a shrug and a nod. "That's good enough for me. I'll wear something that you will be sure to recognize."

I shifted under Haeji's intense stare, urging my cheeks not to betray me and turn red like a lantern.

Chapter 16
Seojun

A LACK OF SLEEP plagued me often. Worries made it hard for my mind to settle, and although Dongbin warned against it, walks around the palace helped me. After a lap around the pond near my quarters, my feet once more wandered to the queen's quarters.

From a distance, I observed Bora. She sat in front of a canvas with one of her attendants seated nearby, the maid posing for the painting, the area illuminated by the lanterns and moonlight. I was too far away to hear what they were saying, but I could see that both their faces radiated happiness, eyes bright like the rising moon above, laughter chiming through the air. The woman appeared relaxed around the queen. Interesting.

Even though I wished to partake in the smiles—to be the source of hers—I decided not to interrupt.

A thump sounded behind me, and my hand darted to the dagger hidden in my sleeve. But when I turned around, a familiar pair of eyes greeted me.

I dropped my hand back to my side. "I told you not to sneak up on me, Minje."

"Apologies, Jeonha, but it was urgent." He stood, taking off the cloth covering the bottom half of his face.

"Lead the way," I barked, and my guard quickly strode down the hallway, my fast footsteps following behind.

He brought me to my quarters, a familiar metallic scent stinging my nose. Another guard slid open the door, and I stormed through. On the floor, Dongbin cradled the head of Gweonho, a young man—a boy, really, no more than fifteen. Blood dribbled from lips, his eyes dulling.

I shouted to the guard at the door, "Go get a physician!"

As that guard left, Minje stationed himself by the entrance while I focused back on Dongbin and the boy.

Upon seeing me, Gweonho smiled feebly, rasping, "Jeonha, I'm sorry."

I rushed to them, my knees slumping to the ground. Taking his hand that was so much smaller than mine, I shook my head. "You have nothing to apologize for Gweonho. I am so proud of you."

"I didn't say anything. I promise," he croaked.

Dongbin jutted his chin down to the boy's other hand where it lay over his stomach. Every fingernail was gone, every finger bent in an unnatural shape. Bile rose in my throat, my blood boiling.

"As expected of the bravest man in Joseon," I said, forcing my gaze to his bruised face.

The boy's breathing grew slower, each inhale wheezing and laborious. Still, he managed to speak, "I heard they plan on intercepting the supplies for Gangwon-do. Councilor Oh will claim bandits stole it, and—"

A coughing fit cut off his sentence, crimson spraying from his mouth.

I stroked his head. "Shh... You are going to be alright." I glanced over my shoulder, cursing silently as the physician had still not come.

When I looked back at Dongbin, he shook his head subtly. Gweonho wasn't going to make it. The boy coughed once more, weaker this time, his strength waning.

I'm going to kill them all.

Gweonho interrupted my dark thoughts. "Thank you, Dongbin, for coming for me."

"Of course. I never leave a man behind," my guard said with water-filled eyes.

Despite his years in the military and then as a member of my Royal Guard, he managed to hold onto his compassion, a softness he protected despite the evil he'd witnessed.

Gweonho's grip of my hand relaxed, slipping from my palm as he took one last shallow breath. Then his chest stilled.

My body began to shake, my teeth clenching together. Although I wished to send guards to each of the councilors' estates and drag them out for execution, the time was not yet right, their influence over the court still too strong, and my evidence against them too weak.

I'm sorry, Gweonho. I cannot avenge you tonight.

Steps stormed toward my chambers.

"The physician is here," Minje announced.

"Send him back," I growled. "He is too late."

Dongbin gently set the boy's body on the floor, and in an unusual show of rage, he threw a ceramic. It shattered against the wall, pieces clinking to the ground.

I crossed Gweonho's hands over his chest, careful with his broken hand despite him not being able to feel the pain anymore.

I stood and reached up, squeezing Dongbin's shoulder. "Go rest." Before he could protest, I turned to Minje. "Go make sure Gweonho's body is cleaned up and arrange for a proper burial," I ordered.

"Yes, Jeonha," the two replied solemnly.

Minje called for two attendants, and a couple of eunuchs entered, unfazed by the dead boy. I grabbed one of my sleeping robes and spread it across Gweonho. As the eunuchs and Minje took away the shrouded body, I followed them out into the hall, pausing outside my doors and watching them disappear around the corner. Soft footsteps sounded to my right, the faint smell of flowers drifting in the air, mixing with the scent of blood. I didn't turn to look.

Haeji rushed towards Dongbin as he stepped into the hall. Scarlet smeared his uniform and coated his hands.

"Is it yours?" the court lady demanded, grabbing his hands and inspecting them.

"No," my guard replied quietly.

"I'll help you wash up," she offered, pausing to look back at me.

I nodded my head, and the two took off towards the guard's quarters.

"Who was that?" Bora asked, coming up next to me.

"A servant."

"I didn't think a servant would warrant such a reaction."

"They do to me." I crossed my arms.

"What was his job?"

"To gather information."

"And he was killed for that?" She tilted her head.

"Overhearing important conversations is as good as having an arrow pointed at someone's head."

For the first time, I was angry at Bora, at her ignorance, at her devotion to that monster. But the scariest monsters were capable of convincing people they were not one. Still, no matter how irrational it was, I couldn't get myself to look at her.

"Goodnight, Mama," I grumbled.

Before I could escape into my room, a hand grabbed my sleeve, anchoring me in place. My gaze followed her fingers, trailing up her arm and finally settled on her face. Her lips were pursed, eyes full of concern.

But she did not inquire if I was alright. Instead she asked, "Shall we go for a walk?"

"Very well."

She released my sleeve, tucking her hands under the long front of her dangui. I wasn't sure who was leading the way, our steps synchronized while we meandered through the palace grounds.

When we exited the winding halls and broke out into the warm night, Bora mused, "Do you ever dream of something else, of *being* someone else?"

My brow rose at the unexpected question. "Like being a farmer or soldier?"

"Yes. For example, I dream of owning a restaurant."

"I find imagining things I cannot become to be depressing rather than inspiring," I scoffed. Such thoughts did me no good—they were a waste of time. I was king, and I had too much to do to be dreaming about a simpler life.

"Tell me about your restaurant," I said, softer this time.

Her voice grew excited as she explained, "I'd serve an equal amount of deserts as meals, and there would be music and storytellers, and every wall would have a painting. I'd have a cooking competition to find the best chef in the capital, so that anyone with talent and imagination could become the head cook."

As she spoke, I was able to picture it, the music beginning to play in my ears, my mouth watering while she described each dish in detail.

"Thank you for sharing your dream with me," I said after she finished.

"I assumed you wanted a distraction," she replied, offering a soft smile.

"A distraction?"

"You didn't ask me how I was feeling when I cried in the rain."

"I didn't think you'd want to share your feelings with me."

She didn't say anything. I must have been right about that, then.

Our feet had taken us back to the Queen's Quarters, and I paused our walking. "Well, in the future, I hope you will also share your feelings with me."

Her shoulders stiffened, and she turned to face me. "Goodnight, Jeonha."

"Goodnight, Bora."

Chapter 17

Bora

ASIDE FROM MY SIBLINGS and Jinyoung, Hanbin had been one of the few people who I felt genuinely cared for me. And concerning the king... Well, I still was uncertain what was an act and what was real, but the way he had looked the other night at the loss of his servant, his face so filled with sorrow and anger, had appeared genuine.

In comparison, Hanbin and his intentions were much simpler. His visits to the palace were bordering on improper, but I couldn't help myself. To turn him away was like turning away the light, the little reprieve I had from the isolating life in the palace. He was not a servant or spy, not some official or their daughters searching for connections. He was just Hanbin, the boy who played games with us in the courtyard and took my side when my brothers picked fights.

I tossed some seeds into the pond, the round lips of the fish swallowing them from the surface. The gaping mouths resembled tunnels. If only I could leap into one and be taken far away from the complicated court.

"Feed me too?" a voice joked behind me.

I twisted around to see the grinning face of my friend. "You're allergic to pine nuts."

"If you're the one feeding me, I'll be fine," he quipped as he sat next to me.

"If you keep saying such ridiculous things, I will give you some just to make you silent," I threatened with no intention of ever following through.

He held out his hand, and I poured some of the seeds from my pouch into his palm.

"You should give these to the birds. My fish are getting too fat these days," I warned with a humorous lilt.

"The fat is what makes them cute. And delicious."

Flinging some food towards the fish, I scoffed, "If you eat one of my fish, I will never forgive you."

"I would never break your heart like that. I can't say the same for the other men in your life," he remarked, his voice growing uncharacteristically cold.

"Do you mean Jinho? He would probably take all the fish from the pond and release them into a lake. Not mean enough to kill them but mean enough to make me cry," I mused, recalling a similar incident that happened when we were younger.

I stared at the swollen cocoon, anticipating the pretty Swallowtail that would bloom from the pouch that resided on the twig in my box. All winter, the little caterpillar had slept in his cocoon, and Jinho chided me for still believing it would hatch.

"It didn't come out before winter, so it never will. You are basically taking care of a coffin," he would say with a haughty tilt of his chin.

But he was wrong. All the caterpillar needed was time and care, and I would ensure it got to the point where it could emerge and fly.

"Just wait and see, Orabeoni," I murmured aloud, adjusting the stick so it would receive more sunlight.

Did they get cold even in their cocoons? Better to be cautious than regretful.

And that was how I left the greenish brown pouch, safe and sound on its twig in a box by my window where winter sun peeked through.

But the next day, it was gone. Not the butterfly. The entire stick and cocoon. Tears rushed to my eyes as I frantically searched my room, asking every servant that passed if they had seen it. From dawn to dusk, I looked for my unhatched butterfly, but to no avail. It was the only day in my life I went without eating anything.

As I sat sobbing on the steps outside our home, praying for my cocoon to show up, my mother hugged me and whispered comfortingly, "Maybe the butterfly bloomed and was so strong it took off with the stick."

It was a lie.

My mother never lied for her own sake but often twisted the truth to spare other people pain. It may have worked when I was six. But I was eleven and knew no butterfly was that strong.

A sudden crash and thump paused my weeping, my mother and I turning our heads to the source of the sound. With a dirt smeared face, Ryu Hanbin—with his chubby cheeks—came around the bushes, and he held a twig in with a little pouch the size of my pinky finger attached to it.

I leapt to my feet and bounded over to him, sucking in the snot that had been pouring just moments ago. As soon as I got a good look, I knew it was my Swallowtail—the body of the cocoon brown and a splash of green crowning the top.

"You found it!" I squealed and threw my arms around him.

From behind us, my mother scolded, "Bora, you are too old for such things. It is inappropriate to touch someone who is not your male relative."

"He is basically another brother," I retorted, too excited by the sight of my cocoon to care about obeying my mother.

She tsked but said nothing else as I released Hanbin, whose face turned red beneath the dirt. I took the stick from his hand and inspected it.

"Thank you," I said, grinning widely, my eyes fixated on the baby butterfly hiding in the pouch. There didn't appear to be any breaks in the lining, and I let out a breath. "Where did you find it?"

He shifted his feet, his eyes darting behind me as he stammered, "Uh..."

I whipped my head around just in time to see Jinho disappear into the house with a look of disappointment on his face. Ignoring my brother was the best way to deal with his pranks, and I turned back to Hanbin, his shoulders relaxing now that the boy two years his senior was gone.

"I didn't want to see you cry," Hanbin mumbled at last.

Hanbin scoffed but made no further comment. Instead, he said wistfully, "I wish we could go back to those days."

My fingers fumbled over the fabric, tracing the gilded dragon on my chest. "So much has changed since we were children..."

"Not you, Bora. You are the same sweet girl who always does as she is told. I wished for once that you hadn't, that you had defied the decree to marry the king."

I lurched forward, my hand covering his mouth and my eyes looked around, praying no one was in hearing distance. Luckily, the group of court ladies that stood far off gave no sign that they'd heard.

"Hanbin! You cannot say such things, especially in the palace," I scolded in a quiet whisper.

He wrapped his fingers around my wrist, gently tugging my arm down. "I mean it, Bora. I can't stand the thought of you being with that tyrant."

In my panic, I had forgotten to use honorifics, but he didn't look offended nor did he mention it. In fact he seemed almost...happy to hear his name? Maybe his mind was also rattled with worry. Such etiquette wasn't important in this moment, as the words he'd uttered were enough to have him killed if anyone overheard and reported it to the king.

We were close as children, but I was still surprised by his dedication to me. He had watched over me when we were young, and he still continued to even now. But I could not allow him to get hurt because of me. The king's temperament changed like the fickle weather of spring, and his unpredictability was what frightened me most.

"I appreciate your concern, but I am fine. Really." I hoped he believed my words even though I could not.

There was always a deep-seated prickling of danger in the palace. My only hope was that my father would save me from any trouble that arose, and I just needed to stay alive long enough for his rescue.

"I'd take you away from here. We could go to Ming. You know I'm fluent, and I could take care of you," he murmured, this thumb brushing against the skin of my wrist.

I hadn't noticed that we were still touching.

I removed myself from his grip and replied with a chuckle, "You joke far too much for a scholar." Before he could say any more treasonous words, I stood. "I should be going, Scholar Ryu."

He frowned at the formality, but stood nonetheless and bowed. "Mama."

I inclined my head and turned to walk back to my chambers, leaving Hanbin behind. Escape was out of the question. The worst thing I could do was run, which would make us both treachers. And a tyrant would never allow his toy to leave. I wouldn't put it past the king to start a war with Ming just to get me, not because he cared for me, but because he hated losing. Not to mention what he would do to my family in retribution.

The king's words echoed in my mind: *I may not always win, but I never lose.*

My body shuddered.

Yes. The safest thing for Hanbin and my family was to stay put, smile, and obey.

Chapter 18
Seojun

F OR SOME REASON, MY steps were drawn to the Queen's Quarters. As I walked down the hall towards Bora's chamber, I caught a glimpse of two figures outside in her courtyard. I stopped, peering out of the corridor window. Bora was sitting across from a man, an omok board between them. All of a sudden, Bora careened back, her head tilted to the sky as she laughed, her hand resting against her stomach as her shoulders shook and the pleasant sound echoed outside.

I leaned forward, my hands gripping the sill of the window until they turned white. My teeth ground against each other as the unknown man reached across and patted her other hand. I never recalled even the hottest summer day making me boil like this, my blood on fire.

"Dongbin," I growled through gritted teeth.

"Yes, Jeonha?" my guard replied behind me.

"Find out who that man is and what his relationship to the queen is," I hissed, my arms shaking and fingers digging into the wood.

There was plenty for me to do, a plethora of responsibilities waiting for me, but my feet refused to budge, my eyes pasted to the scene in front of me. Was she scheming? Was that one of her father's cronies? Why did Haeji allow a random man into the Queen's Quarters? I would have to have a discussion with her later.

Time moved slowly, but at last, the man left, his eyes lingering far too long on the queen. My grip relaxed as I watched him exit on the opposite side of the courtyard. As soon as I was certain he was gone, I switched my attention to Bora. She was walking back to her chamber—towards me. Shoving myself off the window sill, I turned and strode down towards the entrance she would walk through, my thundering steps a match for my storm-filled mind.

Her gold chima fluttered through the threshold, and her plump figure followed. I nearly leapt the remaining distance between us. Lurching forward as she turned, my palms collided with the wall on each side of her. Her nostrils and eyes widened as she gasped.

"Who was that with you? One of your father's followers?" I asked, a bitter suspicion coating each word.

Her face remained blank for a moment before she realized who I was referring to. Her brows and nose scrunched together like a rabbit.

"He is just a childhood friend. He recently passed the Kwago and wanted to share the good news with me," she replied, shifting between my arms.

"Just a childhood friend, huh? Strange he couldn't just send you a message and instead had to meet with you alone in my palace," I scoffed, tilting my head.

"I thought this was my part of the palace? Aren't I allowed to receive guests? Besides, I wasn't alone. I'm never alone here," she mumbled, her eyes going to Haeji and the group of maids waiting a few steps away.

"All of the palace is *mine*, along with the *people* within it," I sneered with a tone I knew I would later regret.

Her eyes flashed with some unknown emotion, and she opened her mouth to retort. But then she suddenly clamped her lips shut and crossed her arms.

Feigning ignorance? Pretending innocence?

She was the daughter of the Chief State Councilor, and I was a fool for forgetting that. At worst, she was conspiring against me, and at best, she was partaking in an affair in my own palace. Perhaps I had been too merciful with her.

"Don't forget where your loyalty should lie," I whispered with a growl.

I stepped back, dropping my arms to my side. Bora looked past me and huffed as she walked away and disappeared into her room.

Haeji started to follow her inside, but I whipped my arm up. "Send some of the others to watch her. I need to talk to you," I ordered gruffly.

She nodded and instructed two maids to follow the queen into her chambers. After the door slid closed, I crossed my arms and inquired, "Who was that man?"

"His name is Hanbin, but the queen didn't say his family name. They seem to genuinely be childhood friends."

"Then that means his father is close with hers," I grunted. I was right about him being one of the Councilor's men.

"Should I bar him from returning, Jeonha?" Haeji asked.

I clenched my fists and commanded, "No. Make sure you listen in on his conversations with the queen. If they discuss anything suspicious, then I can know for certain if Bora is colluding with her father. If they speak of nothing serious, then perhaps Bora is truly ignorant of her father's current scheming."

"And the man?" Haeji inquired.

"Even if they say nothing strange, there is a possibility he is still one of the Min's allies."

"Understood, Jeonha."

And with that she went inside the queen's chambers, leaving me alone with my speculations.

Perhaps the other day had been an elaborate show, a clever trick where Bora pretended to be remorseful and act like she was on my side. Something so complex would fit the Min's methodology. I slammed my palm against the wall, the sting a welcome distraction from the constant war between caution and compassion.

My eyes were drawn to the now empty pavilion. That man—Hanbin—could not be trusted, and I was still not certain Bora could be either.

The next time Hanbin came, I made sure to "accidentally" run into him. I glanced around the corner, watching as he said his goodbyes to Bora. His eyes lingered far too long on the queen's leaving form, and my jaw and fists clenched at the sight.

"Shall I kill him, Jeonha?" Minje asked, observing my radiating irritation.

"No. Bora would be upset."

"We saw him meeting multiple times with the State Councilors. He is obviously planning something," he pointed out, unsheathing his blade halfway.

I shoved the end of his hilt back down until it hit the sheath, clicking shut. "That's not a crime. His uncle is one of the Councilors, after all."

"As you command, Jeonha," Minje dipped his head, stepping back and tucking his sword at his side.

The sound of footsteps drew closer, and I got into position, making it appear as if I had just happened to be walking this way. The timing was perfect, and Hanbin nearly collided with me when he rounded the corner.

"Oh! Jeonha," he exclaimed, dipping at the waist. "Apologies."

Looking down at him, I waved a hand in the air. "No harm was done."

"Then if you'll excuse me..."

He rose and made to leave, but Minje quickly blocked his path. Hanbin's shoulders tensed, and he slowly turned to face me.

"Is there something I can assist you with, Jeonha?" he asked, a slight bite to his words.

"What business do you have with the queen? I hear you come often to see her these days."

He straightened his posture, a smile curling his lips. "We basically grew up together. It is only natural for her to desire comfort in such a—" he paused, gaze roving, "unfamiliar place." He took a step closer, lowering his voice. "It's only natural to cling to the things—or people—we know when life changes drastically."

My eyes narrowed. "How considerate of you."

He shrugged a single shoulder, his smile morphing into a smirk. "She used to like me when we were children. I figured my presence could bring her some joy."

"Well, it is normal for people to outgrow childhood likes. I used to love carrots when I was young," I paused, my eyes dropping from his head to his feet and back up, "but now I get sick when I see them."

"That won't be a problem, since Bora always loves eating."

"Not if the food is rotten."

Rushing footsteps interrupted us, a servant skidding to a halt and whispering urgently into Minje's ear, Hanbin side stepping to avoid them. Minje's eyes widened, his face turning red.

He replied to the servant too quietly to hear before saying loudly, "Forgive me, Jeonha, but there is something important we need to attend to."

Hanbin took the chance to excuse himself. "Jeonha," he muttered, bowing, and turned on his heel, disappearing out of sight.

"Let's go," I growled, storming off towards my quarters.

The pamphlet had been torn at the edges, but the words were clear in the common script, staring back up at me, mocking me. *The fire in Gangwon-do is the wrath of the heavens. The wicked king has brought destruction to our country. Remove the king and appease the heavens!*

"How many of these papers were posted in the capital?" I demanded, crumpling the parchment in my fist.

"We found only ten, Jeonha. But some of the agents in the other provinces sent word that the rumors had spread to them. It seems that the instigator did not bother with written words and simply sent some lackeys to start the fire. Even illiterates would have heard by now," Minje explained.

If Dongbin was my shield, then Minje was my eyes and ears, his network of informants spread throughout the kingdom.

"And how have the people received such lies?" My fingers thrummed against my desk.

"A small riot broke out in Gangwon-do, but it was quickly quelled after the supplies you confiscated from the officials reached them," Minje stated, irritation radiating from his features.

My chest tightened, my fingers curling into a tight fist. The only reason the supplies reached them was because of Gweonho, and the reason he was dead was the greed of the councilors. But I could not let anger cloud my thoughts.

You'll get your justice, Gweonho, I promised before shoving the image of him far back in my mind, refocusing on the matter at hand.

"This reeks of the Right State Councilor. Unlike the Chief State Councilor, he prefers to keep his assassinations to those of character," I commented, disgust dripping from the mention of two of the most corrupt men in the kingdom.

"We could always fight fire with fire," Minje suggested.

"You know that's not how we do things," I chided, rubbing my palms over my face.

"How about using water? We could send messengers to spread the news that the king sent aid to the victims," Dongbin offered, his arms crossed as he contemplated the situation.

"Do it. Minje, send out runners to all the capital cities in the provinces," I ordered, releasing a long breath.

"And what about Ryu Wooseok?" Minje inquired, a mischievous glint to his eyes.

"Rein it in, Minje. We won't do anything until I can catch all the fish at once," I mumbled, interlacing my fingers together, trying to untangle my thoughts.

"Isn't that man who keeps visiting the queen his nephew?" Minje asked, eliciting a sharp shake of Dongbin's head and a gesture to be quiet.

An idea sparked in my mind, though it was not solely founded in logic, was not only a strategic piece in the game between me and the Councilors.

"I think the queen and I should spend some more time together."

Chapter 19

Bora

BEING QUEEN WAS NOT as bad as I thought it was going to be. I wasn't included in court matters and hadn't been invited back to a meeting with the ministers after the previous time. My days were largely spent in leisure, and even the maids were beginning to feel more comfortable around me. They would regale stories of trysts between servants and soldiers or discuss rumors of romance between a wealthy merchant who owned one of the busiest tea shops and one of his cooks. Even Haeji had opened up more, and I didn't find her presence so suffocating.

With a yawn, I grumbled, "I'm going to sleep early tonight."

"Mama, it is your night with the king," Haeji said as she combed my hair.

"Already? I thought it was only supposed to be once a month."

We had yet to spend a night together since our wedding, as the king had made an excuse to avoid the previous month's scheduled night, much to the ire of many ministers who were eager for an heir.

Haeji shook her head while her fingers untangled a knot. "The king commanded that it be once a week that you spend a night in his chamber."

I sighed, since there was nothing I could do. His word was law, and I was at his mercy.

A little brown shrike landed on my windowsill, the sunset gilding its feathers. Leaning forward, I slowly reached out a finger towards the dainty bird, careful not to scare it off.

"Hello, friend," I whispered. "Are you here to wish me luck?" I mused aloud as Haeji made a basic bun and pinned my hair behind me.

In response, the shrike tilted its head, one of its eyes reflecting the setting sunlight. My lips twitched upward despite the knotting in my stomach.

Sleeping with the king...

"Mama, we should be going," Haeji interjected, taking a step towards the exit.

I stood, wiggling my fingers at my feathered friend. "Thank you for stopping by."

As we were walking out, I glanced back once more to the window, but the shrike had already flown off. I wished he could take me away with him. Despite the current tranquility, I doubted it would last long. Uncertainty about the king plagued me, and this new edict only furthered my confusion.

Every step felt like I had stones in the bottom of my shoes. Although I had spent one night with the king, our wedding night was not...what I had expected. Unease danced deep inside me, especially after the other day in the hallway after Hanbin had stopped by.

The king's actions perplexed me. Why was he upset by Hanbin coming to see me? Was he afraid that I was plotting? But who would be so foolish as to plan to harm the king in front of his own servants? Haeji would kill me and *then* inform the king that I was scheming.

Jealousy, then?

No. Definitely not that.

Even if he was at times decent, his actions were not the result of love for me.

By the time we reached the king's chamber, I had still not figured out the reason for his outburst. Ultimately, it didn't matter. He was the king, and he could do as he pleased. The answer could be that he was both good and bad, two sides of a coin capable of kindness and killing. Perhaps that was his volatile side appearing, the tyrant that my father had told us about ever since he had ascended to the throne several years ago.

My father never spoke ill of the previous king though. Didn't that show that my father wasn't that bad? That he was willing to defer to his sovereign so long as he was honorable? I supposed that the current king did not take after his predecessor.

We stopped in front of the door, candles flickering on the other side of the screen. I wrung my hands together, glancing at

Haeji. Was the king still in a foul mood? Was that why he had summoned me more than what was customary? We had yet to consummate our marriage, so why would he call for me once a week?

A stone dropped in my stomach.

Certainly he didn't intend to...

Haeji would offer no answers, her loyalty to her master clearer than a crystal lake. Inhaling, I gathered courage and nodded. Haeji slid the door open, and I quickly stepped through before my bravery faded.

The door slid shut with a soft whisper behind me, and just like that I deflated, my courage leaving me like the shrike flying from my window and into the dusk. The king lounged on his bed on the floor, his eyes closed and one arm propped on the top of his knee.

I swallowed and shuffled my feet forward. Did rabbits feel this way when around a fox? My heart was beating just as fast as one, pounding against my ribs.

"J-Jeonha," I stammered, my foot catching on the heel of the other just as I reached the step that led to the bed of blankets, and I careened forward towards the floor.

My eyes slammed shut as I prepared to meet the ground with a hard smack, but the hurt elbows and wounded pride never came. Something firm held me, and I cracked open an eye to greet the hard face of the king. He peered down at me, the corner of his lip twitching up ever so slightly.

I coughed, and scurried to upright myself. I pushed back misplaced hair that didn't exist, my hands desperate to busy themselves.

"Thank you, Jeonha," I squeaked out, my voice a constant saboteur to my façade of confidence.

The king only grunted in reply before turning and sitting on the bed, reclining back on his palms. Since I had to travel across the palace to the king's quarters, I was still dressed in my normal dangui and chima. But the sleeping robes he wore were unfastened, the fabric sliding off his body and revealing his chest and abdomen. He cleared his throat, refocusing my wandering gaze. The skin of my face warmed, spreading down my neck and to my core, and I looked past him to the painting on the wall.

He cocked a brow, his head hung low between his shoulders. "So, did the Ryu boy come to see you again today?"

Boy? Hanbin was only a few years younger than the king, two older than myself. He was hardly a boy.

"No," I muttered, rubbing a hand along my arm.

The king leaned forward, his elbows resting atop his knees. "Do you enjoy his company? In your eyes, is he handsome?"

What kind of questions were those? They weren't things one asked when they were concerned about potential plots. Was the king mad?

"Umm... Well, we are childhood friends," I mumbled, turning around as my eyes fled his burning gaze and found sanctuary staring at the rafters above us.

Faster than a striking snake, the king appeared behind me, my body freezing as my breath caught in my chest. The heat of his torso seeped through my dangui and into my back.

His breath whispered hot against my neck, my skin prickling. "Is he handsome?" he demanded again.

I shivered as his fingers brushed down my arm.

"Am I so lacking that you must find satisfaction in another?" he questioned, his voice straining.

"O-Of c-course not, Jeonha. I would never blatantly disrespect my king like that. And I have never particularly noticed his looks since we grew up together. He is just like another brother," I stammered, my voice trembling with each word that spilled from my mouth.

The tip of his nose kissed the edge of my ear, and I couldn't help myself, my body acting on instinct and leaning into the king's touch. What was happening? Why were my limbs tingling?

"Jeonha, have I displeased you in some way?" I asked shrilly, twisting to face him.

The king stared at me as he removed the pin from his hair, a black wave spilling around his head, and then he pushed his outer robe off his shoulders, the fabric humming as it fell to the floor. My mouth hung open as I gawked at the sight of his half-naked body. He leaned forward slowly, our faces so close, I could see my reflection in his irises.

My eyes fluttered shut in anticipation.

"J-Jeonha, what do you intend..." my voice trailed off as I heard the sound of someone plopping onto the pile of blankets on the floor.

I flung my eyes open. The king was still in his baji that he wore beneath his outer garments. The heat left my skin, and the buzzing faded from my arms and legs.

"I won't force myself upon you, Bora. Although for the sake of my sanity, we have to keep up an appearance that we are actively trying for an heir. I don't need the ministers pestering me every court meeting about it."

"Oh," was all I said in reply.

Why was I disappointed? Maybe I was the mad one.

The king tucked his hands under the back of his head and closed his eyes, but after a few moments, he opened one to look at me.

"Well, aren't you going to sleep?" he inquired with a teasing lilt that revealed he knew what he was doing all too well.

Fine. If he wanted to torment me, then so be it. I wouldn't miss any sleep over his childish games. I stomped over to the bed and crawled over the top of him to reach the space he had left for me. Although I could have walked around, this would be far more satisfying. As I crossed over him, I paused, enjoying seeing the shock in his eyes and relishing the way he held his breath while his gaze roved from my face and down to my body.

But then the look in his eyes shifted from surprise to mirth, as if I had sparked an ember into a blaze.

He reached up, and I sucked in a breath.

What was he doing?

His fingers wrapped around the pin in my hair and plucked it free, my tresses cascading downward as he tossed the accessory to the floor with a clink.

"Jeonha, you said—"

He pressed a finger to my lips, silencing my stammers. "Careful, Bora. You shouldn't start a game you aren't prepared to finish," he warned, a sultry smirk curling his lips before lowering his hand to the bed.

With a scowl, I finished crawling over him and huffed as I plopped down, positioning myself as close to the wall as I could, although with my full body, it was hard to keep from making contact with him. I stared at the wall where a tapestry of cranes flying above a valley hung. Tracing every stitch helped me beckon sleep, doing my best not to dwell on how it felt when his body was pressed into mine, trying to forget the image of his torso framed by his silk garments. Gradually, my eyelids grew heavy.

Before slumber could claim me, a sound came behind my back.

Turning over, I did my best not to wake the king.

Again, that sound.

"Bora..." he whispered.

My name trickled from his lips as if it were a sweet delicacy. I tilted my head, my gaze following the lines of his face. The tyrant seemed much more tame in his sleep, his hard and sharp features softened by slumber.

What was he dreaming of that he would whisper my name? Was I the source of worry or welcome for him? Maybe neither. Maybe I was nothing to him except a nuisance, a presence he had to bear due to the prominence of my father. But wasn't the king the one who had demanded my marriage? My father had never explicitly told me who proposed it, but I had always assumed the king wanted to use me as a tool to dig at my father.

There were far too many things I was ignorant of, too few things I was certain of, and with each day in the palace, those few certainties decreased.

Chapter 20

Bora

HANBIN CAME BACK OFTEN to play omok or feed the birds, chatting about his studies at the Royal Academy or reminiscing about childhood memories, but every day he visited, the king also happened to demand my presence in his chambers that night. It was on one such occasion in which we were playing another match, when a sudden cold shadow appeared beside us.

Scarlet garbs draped over the king in a luxurious waterfall, gold dragons guarding his shoulders and black ikseongwan gracing his head. He must have just finished a court meeting. But why was he here? I glanced at Haeji for any clues, but her features remained blank as always, not a hint revealed on her stony face.

Hanbin reminded me of my manners when he stood and bowed, and I followed suit.

"Jeonha," we greeted in tandem.

The king ignored Hanbin at first, his hand going to my elbow and pulling me up with a gentle tug. My downcast gaze darted up to his, my eyebrows shooting to the skies. Why was he touching me? He had been touching me more and more as of late, and I hadn't decided if I liked or loathed it. Perhaps I loathed that I liked it. An ember of irritation sparked to life at the sight of Hanbin still hunched over like an old man, waiting for the king's permission to rise.

I cleared my throat and gestured to him. "This is Ryu Hanbin," I explained, hoping the king would grant him permission to rise. Even though his legs were steady, I could imagine how uncomfortable the position must be for Hanbin.

The king, not deigning to look, commanded without a drop of interest, "Arise."

He did not seem shocked when I said Hanbin's family name, even though his uncle—the Left State Councilor—was closely allied with my father. How foolish of me. Of course the king was already aware. Was there anything that he was ignorant of within his palace?

Hanbin rose slowly, his eyes bright despite the inconsiderate length of time it took for the king to acknowledge him. Hanbin's gaze fixated on my elbow where the king's fingers were still lingering. I removed my arm from his hand in the most discreet way I could manage, taking a step towards Hanbin.

"Jeonha, to what do we owe the pleasure of your presence?" I asked, presenting a demure grin and trying my best to act normal. For some unknown reason, guilt pricked my skin like little crawling ants.

The king's nostrils flared, his eyebrow cocked in a way that almost reminded me of a viper preparing to strike. I had seen one once when I was younger. My siblings and I, along with Hanbin, had escaped our family estate and wandered into the forest all because Jinho had dared us to. It had been Hanbin who had saved me, stopping me from being bit as I had unknowingly stepped too close to the well obscured serpent. It had curled its neck, mouth open and fangs bared.

I shuddered at the memory but kept the smile on my face. The king hissed, "We?"

His fiery eyes bore into Hanbin, his displeasure bared openly as his lip curled back, and my mind screamed *danger*.

Stepping forward, I asked, "Jeonha? Is everything alright?"

The king's gaze softened ever so slightly. "I wanted to invite you to dine together," he murmured in a gentle tone that almost made me think his invitation gave me a choice.

My smile widened, and my hands clapped together. "It would be an honor," I said. "And Hanbin can join us too."

The king bristled like a badger's tail, his lips drooping into a frown. "Very well," he grumbled and turned on his heel, sitting at the table under the pavilion as servants scurried about to prepare it for our meal.

The crawling ants appeared once more along my skin, and I rubbed my arms and moved to sit. Before my backside could meet the cushion on the ground, the king darted his hand out and pulled me towards him. My shoulder smashed into his side, my cheeks reddening. The warmth of his body spread to mine as he drew me closer.

Hanbin, much like a river unbothered by a pebble's splash, kept a calm appearance and sat across from us. He brushed aside his wide brimmed sleeves and reached for a ceramic cup of tea, but just as he was about to grab it, the king swooped in and stole it, sipping the tea loudly.

I flinched at the sound, doing my best to give an apologetic expression to Hanbin. He gave a subtle nod in return, his eyes conveying that he did not mind. He reached for a remaining cup, and I released a breath of gratitude when the king allowed him to take it.

An awkward silence hung between us, the king's arm still slung around me like a rope tying me to him. I was thankful when the servants began to bring the dishes out. If conversation eluded us then perhaps eating could fill the uncomfortable quiet that lay heavy like a wet blanket.

With chopsticks in hand, I reached for the pa-jeon, but my hand barely had time to move before Hanbin pinched one of the scallion pancakes with his chopsticks and plopped it onto my plate. I gave a smile and small nod, his own lips mirroring it with a grin.

Suddenly, my plate filled faster than I could eat, the king plunking braised lotus root and grilled pork belly on top of my rice bowl. I glanced up at him, my eyes wide and unable to veil my shock. What was he doing? He had never been so attentive to me before. Was he ill? Did my father particularly irritate him today during the court meeting? It would explain his strange behavior.

"Bora loves jeon, although kimchi-jeon is her favorite," Hanbin said nonchalantly as he brought a scoop of rice and pork to his mouth.

The king stiffened by my side. "She also loves lotus root."

The piece of lotus that I was about to bite dropped back onto my plate. How did he know? It must have been a wild guess.

Hanbin's gaze dropped for a moment before he looked back up and said, "Well, she also loves feeding fish and birds."

The king scoffed, as if it were some common knowledge that all should know. "She always chooses the white omok stones so her opponent can go first," he replied smugly.

Hanbin rolled his eyes, a small ripple that disturbed his serene demeanor. "She smiles even when she cries because she doesn't want people to worry about her."

The king's hand gripped the ceramic cup so tight I feared it would break. "She sings when she walks without realizing it."

Hanbin leaned forward, his pitch climbing higher like a crane. "Her favorite colors for dresses are yellow and pink."

The king leaned forward, his arm that was still pasted to my torso forcing me forward with him. "Her favorite flowers are peonies," he replied with a hint of a growl.

I stared down at my plate, the lack of steam creating a heat inside me. My food had gone cold, and I was tired of whatever competition the two were engaged in.

"Enough!" I shouted, slamming my chopsticks down, the bowls and plates on the table rattling.

Both of the men sat back with wide eyes, the grips on their utensils loosening.

"What's the matter?" they asked in tandem, the first and likely last time they would ever do something together.

I forced my shoulders to relax and smiled, pointing to the delicious array of dishes on the table. "Let's just eat before the food is colder than winter, shall we?"

What was wrong with them? They had been locked in their own match, but I had no idea what game they were playing. With a sigh, I shoved a scoop of rice into my mouth. Thinking was always easier on a full stomach.

Chapter 21

Bora

THE LOTUS LANTERN FESTIVAL was an annual celebration at the end of spring, and I was unable to attend the previous year, as my father had determined it inappropriate for a betrothed woman to go. But this year, I was not betrothed, and I would be there with my husband.

The thought of all the food that the festival vendors offered reminded me of Jinyoung. She loved mandu best. A pang of pain rang in my heart. At last, I was ready to admit that she tried to assassinate the king and that my father had sent her to do so. He had tried to get me to kill the king too, and if he was capable of it once, he was capable of it multiple times. My only hope was that after my failed attempt, my father would forfeit his ambitions.

I also tried to comfort myself that even though all of that was true, she had cared for me. All those evenings of stolen desserts and doing my hair over and over just because I liked it, those had been real. I refused to believe otherwise.

"Mama, we have arrived," Haeji hollered through the palanquin curtain.

I shoved away the sadness and sorrow-tinged memories. There were not many opportunities for me to leave the palace, so I wanted to savor this night. And maybe I could even pretend that I was just another young woman in Joseon, enjoying the floral décor and leaping lights above. The promise I'd made to Hanbin sat in the back of my mind. It couldn't be that hard to slip away from our entourage in a crowded festival, right? I glanced down at the gold dragon embroidered in the middle of my dangui. Maybe it was easier said than done...

I could always figure out an excuse later.

Careful not to hit my head on the top of the palanquin, I stood, slightly bent, and shuffled outside where Haeji waited with her hand outstretched. As I stepped down, I stared at the meadow of color and commotion splayed before me.

Red, yellow, and pink lanterns were strung from railings and rafters, light cascading like a spill of stars in the twilight, illuminating the streets of the capital. Children ran to and fro, giggling and gripping animal-shaped sugar. Couples allowed themselves to show public displays of affection on the festive night, and the smell of fried mandu, honey-dribbled yaksik, chewy yeot, hwa-jeon topped with fresh spring flowers, and smoked chicken wafted through the air and made my mouth water. My stomach did a little leap, eager to begin eating.

Haeji suddenly turned to someone behind me, and I pivoted to look, my heart beating like a crane's wings, thumping against my chest as it tried to escape its cage.

"Jeonha," I called out.

The king spun around, his eyes sparkling and his face lighting up brighter than the lanterns that hanged over our heads. A smile spread across his lips as he swiftly strode towards me. Why was he so happy?

His hair coiled atop his head, covered by a black gat, and a peacock feather dangled from the top along with a golden tassel while ornate beads in a rainbow of color hung from each side, framing his face. Instead of his usual robes, a cobalt jeonbok with a gold dragon embroidered on the chest and shoulders billowed from him, and a white po and baji peeked out from beneath the ocean of dark blue fabric. The sharp lines of his face were highlighted by the lanterns, his eyes dusky as they peered at me from under his wide brimmed gat.

Once again, the celestial beauty he possessed struck me. He would be a welcome muse to many artists. I should try painting him someday.

It took me a moment to realize the king had spoken to me.

I shook my head and stammered, "What did you say?"

A smirk pulled at his lips, and he restated his question, "What would you like to eat first?"

A sheepish smile formed on my face as I suggested, "Hwa-jeon?"

"To the hwa-jeon stand then," he affirmed with a nod and grin.

We walked side by side into the bustling crowd, Haeji, Dongbin, and another guard that I heard the others call Minje trailing behind us. I was keenly aware of the space between the king's shoulder and mine, or more like the lack of it. The river of people around us forced us to wade through them while touching, each contact like a spark. The festive atmosphere must've been getting to me.

At last we arrived at a stall that sold the sweet, fried, rice-flour cakes.

The owner's eyes widened to the size of the lanterns hanging overhead. "Jeonha, Mama, it is an honor to be graced with your presence," the vendor gushed.

A grumbling sounded from my stomach, and my cheeks immediately reddened.

The king just smiled and said, "Give us seven."

The vendor nodded and scrambled to gather seven hwa-jeon and bundle it in a cloth. I grabbed the food with an eagerness that did not befit my station, but the sweet smell mixed with just a smidge of oil was too tempting. After shoving one into my mouth, the azalea topping the cake sticking to my teeth, I handed one to the king, Haeji, and each of the guards.

The king cocked a brow and jutted his chin towards my treasure trove. "Are you going to eat all three?"

Did he think I was eating too much?

I removed the hwa-jeon from my mouth—a large crescent bite taken out of it—and mumbled, "Well..."

Before I could finish speaking, the king turned back to the vendor and held up four more fingers. "Two more for me, and two for the queen to have later."

I smiled and took another bite.

While snacking on a mixture of sweets, we wandered through the sea of people towards the center where a stream cut through the capital. Even from a distance, I could spot the lotus lanterns that peppered the water, as if the stars had fallen to earth and nestled themselves inside the pointed petals.

"Haeji, buy two lanterns," the king commanded softly, his eyes lingering on the water, a wistful look washing over his face.

What was he thinking of?

Before I could ask, Haeji returned with two lotus lanterns, handing a pink one to me and a yellow one to the king.

We each cupped the little, flower-shaped lanterns in our hands, a small candle nestled in the center making it glow like a drop of sunlight. Crouching down beside the stream, I closed my eyes and prayed for wisdom and discernment concerning the king, the court, and my father.

"I don't think the king is all that bad, but I can't fathom my father lying to us. There must be some truth to the tales he told us. But my eyes do not deceive me. Am I unfilial for disobeying my father? But fealty to the king is the greatest loyalty, right? No matter what I do, I am betraying someone," I whispered to the heavens so softly that I was certain not even the king could hear my words.

When I opened my eyes, I turned to the king, who gazed at me with such intensity—golden light gilding his irises like glowing embers—that almost made me think I had been the object of his prayers. We stood slowly, and I succumbed to some sort of trance, unable to look away. For a moment, I felt like I was the woman in one of the romantic stories, the hero about to confess his undying love for me.

The king's hand reached towards me, slow like a gentle current, his finger hovering just in front of my face like a bee above a flower. I sucked in a breath, my chest refusing to move until he did. At last, under the lantern light, he brushed his thumb against my skin, just next to my lips.

Was he going to...

He removed his finger, and with a small smirk, he showed me the chunk of rice cake that had been left from the hwa-jeon. I exhaled, surprised at my own thoughts—and disappointment.

The king gave a low chuckle and licked the crumb from his finger. "You look hungry, Bora," he teased.

Heat crawled along my neck, my hanbok feeling hot and sticky. "I'm not. We have eaten a lot..." my voice trailed off.

"I wasn't referring to food," he murmured in a sultry voice, a lilt to his words that sounded far too seductive for a public place.

The creek was suddenly very appealing, the heat of the summer night compounded by his flaming gaze.

The mirth-filled look left the king's face, his expression turning earnest, his voice low and strained. "Bora, I need to tell you something. The reason I was so irked by Hanbin was—"

Hanbin! I dropped the snacks in my hand and covered my mouth. I had completely forgotten about my promise. The king had stopped mid-sentence, a frown forming as his brows furrowed. It was best to just get the meeting with Hanbin over with, then I could return to the king and enjoy the rest of the festival. And hear the rest of the sentence.

Before the king could speak, I interjected, bunching my chima in my sticky fingers. "I'm sorry, but there is something I need to do." As soon as the last word left my mouth, I took off, wading through the crowd with the deftness of a fish swimming in a stream.

I couldn't tell him about my meeting, for he would never allow such a thing. If he found out, he might take out his ire on Hanbin, so I couldn't allow him or Haeji to see us meeting. And if fortune didn't favor me, then I would beg for forgiveness later. Perhaps if he ate another hwa-jeon, his anger would ease. If not, I could paint him a picture and give it to him as a present.

Turning to check if he was following me, I caught sight of Haeji slithering through the ocean of people, and her expression made me think I would need to paint something to gift her too. She would be difficult to lose, so I had to be quick. Hanbin had never dictated how *long* we had to meet. I could say a brief greeting, wish him blessings, and then head back to the king.

A promise was a promise, and if I didn't intend to keep it, I shouldn't have made it in the first place. At the time, it seemed innocent enough, but seeing how the king became when Hanbin came to the palace, it was not a good idea to continue meeting him. I jutted my head as best I could above the crowd, searching for Hanbin. I needed to fulfill my word and tell him not to come by the palace anymore.

There.

I recognized the tie around his hair as the one I had given him when he took his first Kwago—teal with white feathers embroidered down the middle. It was impossible to be anyone else, since I had sewn it myself, the feathers jagged and uncentered. My painting skills were far superior than my embroidery. The crowd was thick, but I managed to weave my way towards him. Just as I was about to call out, he moved, disappearing into a side alleyway. With a huff, I followed after him. Why was he going there? Was he also worried about the king's wrath if he found us?

The light of the festival grew less and less as I walked down the path, the sounds of the people growing dim. Where did he go?

An uneasy feeling sprouted in my stomach.

The sound of footsteps behind me made my skin prickle. It was either Hanbin or Haeji, right?

I spun around, but a hand clamped over my mouth. I tried to punch, kick, and scream, but another person had arrived, and my arms were pinned to my sides. There was some sort of cloth over my mouth and my vision was darkening.

At the end of the alley, I could make out the blurry figure of Haeji. I wanted to call out to her, but I couldn't move, couldn't speak.

I was so, so sleepy.

Chapter 22
Seojun

Now that Bora was gone, I could think straight. Her beauty attacked my senses, and she made it hard to think. But her absence was even more peeving. I'd rather be reduced to a bumbling idiot than be apart from her. I'd been denying my feelings for her, denying the true reason seeing Ryu Hanbin in her pavilion bothered me.

Her sudden disappearance was unusual, but maybe she saw something she wanted to eat or buy. No matter the reason, I was disappointed that my confession had disappeared with her. When she returned, I was definitely going to tell her what she meant to me. Not the daughter of my enemy, not just a political marriage, but a woman I had grown to love.

I sensed someone approaching, and I spun, expecting to meet the soft face of my queen. But it was Haeji.

My insides froze.

Bora wasn't with her. Red seeped from a cut on her forehead.

Dongbin and Minje helped her towards the wall of a nearby building, the former's lip pursed and brows pinched while his concerned eyes fixated on the court lady.

I felt bad for the harsh way my words came out, but worry gnawed at me, panic prickling my skin and fraying my patience. "Speak. Quickly."

I couldn't hear what she said—didn't *want* to process what she said.

The nightmares of losing those I cared for, of my father, of my mother, Gweonho...of Bora. Ghosts of those who I failed to protect haunted me. Bora could not become one of them.

My heart was pounding, blood rushing like a river and roaring in my ears. Haeji was leaning against the building, a trickle of crimson creeping down her face, the area around the wound swollen like an egg.

"What did you just say?" I asked, a cold sharpening my tone as if winter had never left.

"Forgive me, Jeonha. The queen is gone. Someone must have taken her," she said through panting, wincing with every word from the pain.

I gritted my teeth and clenched my fists. "Minje, take Haeji back to the palace and call for the royal physician."

Haeji pushed herself off the wall, limping a step towards me. "Jeonha, I am fine. Please allow me to look for—"

"No."

An order. It was not a punishment though. She was too injured to be of use and would impede our efforts.

"Haeji, please don't worry. I promise to find her," Dongbin said, his hand reaching out to grasp her forearm with a gentle squeeze.

"Go. Now," I commanded, and Minje saluted and dragged a reluctant Haeji back towards the palace.

"Shall we lock down the capital?" Dongbin asked, his brows bunched together.

"Yes, but only the Royal Guard will join us in the search for the queen. I do not trust that the city guards are untainted by Min spies," I replied, turning and stalking back towards the palace.

Dongbin's tone came out unusually dark for the normally optimistic man. "Do you think Chief State Councilor Min is the cause of this?"

"Nothing nefarious is done in Joseon without his influence," I hissed, cursing myself for being too arrogant, for not seeing this coming.

It felt like I was always one move behind him, every advance I made matched with his own. He wouldn't win this time. I would tear down the entire city to find her, and if she was found harmed...then the history records would remember this night as one of great bloodshed.

As I led a retinue of Royal Guards back into the capital to search for Bora, an arrow flew through the air and landed in a tree trunk several strides away.

"To the king!" Dongbin shouted, and the soldiers surrounded me in a wall of bodies.

I scanned around but could not see anyone, granted in the darkness, the perpetrator could be hiding anywhere. But no more arrows came, the area around us silent and serene.

Gesturing with my hand, I gruffly ordered, "It's fine."

Pushing past the circle of guards, I strode towards the tree. Wrapped around the arrow shaft was a note, and I untied the string and uncurled the paper.

Eastern forest. Come alone or the queen dies.

I swore and crumpled the paper in my fist, my grip tightening around the hilt of my sword. It had been a long time since I had held my weapon, and my blade was begging to be used tonight.

"Jeonha, what is it?" Dongbin asked, appearing by my side.

I planted the crumpled paper in his chest, and he scrambled to open it. His eyes narrowed as he read, his knuckles turning white.

"It's a trap," he hissed.

"Indeed," I growled, already heading in the direction of the eastern forest.

"What's the plan?" Dongbin asked while he motioned for the rest of the soldiers to follow.

I paused, turning to face him. "Get bows and follow my trail. Whether it is a cave, home, or just in the middle of the forest, you need to surround them. I'll get the queen while you take care of the rest."

"That's it? That's the plan? I mean no disrespect but—"

I cut him off with a glare, one full of warning that he had better stop talking and just follow my orders. "That's what you're for, Dongbin. What makes me a good leader is surrounding myself with capable people who are smart enough to be flexible and think on the fly. Do your job. Now go," I ordered and took off towards the woods, not bothering to look back.

Dongbin would follow my commands, even if he disagreed. He worried about my safety, but mine was nothing compared to Bora's. I had an army to come rescue me. She only had me. Her snake of a father would never help her and was in all likelihood the mastermind behind this trap. His end goal could be to kill her along with me. Nothing was immoral to that serpent.

Glancing to the star-splattered sky, I prayed for Bora's safety, begging the heavens to guard her until I could arrive.

Jogging brought me to the forest in less than an hour. I slowed to a walk and crouched to catch my breath and check for any signs of people. Amidst the foliage, something shimmered in the moonlight, a flash catching my eye when I turned my head. Twigs snapped under my feet as I approached. Leaning down, I plucked the object from the ground. My hand began to shake, and my nostrils flared. Bora's pin. Whether it had fallen accidentally or was purposefully left behind to lure me in the right direction, I didn't care, my feet stomping forward to where she was waiting.

I'm coming, Bora.

Chapter 23

Bora

DARKNESS AND A MOIST must assaulted my senses as I slowly opened my eyes, my head aching. I blinked until my blurry vision cleared. What happened? I looked around, trying to figure out where I was. My skull was pounding from whatever drug had been used to knock me unconscious. I tried to stand but couldn't, and it was then that I noticed my hands were tied behind my back, a rough rope rubbing against the skin of my wrists.

My eyes scanned the room. Only the faintest streams of moonlight filtered through the thatched shack, darkness consuming the majority of the space. Scattered straw on the floor poked my legs, and I grumbled to myself, frustrated at my inability to scratch my itching thigh. I jerked around, trying in vain to free myself of my bonds.

After a few futile tries, I gave up. There was no use wasting my energy. Panic started to sprout, my heart beginning to beat faster. Taking a deep breath, I forced myself to calm, coaxing the anxiety back to sleep.

What would the king do?

The king wouldn't have gotten himself into this mess in the first place...

I shook my head, which helped extinguish the last of the fog clinging to my mind. Self-deprecation would solve nothing. Perhaps if I figured out who took me, I could at least be prepared and plan on how to escape. The last thing I remembered was calling out to Haeji when someone came up behind me and covered my mouth. Then everything went black.

I opened my mouth to shout for help but thought better of it. It would only alert my captors that I'd awoken. But suddenly, the doors ripped open, revealing men possessing torches and malevolent expressions. Chills ran down my spine despite the warm spring night.

"Who are you?" I asked, my trembling voice betraying me and any desire I had to appear strong.

The man who had opened the door frowned. "I'm sorry about this, Mama."

"Then you know who I am. You should let me go. I promise I won't punish you," I stuttered.

The man shook his head. "I'm afraid I can't let you go until the king gets here. It's nothing personal."

Tears began to well in my eyes, and my head fell to my chest. "The king won't come for me. I'm the daughter of the Chief State Councilor. He will probably thank you for killing me for him."

Hopefully, my words were true. I couldn't bear the thought of the king walking into a trap all because of me. After failing my father, I didn't want to fail the king too.

One of the men holding a torch spoke, his voice muffled by the cloth covering most of his face, "See! I told you we shouldn't have accepted this job. If he won't come, we might as well have some fun with her and be done with this."

The first man snapped, "No! That's not what we were hired for."

"Someone's approaching from the forest!" a voice shouted from outside, saving me from the ill intent of the masked man.

The man with the torch hollered triumphantly before reaching down to grab my arm. He tried to yank me up, but I willed myself to be a heavy rock. He grunted and pulled again, but I refused to budge.

I looked up at him and said in as soft and unassuming a voice as possible, "I'd be able to get up if my hands weren't behind my back."

The man's brows contorted as he contemplated for a moment. The rest of the men, who had already rushed outside to set whatever trap they had planned, shouted for the torch-wielding man to hurry. He mumbled some words to himself and pulled out a knife and crouched. He sawed at the ropes behind me until I felt them fall and the air kiss my wrists.

I had never been so happy to weigh so much.

He didn't return the knife to his waistband, instead keeping it pointed at me as he ordered in a gruff voice, "Up."

I clambered to my feet, my mind racing over what I should do. Someone was coming, but it wasn't necessarily the king. Why would he risk his life for the daughter of his enemy, the woman who had once tried to poison him?

"I think I can see someone," one of my captors hissed to his comrades.

I prayed it wasn't the king.

We stepped out of the shack and into the moonlight, and I peered at my surroundings. A makeshift log barrier guarded a house and the shack I had just been in. Men, all armed with swords, knives, or wooden spears, had gathered around the entrance of the wall. The sound of someone approaching from the forest that surrounded us grew closer and closer, leaves and twigs cracking and crunching under the unknown person's footsteps.

Please not the king. Please not the king.

A cobalt jeonbok with golden dragons appeared in the moonlight.

He had come.

I waited for a retinue of guards to follow behind, but nothing, not a single sound of an army approaching.

He was completely alone.

The king had a sword in his hand, his eyes hard and cold, holding the promise of death in their dark pits. "How dare you kidnap *my wife*," he growled.

But suddenly his eyes flashed with fear, and I felt cold steel against my neck.

"Drop your weapon," one of my captors yelled.

His brows drew together as he frowned and stalked forward.

"Not a step closer or we'll slice her throat," the man holding the blade to my neck shouted.

He froze, and I could see he was analyzing the situation. His grip began to relax on his hilt.

"Don't drop it. They want to kill you," I said as loud as I dared, hoping the movement wouldn't cut my skin against the sharp weapon.

That was the only way this all made sense. Why kidnap me and not kill me? The men had even admitted that I was the bait to lure out the king from his well-guarded palace.

His fingers tightened their grip on his sword. He took another step forward, but halted abruptly when I hissed in pain. My neck stung, and I felt something wet slide down my skin.

"I mean it! I'll slice her throat if you come any closer," my captor warned in a shrill voice.

The king's arm swung back down and hung by his side. Understanding washed over me, and my heart dropped to my stomach.

"No," I whispered, afraid that if I spoke too loudly the blade would dig deeper into my neck.

His sword fell to the ground with a thud, and the rest of my captors swarmed the king, circling him like a pack of wolves. Water formed in my eyes, and my vision blurred as my chin quivered. However, his face was calm, his eyes never once leaving me even as his shoulders drooped in resignation.

One of the men kicked the back of his legs, and the king's knees collided with the ground in a hard smack. The man holding the blade at my throat relaxed just a bit, and a cry escaped my throat, the king wincing from the pain.

"SEOJUN!" I screamed, a high pitched wail that shattered the twilight.

Another knee slammed into him, eliciting a deep grunt from Seojun's throat.

"No! Please don't hurt him," I begged, tears sliding down my cheeks.

Seojun's gaze locked on me, and he smiled. "Don't worry, Bora. I may not win, but I never lose."

Those words must have ignited a fire in the men, for they all started to beat him in a furious flurry. Seojun grunted as each hit and kick landed, blood dripping from his lips after a man smashed his fist into his mouth. He fell onto his hand, his other clutching his side as the assault continued.

"Stop! Please, I'm begging you! Stop hurting him," I screamed, thrashing in the grip of the man holding me.

Even as he was beaten, a cracking sound echoing after a hard kick to his ribs, he never took his eyes off of me. Sobs racked my body, my chest heaving up and down while I pleaded for his life, my wails meeting a stone cold wall of indifference.

"Close your eyes, Bora," Seojun rasped, his face already swelling and turning red.

I shook my head. How could I shield myself from the horrific sight when he had sacrificed himself for me? I cursed myself for being so useless. I was helpless, unable to do anything to stop the attack on Seojun.

Without warning, a whizzing sounded through the air, and the men beating Seojun slumped to the ground, arrows protruding from their bodies. Shock froze me for a breath before I processed what was happening. I gritted my teeth and flung my head back as hard as I could, pain exploding through the back of my skull as I made contact with the face of my captor. It was enough to make him stumble back, his knife-holding hand falling to the side, his other flying to cover his bleeding nose.

My fingers flung to my throat, checking that there were no more cuts. I let out a long breath in relief that my neck remained intact. Seojun jerked his head up and reached for his sword that lay nearby. He wrapped his fingers around the hilt and sprang forward. I turned my head just as he reached the man who'd been holding me hostage. He had recovered from the hit to his face, but Seojun was faster, the tip of his blade pointed right at the man's throat.

The man dropped his sword immediately and lifted his hands in surrender.

"Who ordered you to do this?" Seojun demanded with a hiss, his words dripping with venom.

Just then, several guards appeared, but one of them had a bound man, a cloth obscuring his nose and mouth. But those eyes looked familiar, and wrapped around the hair on his head was a strip of cloth with jagged feathers...

Seojun limped toward the masked man and ripped the cloth from his face, and my suspicion—my horror—was confirmed. Hanbin stared at me, eyes full of fear and something else I could not read. But I did not care. My blood rushed through me, a beating drum demanding retribution.

Lifting his bruised and bleeding arm, Seojun pointed his sword at Hanbin's neck. "Did someone put you up to this?"

I winced, knowing that the "someone" that Seojun suspected was my father.

Hanbin shook his head before fixing his eyes back on me. "No. No. *No.* You weren't supposed to come, and on the off chance that you did, they were supposed to stop you before you got here. Bora was supposed to see how little you cared for her. *I* was going to rescue her!" His words grew louder and shriller the more he spoke, desperation dripping from his eyes, begging me to understand.

"That's not what *they* said," I hissed, pointing to the bodies on the ground. "They said they took me in order to lure the king here. They threatened to kill me."

Hanbin's eyes were as wide as the moon above us. He tried to yank himself free of the guard's grip but to no avail. "That wasn't what we discussed. That wasn't what was supposed to happen!"

Without thinking, my legs brought me forward, and my hand collided with his face in a thundering smack, his head jerking to the side. The shape of a red palm remained on his cheek, and I backed away, seething.

"Bora, wait. I love you. Your father promised you to me when we were children. *You* promised me! You were supposed to be mine," he said, eyes wild and nostrils flaring. He whipped his head towards Seojun. "You! You stole her from me."

Seojun leaned forward, rotating his sword so that the sharp side nestled against Hanbin's chin. "Her father forced her onto me, but I intend to keep her."

He whispered something in Hanbin's ear that I couldn't hear, but whatever it was enraged him, his face turning as red as the handprint I left on his face, his eyes bulging. Hanbin cursed and writhed, but he could not escape the guards. Seojun waved his hand in the air as if swatting away a pesky fly. The guards nodded and dragged my old friend away, his feet dragging in the soil where my affection for him would be buried.

My heart ached at the pitiful sight of my childhood friend, but as I turned towards Seojun, the sorrow mutated into rage. Hanbin had hurt him, but he had only been able to hurt him because I was so useless, so naïve. I had allowed Hanbin into the palace and had agreed to meet him during the festival.

Tears poured down my face once more. I leapt towards Seojun, my arms wrapping around him and squeezing as I cried out, "I'm sorry. This is all my fault."

Seojun let his sword clatter to the ground and embraced me, one hand patting my head. "It's not your fault that I got injured, but it is your fault for squeezing me while my ribs are broken," Seojun croaked.

I reeled back, wiping my nose and face. "Oh, I forgot. I'm sorry," I mumbled as I scolded myself, my head dragging down to the ground.

I was causing him even more pain. He shouldn't have come for me.

A warm hand gently grabbed my chin and lifted my face up. Seojun gazed into my eyes, his irises glistening in the moonlight. He paid no heed to the fact that some of his guards were still present, and he whispered, "This will be the only time in your life that I will reject your touch. Next time, you'll never get me to let go."

Then his lips pressed into mine, and the taste of metal filled my nose and mouth. But I didn't care. I leaned into him, enjoying the embrace of our mouths and the way my body warmed and tingled, washing away the bad memories of that night. My hands, seeming to have a mind of their own, reached towards his torso and gripped his clothes.

All of a sudden and all too soon for my liking, he pulled back. He winced, and my heart plummeted to my stomach. Was it displeasing to him? Was I that bad at it?

Gently, he grabbed my forearms and pulled my hands away from his body. "My lips are sad to part from you, but my ribs are begging for your hands to stay away," he said with a chuckle and a wince.

An awkward laugh burst from my throat as I tried to apologize. "I'm sorry. I keep forgetting."

He leaned forward and pressed his lips to my forehead. When he pulled away he said, "Let's go home, Bora."

Home. I was already there. Where he resided, that was home.

Whether we were in the palace or in the middle of a forest, so long as he stayed with me, it was safe. He was the land, the barrier between me and the Dragon King who wanted my liver. I smiled and interlaced my fingers with his, indifferent to the dirt and blood crusting his hand. As we walked out of the little walled hut and into the twilight forest, guards surrounding us, I pressed my body against his. He was alive, and even more than that, he had come for me. There was one man in this world who would tear down cities and mountains to find me.

Chapter 24

Bora

AFTER ARRIVING AT THE king's chambers, I ordered the servants to draw a warm bath, and as soon as we were alone, Seojun swept me into an embrace despite his earlier protests of pain. I returned it, careful not to touch his ribs. Beneath the smell of blood and soil, the scent of incense and citrus still clung to him, comforting me in its familiarity. My mind wandered to the feeling of his lips against mine, and a warmth in my stomach blossomed all throughout my body.

My face turned hot, heat sprawling along my cheeks to my ears and down my neck, and I tucked my head to hide from his gaze. Gentle fingers gripped my chin with a feather-light touch as Seojun lifted my face. His eyes were filled with a glowing ember of longing, and my heart leapt in my chest as they burned into me. It was not the same way that it burned when I first met him, like the way the freezing winter digs deep into your bones. It was the burning sun on a cool spring morning, a comforting heat that tempted you to stay in its welcoming rays as it kept the chills at bay.

"I hope you know that I would tear apart all of Joseon to find you, Bora," he whispered, his fingers lingering on my face, reluctant to let go.

His face drew closer to mine, and I inhaled, my body buzzing and my stomach full of flapping wings. Just when our lips were about to meet, the door slid open, and servants entered. We both took a jarred step back, his phantom touch lingering on my skin as I cast my eyes to the ground.

"I'll—I'll wait for you here," I mumbled, my fingers wringing together.

"I won't keep you waiting long," Seojun said, sending me a smirk before exiting the room, servants trailing behind him.

After they left, Haeji entered, her footsteps fast and her lips pursed, carrying a box overflowing with bandages and containing clinking ceramics of what I assumed was medicine. She collapsed at my feet, pressing her forehead—a red egg of a welt just above her eye—to the floor and wailed, "Mama, please forgive me. I failed to protect you."

I reached down and gripped her elbows, gently tugging her up. "You did nothing wrong. And I am fine, so there is nothing to be sorry about."

Haeji rose, scooting closer on her knees, her hands grabbing my chima. "Are you injured at all? Shall I send for the physician?" she asked with a voice that reminded me of my mother, her eyes scanning my face and body, searching for any wounds.

Offering a smile, I patted her shoulder. "I'm fine, really." I did my best to fill my voice with sincerity, because although my body was unharmed, my heart wrenched into two.

Seojun had gotten hurt on my behalf, had almost died for me, and my childhood friend had betrayed me, had done something so selfish and cruel. All of our shared memories were tainted, and tears welled in my eyes as I thought of the sweet, young Hanbin, so different from the man from tonight. And the true instigator behind tonight's events...

Instead of focusing on such things, I turned my attention to Haeji. Even though she was Seojun's spy, a genuine look of concern formed on her face. The way her shoulders hunched with shame and her eyes filled with sadness, her brows dragging with guilt, was not something that could be easily faked. Even if I had started as an assignment for her, she cared for me.

"You have never once harmed me nor failed me. The king won't hold it against you either," I said softly. "How is your head?" I pointed to the bump protruding from above her brow.

"I've been through worse," she said, giving a hollow chuckle and shrugged.

The doors slid open and Seojun stepped through, his raven hair wet, water dripping onto the wooden floor. He was clad in nothing but white baji, his white jeogori untied, the strings dangling loose at his sides and fluttering like ribbons in a breeze as he walked forward. Haeji's head whipped back and forth between Seojun and I before she leapt to her feet, bowed, and made a hasty exit while mumbling some words I couldn't bother to listen to.

Seojun brushed past her as she exited, his eyes firmly fixated on me. The lantern-light softened his face, but perhaps it was not that he had changed, just that my perception of him had. He sat next to me on the bed, and now that we were so close and he was clean from the bath, I could see the bruises and red wounds from tonight that would take weeks to heal, months if he had broken any bones like I suspected.

I reached down to the bandage-filled box Haeji had left and pulled out a strip of cloth. I glanced back at Seojun, my cheeks reddening. "I'm not sure which ointment to use."

His lips twitched up, and he gave a soft chuckle, a sound like a warm, sunny spring day. "It's alright. I'll pick the correct medicine, and you apply it for me."

I smiled and nodded as he leaned down and pulled out two tiny jars.

He handed me a pale teal one and explained, "This is for open wounds." Then he placed a brown clay container in my hand. "This is to help numb things, which I desperately need on my ribs right now."

He said it like a joke, but he winced when he spoke. I frowned and my hands went to work applying the ointments over his torso. As I dabbed the medicine on his skin, I noticed white scars, pale from age, dotted along his body. I glanced up at him from under my eyelashes, his own staring down at me, and I was certain his gaze had never left me the entire time. For a moment, I thought perhaps this was all a dream and I would wake back in the shack, Seojun's lifeless body on the ground and Hanbin's victorious face leering over him.

Without realizing it, I had started crying. Seojun lifted his hand, his finger wiping away the wet spots on my face.

"I can't help but wonder how much you have suffered, and I don't desire to know who inflicted it upon you," I whispered, my voice cracking as I cried.

I knew who had caused much of his pain, but there had been a deep-seated reluctance to admit it. I couldn't ignore it anymore though. It stared me right in the face, a canvas covered in crimson and dark purple depicting the treachery of my father. He had done horrible things, and greed was a disease that affected generation after generation. Was there any government that was able to avoid it? Did a nation without corruption exist? In the past, I was naïve, but I knew now that such a utopia was a dream, something unattainable in this life.

I had even thought that Seojun prevented Joseon from being such a place, but how foolish I'd been, blinded by my fealty to my father. All those stories my father told me had been perverted versions of the truth. The man in front of me wouldn't harm anyone who was not deserving of it. Jinyoung, all those ministers—they were guilty.

While my fingers continued their work, I whispered, "Why do you pretend to be bad? Why don't you just remove all the dishonest officials and let people see how kind and generous you are?"

For a few moments, he said nothing. I wondered if I offended him somehow.

"I'm sorry," I mumbled.

Seojun shook his head. "You didn't say anything wrong. It's just that I don't want to hurt you by speaking ill of your father."

It hadn't stopped him before, but maybe now he was more concerned with how such words would affect me. But I did not wish to run from the truth anymore, no matter what it cost me. My fingers dabbed a dollop of cream onto one of his cuts, and he hissed, gritting his teeth from what surely stung like a thousand needles.

"It's okay. Speak freely." I blew on the wound, hoping to chase away the stinging pain.

Seojun sighed. "You know your father is the Chief State Councilor, and he had that position since my father's reign. My father was too indecisive and trusting, and he was degraded into nothing more than a puppet for the State Councilors. I learned early on that if I wanted to possess the power of the throne, I had to be more clever than my father, had to make sure that if they refused to love me, they would fear me."

"Isn't it good to have the people's love and respect?" I asked.

"You can have the love of the people or the love of the nobles, but not both," he said and closed his eyes, leaning back on his palms.

He continued, "Better the nobles hate me than the people, better they fear me than attempt to control me. This façade of indifference to their pleas and a volatile disposition are the only shield between me and them. Good kings are often killed for their naivety, for their blind trust in the innate goodness of men, but the tyrants, those who rule with fear instead of love, they live to make a change—for better or for worse. Certainly a handful of the ministers are good and loyal, but the majority are serpents in silk garments, ready to strike their sovereign, slithering in the shadows of secret meetings and solidifying alliances while severing others. Better to be a falcon rather than a dove, better that history write harshly of me than I die before it can be made. They can curse me, revile me, and even remember me with a ruined reputation, but the common folk will be well fed, well looked after, under my reign."

The sentiment was noble, but I still didn't understand why his methods were necessary. "But, if the people are on your side, doesn't that mean the nobles and ministers can't hurt you, less they incur the wrath of the commoners and start a rebellion?"

He shook his head, sighing. "No. The nobility have done their best to ensure that the lower class is too busy surviving to retaliate. Even some past kings have tried to keep the commoners in a strict caste and limit access to advancement. It wasn't until King Sejong that reading became possible for most. Peasants with pitchforks do little against a well armed military anyways."

How unfair the world could be. How wicked people could be.

Seojun's voice deepened, his gaze glazed over as he stared off into a place I could not follow, "I will be all the darkness so that they may live in the light. I am the wall between the greedy and the common folk. I will bear the blows, endure the scheming and scorn, all to keep them safe."

Safe from people like Hanbin, like my father.

"You're not the darkness, Seojun. You're the moon, reflecting the light even in the night, a lantern illuminating the path," I murmured and reached to grab his hand.

He had forfeited his name—his legacy—for the people of Joseon. Aside from the little village of children, I doubted that the commoners had a good image of the king. Any credit from a benevolent action would be stolen by the officials as they accepted the people's praise while slandering the king.

In that moment, I vowed to myself that my name would be associated with his, that whether it was praised to the heavens or dragged through the mud, it'd be alongside his.

Chapter 25

Seojun

THE SOFT AND WARM presence of Bora in my arms made me reluctant to get up, to even move lest I wake her from her slumber and bring an end to this moment of tranquility. Gently, I pressed my lips to her forehead. With my hand, I ran my fingers through her dark hair, inhaling her scent. If I could have stayed like that forever, I would have. For a moment, I considered passing a law that the queen's presence was required for court so we would be together throughout the day.

However, I knew she would not enjoy it. She was smart, more than she gave herself credit for, but she had no desire for politicking. I loathed it too, but it was a necessity. Another idea, more sensible than the previous one, sparked in my head. I would invite Bora to stay in my chambers. Or I could stay in hers. Whatever she wanted.

All I desired was to never be apart.

As her eyes fluttered open, I looked down at her and smiled.

"How are you feeling?" she asked, yawning with a groan.

My head throbbed, my ribs demanded a strong sedative or at least a bowl of wine, and my knees begged me not to move.

"Fine," I replied, ignoring my body that screamed its displeasure at me. "How are you? Did you sleep well? Any nightmares?" I questioned, brushing her hair back behind her ear.

"I'm fine, too," she said, a smile dusting her lips.

She was a terrible liar. She smiled even when she wasn't alright. In the middle of the night when I awoke from my slumber due to the terrible throbbing in my ribs, soft sniffles and muffled sobs had sounded next to me. It must have been so hard for her, the betrayal and the confrontation of her father's undeniable guilt. I wondered if she knew how strong she was.

"Bora, you wear your smile like a shield, but if you will allow me, I will be your palace walls. I will be the sanctuary where you can unleash the tears and speak of your fears. I don't care if you cry every day. I will wipe your face and hold you all the same."

She sucked in a breath, water welling in her eyes. When she spoke, her voice trembled, "I was so scared last night."

As the salty rivers streamed across her nose and down to her pillow, I reached a hand towards her face, my finger tracing the wet lines. "I'm sorry that I failed to find you sooner. I'm sorry for not following you faster at the festival," I whispered, my voice breaking in the middle of the sentence.

She sniffled. "I'm not talking about that." Her palm cupped my cheek. "I was afraid that you were going to get killed."

My body stilled, my heart skipping a beat. "You were scared for me?"

She nodded, her finger going to the bruises that I was all too aware of on my face. I winced as she accidently pressed too hard on one of them.

Yanking her hand back, she cried, "It's all my fault. I left you and Haeji to find Hanbin. Because of me, you were hurt."

I did my best to shrug while lying down, fusing a lightness to my words. "That's just part of being king. It's my duty to help my subjects."

The joke didn't appear to ease her guilt at all, and she sniffled again.

"Well..." I began softly, "You could always stay with me every night instead of once a week. Then you could make sure I am always safe."

She gasped, her eyes widening and mouth parting. "I–I don't think I am ready for that."

A weight pressed on my chest, crushing my excitement. I was disappointed, but I understood. "I'll wait for you, Bora."

I removed my arm from beneath her neck and slowly leaned up with a groan. My body insisted that I lay back down, but defiance was one of my better traits.

"Where are you going?" Bora demanded as she bolted upright.

"I need to meet with some officials," I replied with a wince, my ribs and stubbornness wrestling with each other.

Bora crawled past me and stood in front of me. "No," she said firmly. "You need to rest. Invite the officials here to speak with you."

"I can't let them know I am hurt, especially with your father's schemes getting bolder," I retorted a little too rough due to the pain.

Bora grimaced. "I understand, but you have me, for what it's worth, and Haeji and Dongbin and Minje. If you push yourself too hard now, you won't heal properly and will be weak for longer."

I sighed. "Fine. But I expect you to at least check on me before you go to sleep," I replied with a smirk that caused almost as much pain from the bruises on my head as it did pleasure at seeing Bora blush.

"R-right," she mumbled and spun and nearly ran out the door.

After she left, Dongbin entered, glancing back to where the queen had just hastily escaped.

"Call for Inspector Kim from the Inspector-General Office," I ordered, wincing again as I laid back down.

The knife in my hand sliced the top of the wooden circle with ease. Laying down with nothing to do felt torturous. To keep my worries away, my hands needed to be doing something.

"Any updates on the investigation, Inspector Kim?" I asked from my bed, wood shavings sprawling over my lap.

The inspector bowed, his lips drawn in a straight line. "No, Jeonha. The few men left alive from the forest all pointed their fingers at Hanbin. Although Hanbin alluded to the Chief State Councilor's participation, he refused to provide any more details. If we brought the case to the court meeting, one could contest that Hanbin was trying to pass the guilt along to spare himself. I do not think there will be sufficient evidence to arrest the Councilor."

A chunk of brown went flying as I gouged the wood. "There has to be something. He can't possibly be erasing all evidence. There is always something left, some crumb, some thread to follow," I growled.

The inspector slowly stood, rubbing a thumb against the thin stretch of facial hair that dusted his jaw. "I think that it would be beneficial to include the queen in the investigation. Perhaps there is something she is privy to—"

My hand holding the knife froze. "Are you suggesting she is complicit?" I asked icily.

"No, Jeonha. But if she was aware of the extent of his crimes and scheming, she may be able to recognize things that appeared innocent enough but in hindsight were suspicious. She may even be able to visit home and search for any evidence."

"It could be dangerous for her. I would not put it past Min to harm his own daughter in his pursuit for power," I grumbled, slicing at the wood.

The previous evening's kidnapping was not to harm Bora, but rather to bait me. I was the only target to be killed. For now.

"Then I am afraid our investigation will be drawn out. Please, Jeonha, reconsider—"

I hissed, a red line forming on my finger from where the blade had made contact. "Do not bring up the matter again," I ordered in an icy tone. "Although I am confident she is on our side, he is still her father. It is one thing to ask her to not interfere, it is another to ask her to actively attack him."

"As you wish, Jeonha," the inspector muttered and bowed.

I had Bora's heart, but I wasn't certain she could handle being part of the plot to arrest her father. She was too kind and a terrible liar. And if she stirred the nest of the snakes, they were bound to bite her. I could not lose her again.

Chapter 26

Bora

THE MOUNTAINS SPRAWLED IN an unnatural shade of teal, but I thought they complimented the red and white cranes and peach blossoms. I had run out of pink paint though, and I had to wait for Haeji to fetch some before finishing the grove of trees nestled at the bottom of the mountains. Footsteps approached, and the door slid open with a whisper.

"Oh, good timing, Haeji, I was just—" The flow of my words stopped at the sight of the surprise visitor.

"Oh, Dongbin. I wasn't expecting you. Is there a message from the king?" I asked.

His eyes searched the room for something—or someone. "Uhhh... No, Mama. I was just wondering if Haeji was here?"

It was then that I noticed something in his hands, a ceramic that resembled one that a physician would possess.

Doing my best to smother my smile, I replied, "She went to get me some paint, but she will be back shortly. You are welcome to wait for her return."

His feet shifted beneath him, and he scratched the back of his neck. "That's alright. I can just come back later." Dongbin turned on his heel to flee, nearly crashing into Haeji, who almost dropped the paint in her hands.

Her eyes widened, but she quickly recovered her composure, taking a step back and inclining her head. "Is something wrong with the king?"

Dongbin shook his head, his mouth opening and closing like fish. At last he found the words to say, "This is for your bruise." He jutted the ceramic towards her, his finger pointing the blue oval above her brow from the night of the festival.

Haeji reached out and accepted his gift, and for the first time I had witnessed, she stammered, "Thank you."

As soon as she finished saying those words, the normally confident guard scurried off. Seeing two of the most calm people I knew lose their composure made me want to laugh. Haeji kept her eyes on the hall, in what I could only assume was her watching the guard running away. A smile tugged at the corners of her mouth. Was there even a faint blush to her face?

Finally, she entered, the paint I had requested in one hand and the medicine in the other.

"Is there something going on between you and Dongbin?" I asked, returning to my painting.

"Who? Oh, the guard?" I had never seen Haeji so flustered. She continued, "Dongbin is just...a colleague. Our mutual service to the king forces us to work together sometimes."

"He is handsome though."

"Indeed he—" She cut herself off with a cough. She cleared her throat. "I never noticed."

I tried to stifle my smile. "Although it is not normally allowed for court ladies to get married, I happen to know someone who could change the rules..." my voice trailed off as Haeji's face got redder.

She placed the pink paint on my table, nearly knocking the others over with the rushed movement, jars clinking together like music.

"That won't be necessary," she mumbled, but her eyes were bright and soft as she opened the medicine, bringing it to her nose for a sniff.

I dipped my brush and stroked it against the paper. "Well maybe you will change your mind. You weren't attached to me at first either."

"That is not true, Mama," she retorted.

"It is okay to admit it. From your point of view, I was a threat to the king. You had no way of knowing otherwise."

"I cannot deny that I was cautious in the beginning. But then you grew on me. Like fungus on a tree."

"Oh. Thank you, Haeji. That is very...touching."

It was Seojun's first court meeting since the incident, and while I waited outside the main palace, shifting my feet and chewing my lip, I couldn't help but worry. Had the meeting aggravated his still healing body? Was he in a lot of pain? Had the officials been extra difficult today?

He should have waited one more week like the royal physician and I—

"Lovely day for a walk, is it not, Mama?" a voice I was intimately familiar with sounded from behind me.

My muscles tightened, and I spun around to see my father, garbed in his court attire, the ivory scepter still in his hand.

My stomach twisted, but I smiled nonetheless. "Yes, indeed. I came to see if the king wanted to take a stroll with me," I lied.

I had never lied to my parents before.

"Mama, if you would please take a moment to speak with me," my father requested, gesturing towards an area barren of others.

"Let us go to my pavilion," I said flatly.

Not a suggestion, but an order of the queen, of his superior.

He cocked a brow, and I was certain he would refuse, would be displeased that I dared to dictate another option and not immediately follow him. To my surprise, he nodded, and I led the way down the path and around the corner towards my chambers. A heavy silence hung between us, sweat forming on my back. I felt like I was going to be sick. I did my best to lull my stomach into calm, praying that I wouldn't vomit. Haeji's presence brought me some comfort.

I led him to the pillared pavilion and sat at the table, the omok board still nestled on its top. My father sat adjacent to me, his eyes glancing at Haeji. Clearly, he wanted me to dismiss them, and he would not speak his true intent until they were gone.

With a sigh, I waved my hand and ordered, "Please give us some privacy."

Haeji wouldn't like it, but I was grateful she left without a word—that she trusted me— the trail of maids following her and standing out of earshot.

After we were alone, he dropped all honorifics, his voice filled with the authority of a father speaking to his daughter instead of a subject addressing their queen. I had mistaken his previous usage of informal speech as an affection for his daughter instead of what it truly was.

"Bora, I won't ask why you failed to follow my instructions, but you must obey me this time. The king is getting more volatile. He ordered an investigatory raid into one of our family businesses in broad daylight. He is going to ruin our family and my plans for Joseon."

A few months ago, I would have believed those words with complete sincerity. I would have trusted my father, that he was trying to improve the nation and help its people and that the tyrannical king was impeding his efforts. I would have believed that the cruel man on the throne wished to reduce my family to nothing.

"Play a game with me, Abeonim," I said, my tone matching the still calmness of the pond next to us, and gestured to the board on the table.

His nostrils flared, his eyes narrowing for a moment before acquiescing. "Alright," he grumbled.

Before he could reach for the small wooden bowl full of black stones, I grabbed it, withdrawing a piece and placing it on the middle of the board. My father's hand folded into a fist before relaxing, and he grabbed the bowl of white stones. He placed his white piece directly above mine.

He opened his mouth to speak, no doubt to give his next instructions for me, but I spoke first. "I have something I'd like to know... concerning Jinyoung." I placed a stone diagonal to my first.

He sighed, chest heaving with what was surely frustration. "What is it?" He shoved his piece right above his previous one, the white orb making a sharp click as it hit the wood.

"Did you send her to kill the king?" I asked, urging my voice to remain steady as I gently set down another stone to create a triangle.

He didn't even bother to keep his voice down, to try to deny it, to create an elaborate reason as to why he felt it was necessary. He simply replied, "Yes."

He had three in a row now.

Setting my piece at the top of his line of stones, I nodded. "I see."

Seojun was right. I'd known it too, deep down, but didn't want to admit it to myself. I needed to hear it from him—to confirm his lack of remorse and his determination to continue trying.

"Now that we have gotten that out of the way, I need you to focus on this next task. During the Summer Hunt, you must lure the king—"

"No."

Silence.

"What did you say?" my father asked, a low threat tinging his tone, the fingers that held his white stone hovering over the omok board as the game held its breath.

I inhaled, shoved my shoulders back, and met his gaze. "I said 'no.' I will not hurt the king, and I ask that you cease your scheming. He is my husband, your son-in-law, and most importantly, your sovereign."

"Can't you see firsthand how wicked he is? You saw how he stole from the ministers. I told you he is conniving and clever. He is manipulating you, Bora," my father urged, leaning forward and gripping my hand.

Placing my other hand over the top of his, I said with a small smile, "He is actually quite nice. I think there was just some misunderstanding between the two of you. Perhaps if you two can reconcile—"

He withdrew his hand, his two fists hitting hard against the table. "Bora, this is my final warning. You cannot allow yourself to be fooled by him. You need to adhere to my plan, for the good of all Joseon. For the sake of your *family*."

"I will not harm him, nor will I allow you, Abeonim," I replied with a steel that surprised even myself.

But Seojun was worth weathering the wrath of my father. After all, I was still his daughter, certainly that had to mean something, to hold some weight. He would not hurt me, not intentionally. If I stood between him and the king, he would not strike.

I added, "I am asking both as your queen and as your daughter."

He leaned back and tucked his hands in his lap. "I understand," he growled. Then he stood and bowed as shallow as a puddle. "Have a good day, *Mama*," he said through gritted teeth.

He did not wait for a reply, did not wait for me to dismiss him, before turning and leaving. I watched him disappear around the corner and turned to look down back at the board.

I'd almost beaten him—four black pieces in a row with open ends.

Following the conversation with my father, I rushed to the king's chambers.

Haeji scurried after me. "What's wrong, Mama?" she asked between breaths.

Wishing to conserve my energy, I did not reply, not wanting to lose any time as I ran past doors, flashes of pillars and gardens blurring out of the corner of my vision as I headed inside. I wound through the halls, my footsteps smacking on the wooden floors.

"Jeonha!" I hollered as I neared the doors of the king's chambers.

Dongbin stood outside, and I could see him open his mouth to say something through the screen.

I slowed to a stop, my chest heaving up and down and gasped, "I have to see the king, Dongbin."

The door slid open, and Seojun loomed over the threshold. His eyes—a rainbow of bruises that not even cosmetic powder could fully hide still coloring his face—were scrunched as he scanned me. "What's wrong?" he asked, his voice coming out strained, his hands reaching out and pulling me inside. His eyes darted to Haeji, "What happened?"

Haeji shook her head from outside in the hall. "I am not sure, Jeonha. Chief State Councilor Min came and spoke with the queen, and right after he left, the queen ran here."

As soon as I had swallowed enough air, the words began spilling out. "My father is going to attempt another assassination during the Summer Hunt."

Time stopped. Everyone froze.

Dongbin moved first, the guard's hand gripping the hilt of his sword as a string of curses against my father left his mouth. Haeji did not speak aloud, but in her eyes, she shared the same sentiment as the guard.

Seojun scowled. "Dongbin, I can't say I don't share that opinion, but please refrain from such comments in front of the queen."

"Yes, Jeonha," he grumbled. Bowing towards me, he muttered an apology.

"Seojun," I whispered in a worried tone. "What are we going to do?"

"Don't worry, I will make a plan," he said comfortingly and cupped my cheek, his thumb caressing my skin.

"But—"

"I may not always win, but I never lose," Seojun said with steely eyes and a smirk, and I was inclined to believe him.

His confidence was enough to overcome my own doubt. The king had navigated many similar situations and came out alive. This time would be no different. As my worries over the hunt eased, another one came to mind. I wasn't sure if Seojun would like me intruding upon his affairs, but it concerned me too.

"What are you going to do with Hanbin?" I asked hesitantly.

"Why do you still care about him?" Jealousy lit up Seojun's face.

"It's not that... Just..." I glanced at Dongbin and Haeji for help, but they were already retreating from the room, a half-suppressed smile on their faces.

Seojun gently grabbed my chin, guiding me to meet his eyes although I so desperately wished to look away. "Do you like him?"

"Not in that way."

"Are you unaware of how he looked at you?"

"Like what?" I stammered.

His voice dropped low, and he murmured, "Like a starving wolf presented with a fawn."

A strange courage came upon me, and I asked, "And how do you look at me?"

His eyes burned as if a glowing ember resided in his irises. "Like a man in a desert who just found the oasis that will save him."

And then our lips were together, fingers tangled in each others' hair as thoughts of Hanbin melted from my mind. Seojun's warm lips and body consumed me, leaving room for nothing else. Suddenly, I understood his analogy of a thirsty man in a desert.

Chapter 27

Bora

THE DAY OF THE Summer Hunt had arrived, and the sweat coating my skin was equally due to the scorching sun and the nerves riling inside me. My father hadn't told me of his plans, and I scolded myself for not playing smarter. I should have let him share his scheme with me before speaking up, so then I could have known how to foil it, to prevent Seojun from getting hurt. Due to my ineptitude, I had no idea what exactly my father intended to do, but I knew he would attempt something today.

That was the only certainty.

Birds chirped, cheers ringing through the air as a soft breeze danced in the branches of the voluptuous trees that waved in encouragement. The horse beneath me shimmered in the sunlight, a serene scene that did little to keep the worry that gnawed on me at bay. I glanced towards Seojun, cobalt jeonbok reflecting like a sapphire in the rays of sun, his gold hairpiece shining like lanterns. Last time I'd seen him wearing it, he'd gotten hurt because of me. I prayed today would not be a repeat of that.

His eyes were narrowed slits, scanning our surroundings while he and Dongbin whispered back and forth, their words too soft for me to hear.

My own eyes darted around us as I shifted in my saddle. A group of assassins? A poisoned arrow? A wild pack of wolves unleashed upon us? All the different ways to die flashed in my head, increasingly creative as my thoughts became muddled with panic.

"Bora," a soft voice said beside me.

I turned to Seojun, his face calm as a wide river, but beneath the deceptive surface, there roared a strong current.

He reached out a hand to caress my forearm. "Don't worry. Everything will be alright."

"You can't be certain. Unless you have a guard in every tree in the forest, there will be danger at every turn." My shoulders folded inward, my gaze cast down to the neck of my horse, its mane fluttering in the breeze. "Can't we just cancel it?"

Seojun laughed softly. "It's a little late for that. Besides, it's tradition, and if I canceled it, it'd be a sign of weakness, a concession to *them*."

I shifted in my seat, mumbling, "I suppose you're right."

"What do I always say, Bora?" Seojun asked, a gentle hand lifting my chin up.

"You may not always win, but you never lose," I said with a faint chuckle.

"That's right," he paused to lean across and kiss my cheek, "so don't worry. Just enjoy the scenery." He straightened in his saddle and grinned. "You're the perfect example. Your father thought he would win by making us get married, but I gained the most beautiful and kind woman in all of Joseon."

I gave him my best smile—his sweet words not enough to calm my concerns—and nodded, my fingers tightening on the reins. No need for him to know just how nervous I was.

"Minje, stay with the queen at all times," Seojun ordered, his voice low and deep, each word dripping with confidence and authority.

He was sure of himself, sure of his plan.

However, he had honor, and my father did not. Seojun had lines he refused to cross while my father never dined with integrity. My only hope lay in that he wasn't so depraved as to harm his own blood.

The string that connected me to Seojun coalesced in my mind, a thin red thread that bound me to him. He would be willing to cut it if it meant saving me—protecting me—but I wasn't willing. I would cling to him with all my might and share his cup of fate.

A horn echoed in the valley, its call bouncing around the trees and ricocheting between the mountains. My heart skipped a beat as our horses moved forward into the forest. I prayed that Dongbin and the rest of the guards would be diligent, their swords swift, and their aim with their bows steady. While the king was hunting prey, the loyal guard would need to be on the lookout for bears, wolves, and boars. How clever and dangerous predators humans were...

Twigs snapped under the hooves of the horses, and the scent of moist soil and summer foliage permeated the air, a nearby stream trickling like chimes. My heart stilled, my breath trapped in my chest as a flash of brown crashed through the brush. Seo-jun lifted his bow and with a twang, the arrow hit the creature. A servant dismounted and walked towards the carcass, and I spun my head around. When we were distracted with a catch, it would be the perfect time to strike.

Nothing.

Exhaling, I forced my shoulders to loosen. Was I being too paranoid? Perhaps my father had a change of heart. Maybe nothing would occur, and I should just enjoy the day in the woods.

My heart plummeted, dread creeping through me like a winter chill.

I wasn't sure how, but I saw the arrow whizzing through the air, and my body moved of its own accord, the heavy sense of danger sending tingles through my limbs. It happened so fast, and I could at last confirm what I'd heard about soldiers going into shock.

It did in fact hurt. *A lot.*

As the arrow pierced my flesh, a blazing agony rippled through every part of me. I shouted, the pain excruciating. Burning. My skin and muscles burned like fire.

My dangui quickly grew wet from the blood pouring from the wound on my bicep. Had it gone straight through and into my ribs? I wasn't sure. Pain thundered through my body, my head and heart pounding as my vision clouded. I felt myself tipping, but just before I collided with the ground, a pair of arms caught me with a grunt. I couldn't hear anything at first, my ears roaring, but I could see Seojun's face contorted with a mixture of fear and rage, his brows pinched together and eyes filled with water. A scarlet-coated hand reached up and touched my face.

Was he injured? Had another arrow been fired?

With shaking hands, I grasped his arm and tried to inspect his hand. "You're...bleeding," I croaked.

He shook his head, offering a smile that didn't reach his eyes, his bottom lip quivering while a tear slid down his cheek. "No, no. I'm fine. It's not my blood."

Not his? Then it must be mine. I was bleeding. I was dying.

My vision began to dim, and my breathing was slowing. Everything felt heavy, but at least the pain was beginning to fade. My arms dropped and fell limp against the ground.

Using the little bit of strength I had left, I rasped, "I love you, Seojun."

The last thing I heard was like a roar of a tiger, a shriek of fury and grief that casted itself all the way to the heavens.

Then everything went dark, and the pain ceased.

Chapter 28
Seojun

SOMEONE WAS SHOUTING. My own words felt hollow, as if they were coming from someone else. Bora lay limp in my arms, blooding staining the silk of her garments and turning the dirt beneath a dark burgundy.

"Minje! Go after the shooter. Dongbin, help me get the queen onto my horse," I barked out, each word sharp as a sword.

Minje took off, his blade a slice of silver amongst the green leaves, two more guards trailing after him. He better run someone through with it. Dongbin rushed to my side, tearing a piece of his cheollik off and wrapping it around the wound, the arrow still protruding from her arm. As soon as he finished, we grabbed Bora and dragged her to my horse. Thankfully, she was unconscious, as the method to get her on the horse lacked any elegance. A bit of embarrassment was better than death. I launched myself up onto the saddle and wrapped my arms around her, cradling her atop the horse. The metallic scent of blood filled my nostrils, sparking urgency.

Without waiting to check if Dongbin had mounted, I kicked the flanks of my horse and flicked the reins. I had been with my horse for years, and I trusted him to weave through the trees while I focused on keeping Bora upright. My heart pounded in tandem with his hooves, flashes of green and brown whipping past me.

Too slow.

We were taking too much time, time Bora didn't have, especially if they'd poisoned the arrow. I pressed my cheek against hers, an unsettling cold greeting my skin.

Faster, faster.

I pressed my heels into my horse, desperate for him to sprout the wings of the mythical chollimas so we could fly all the way back to the palace. As the wind yanked at my robes, so did guilt bite and pull me with its sharp claws. It was my fault. I was overconfident in thinking the increased number of guards would be enough to deter any assassin. I should have moved the hunt closer to the palace. Although I had brought a physician with us, he was of little use out here without all of his tools and medicine.

The arrow meant for me now protruded from her arm. It felt like I had been shot in the heart.

I sat on one side of Bora, hand firmly gripping hers, while the physician kneeled on the other side, tending to her injured arm. After cleaning the wound, he'd wrapped it in bandages, ribbons of white curling around her bicep. Now he held a finger to her wrist, checking her pulse.

"Well? How is she?" I demanded, my words coming out harsher than intended.

The physician shifted, bowing his head. "The queen will most likely survive. It does not appear that the arrow had any substances on it, but she's lost a lot of blood. It may be awhile until she wakes up."

At last, the tension in my shoulders dissolved, and I whispered many thanks to the heavens that the arrow had not been poisoned. If it had, then Bora...

I refused to imagine it.

"You did good. You may leave," I ordered the physician without looking, my eyes fixated on Bora's face.

Days passed, and each time I had to attend to my royal responsibilities, I would rush back, hopeful that her eyes would be open and she'd be smiling. That bright smile that could outshine the sun was a lantern that lit my path. But every time, I was left disappointed. I wasn't sure how many nights had gone on like that, an eternity seeming to stretch on as I sat beside her bed. She had to wake up. I had endured much in this life, but losing her was not something I could recover from.

Laying down next to her, I lifted a hand, gently stroking her hair. My gaze soaked in her features, my heart ringing in pain.

"Please wake up, Bora. I need you," I whispered, my voice cracking as my throat tightened.

Sleep must have claimed me, and when I slowly blinked my eyes open, I felt something brush against my forehead. Lifting my head, I gasped. A round face and songpyeon-shaped eyes peered down at me.

I scrambled onto my knees and enveloped her hand in mine. "Bora," I rasped. Once more with all my eagerness and jubilation infused into that single word, I nearly shouted, "Bora." Leaning over, my lips pressed against her forehead, the skin warm and soft. Sitting back on my heels, I brushed the hair from her face. "How do you feel?"

She glanced down at her bandaged arm and winced. "Sore."

"I'll call for the royal physician. He can get you something for the pain, and he should check you once more just in case. And—"

"Seojun," she groaned as she sat herself up.

My hands supported her back, and she carefully adjusted herself in a seated position.

"I'm fine," she whimpered, her eyes fixated on her fingers, avoiding my gaze.

"What's wrong? What hurts?" the words tumbled from my lips.

"He...he still did it. Even after I asked him not to..." Her voice trailed off as it began to crack.

"It's okay to cry. Tell me what you need from me," I whispered, stroking her hair.

Still she smiled; even when water welled in her eyes and her bottom lip quivered, she kept her mouth upturned. "I'm fine," she stated, her voice shaking while she did her best to hold onto those words, to the lie.

This was a death of sorts: a death to the dream, to the desire for love and protection from the man who should provide it to her. The relationship between daughter and father completely unraveled, each thread removing its place in her heart with a painful snap.

"W-why, w-weren't we enough?" she blubbered, her chest heaving as she choked out each word. "Why did he need more power? Why didn't he choose us?" Her hands curled into tight fists by her sides.

Careful not to put pressure on her wounded arm, I pulled her into me as she wept.

"My father... He was going to kill you today. It didn't matter that I begged him not to," she sobbed.

I didn't know what to say. Her father had done many terrible things that I couldn't deny. He had tried to kill me on multiple occasions. All I figured I could do was hold her and keep him from hurting her again.

When her weeping ebbed, she uttered words that I wouldn't have ever imagined coming from her lips a few months ago. "Do what you must. Do not allow my relation to him stop you."

I pressed my lips to her temple. "I love you, Bora. Thank you for choosing Joseon. For choosing me."

She didn't reply right away.

To break the silence, I asked in a teasing tone. "When did you start falling in love with me?"

"I-I don't know. I think it started the day you covered me from the rain. You didn't ask what was wrong, just comforted me in a silent way," she replied, wiping her eyes.

Her ears were turning red, and I smiled. That day remained in my memory, although I didn't recall the reason I went to her palace. There were many times I found my steps wandering to her, stopping myself just before we made contact. I didn't stop myself that time. She looked so sad, and I was very familiar with what it was like to hide my tears in the palace. No one comforted me when my mother was gone, nor when my father left this life. Even if she was thinking of ways to kill me, she didn't deserve to cry alone.

"And me?" she inquired sheepishly, fumbling with her fingers.

"You? Well at first I just hoped you weren't my enemy. But love... It was slow like a blooming flower, being rained upon by your smile and kind words to the servants. But what started it all was when we went into the city. At the time, I hoped to simply turn you into an ally, but the way you interacted with the children..." I paused and gazed at her as if she was a breathtaking painting, my eyes tracing every line of her face, content to study her for all of time. "You are kind and strong, Bora, in so many ways, and I knew that even if you were the death of me, I'd keep you by my side."

"I am sure Haeji, Dongbin and Minje were not very happy with that idea," she joked, chuckling softly.

"Well, thankfully you were a terrible assassin, nearly poisoning yourself in the process," I teased.

"Was that when you started trusting me?"

"Yes. As a man, I was ready to be devoured by you, to drown in your arms, but as a king, I could not allow myself that luxury, could not be drawn into the dangerous waters that were you. I resisted, which was made easier by the constant attempts on my life by your father."

I regretted the last sentence as she stiffened beside me. To me, he was an enemy, an evil entity I was determined to end, but to her, he was a father who housed and clothed her, had given life to her. There was an innate desire for a loving father that for many was left unsatisfied in life. Victory for me meant mourning for Bora. Even if she was on my side, dedicated to seeking justice and removing the infestation of corruption, it would not be easy, like each step towards that goal was taken on a path of hot coals.

"Sorry," I mumbled.

"No," she breathed out with a sigh. "I should get used to hearing such things. I am sure every day there is a commoner cursing his name."

I stifled a laugh. Clearing my throat, I replied, "You should get some rest. I have something important to ask you later."

She twisted her head to look up at me, her eyes red and puffy. "What is it?"

Pressing another kiss to her forehead, I whispered, "Later. For now, you should rest."

Chapter 29

Bora

A STRANGE TIGHTNESS PULLED at the skin around the wound, and the itching was going to drive me mad. Every time Seojun caught me scratching, he scowled and threatened to call the royal physician to give me one of those foul-smelling ointments. While we waited for the official he'd summoned, I glanced towards Seojun, making sure he wasn't watching. I slowly lifted my hand to my upper arm, fingers ready to attack the irritating scab.

"I think the physician left some ointment for you," he threatened.

With a huff, I lowered my hand.

Seojun leaned over and whispered in my ear with a sultry drawl, "I can offer you a distraction."

Heat crawled along my skin, and I shifted in my seat. Just then, a man garbed in burgundy entered the king's quarters.

Wonderful timing.

I casted a glare at Seojun, promising revenge, but it only served to widen his grin.

"This is Inspector Kim," Seojun explained, gesturing towards the official who bowed before us, facial hair dusting his jaw and around his mouth.

He was young—perhaps the same age as Jinho.

"He is one of the new appointments to the Inspector-General Office. He is a good man with integrity."

"The king flatters me," Inspector Kim replied.

I nodded in greeting, offering a smile. "Pleasure to meet you."

The inspector bowed and spoke with a deep voice. "It is truly an honor, Mama. The king always speaks highly of you."

I glanced at Seojun, a brow cocked. The perfect opportunity for revenge. "Really?" I asked in a teasing lilt. "Even back when he thought I tried to have him assassinated on our wedding night?"

Inspector Kim's eyes bulged from his head, his mouth hanging open at what he surely thought was an improper conversation.

Seojun crossed his arms, his lips puffed in a pout. "You thought I was going to kill you that night too."

Leaning towards him so only he could hear I whispered, "You should search me again tonight, Jeonha."

Red slowly crept along his neck and face, his ears the color of berries. I wanted to nibble them. I covered my mouth as I chuckled, a little sorry for the poor inspector standing opposite of us, but there was satisfaction in making the king of Joseon blush.

Just when I thought I had been victorious, Seojun whispered back, low and lilting. "I warned you about starting games, Bora. I'll show you how I finish one tonight."

My lips folded on themselves, heat blossoming in my core.

Inspector Kim cleared his throat and straightened his posture, tearing our attention away from each other and back to him and the matter at hand. Albeit, I wasn't actually sure what that was.

"Jeonha, did you call for me to include the queen in the investigation?" he asked with a seriousness that implied he was eager to move on.

"Investigation?" I asked, turning to look once more at Seojun.

He nodded, a darkness sweeping over his eyes. I would banish such shadows if I had the power.

"Yes. My father, late King Changwon, did not die of natural causes. Someone, or a group of people, poisoned him," Seojun said solemnly, his shoulders dragging.

I gasped and reached out to grab his hand. My heart hurt, but my head knew it was the truth. "My father is responsible, isn't he?"

Seojun only nodded.

In his stead, Inspector Kim spoke, "We believe so, but we have no evidence to convict him."

"Seojun is the king. Can't he just order his imprisonment?"

Certain words clogged in my mouth. We all knew the real punishment that awaited such actions.

"It is not a matter of *could* but *should*. The king has been working hard to clean the court of corruption while also adhering to proper procedures. It is no easy task and at times he has chosen to conduct justice in some unique ways. However, he has never killed or exiled anyone who didn't deserve it, and the evidence is always recorded in the Office of Records," the Inspector explained.

"Sometimes, I don't share the records with the other officials. It helps keep up appearances," Seojun commented, a smug expression painting his face.

In lieu of twirling my hair that was pinned, I chewed my lip. It took me a few moments, but at last I arrived at the reason for this meeting.

"You want me to investigate my father?"

Seojun turned, grabbing both of my hands in his. "If you say no, I will never ask you again. But for the sake of not only my father, but for all of Joseon, I ask this favor of you, knowing how hard it will be, how it will break your heart."

My gaze lowered for a moment before I looked back up, my voice full of a mixture of emotions. "I–I will do it. It is my duty as a citizen of Joseon, as its queen, and as your wife."

At the use of the word, Seojun beamed despite the dark matter we were discussing, and it eased the aching in my heart ever so slightly.

Taking a deep breath, I put a smile on my face and asked, "What do I need to do?"

Seojun squeezed my hand and stated, "I think it's time for you to make another trip home."

Chapter 30

Bora

IT WAS A FORTUNATE thing that I had broken tradition by visiting my family home previously, as it made my current visit less suspicious. Under the guise of wishing to see my siblings and parents, I visited the Min Mansion with Haeji and Minje, who were waiting outside with our palanquin and its carriers.

I hadn't announced my arrival ahead of time, and I slipped inside before anyone came out to greet me. The heavens granted me favor, and I somehow managed to avoid being seen while I made my way to my father's study. The room had always been off limits to me, and even as a child, I had never dared to disobey and enter. The fact that it was all unfamiliar to me made it much more difficult to investigate. I didn't know where he stored his business records nor his correspondence, or if kept such things at all.

My muscles tensed, and I peered around the room, walking around the perimeter like chicken, my head bouncing up and down as I checked every crevice and ridge. I flipped through all the pages of the books on his shelves, but there was nothing out of the ordinary, nothing nefarious. I went to the cabinet behind the desk and crouched down.

Inside were stacks upon stacks of papers. My fingers brushed against the letters, my eyes trying to consume as much information as possible before someone entered. My heart beat faster than a bird's wings, and my blood roared in my ears, urging me to go faster. Messages from other ministers about taxes, copies of old memorials to the king, and accounts of our family's finances were the only content I could find. Nothing out of the ordinary, and definitely nothing depicting dangerous matters, was present in the documents.

I sighed, my fists curling and teeth gritting. There had to be something. Did he have a secret study? No, those were mere fiction, something that only existed in stories. But what about a secret compartment in a table or wall? That seemed more realistic.

My fingers prodded the wall, my eyes scanning for even the faintest crack that would allude to a secret compartment. Nothing. I turned to his desk, a large, thick thing carved from cedar and imported from Ming. I kneeled down and tilted my head to look under it. My eyes were greeted with a crane curled into a circle, its wings protruding just enough to grab. I reached up and tried pushing it. Nothing. I bit my lip and twisted it, praying it would work. A soft click emitted from the wood. I gasped, my heart skipping a beat.

I scrambled back and smiled at the sight of a hidden drawer had opened. My eyes glanced towards the entryway while my ears strained to listen for the sounds of anyone approaching. Silence answered, and I returned my focus to the secret drawer. Pulling it open, a stack of parchment lay nestled in the wooden box. I yanked them out, my eyes devouring the words written like a starving man.

"The Crown Prince is of age now, and he has been insisting on intruding in political matters. The king is starting to listen to his son. Steps should be taken to ensure the crane is caged."

My hands trembled, my mind working to decipher what the message meant, but it wasn't hard to understand that the intent wasn't good. I shoved the paper to the bottom and read the next, my heart beating hard and loud like a gong.

"The king is fond of yakgwa. One of the eunuchs of the king is Ryu's men. He may be useful in clipping wings."

My mind and heart were racing in tandem as I flipped to the next note.

"A daily dose to weaken. The Crown Prince is refusing our guidance. Next step—"

The sound of footsteps thundered closer. I scrambled to stuff the papers into my waistband and shove the secret compartment closed as quietly as I could. As I stood, the door slid open to reveal my father, his eyes widening in shock, then a flash of suspicion and irritation, all gone within a few breaths before his face settled into its normal expression of feigned fatherly affection.

I had never thought of it as a façade, but now I was certain. My father viewed me as nothing more than a tool, a weapon to be wielded and discarded upon his whim. Memories flooded my mind, but a gloomy haze washed over them. Every gift, every compliment, every smile, everything seemed suspect to me now. Had there ever been a genuine moment in which he loved me?

"Bora, what are you doing here?" he asked, but his tone couldn't help but convey some level of cynicism.

My heart beat rapidly, but I willed it to calm, lest my father detect my mutinous intentions. *Everything is fine, Bora. Breathe.*

"I wanted to surprise you with this," I said, putting on my best grin as I lifted a painting that I'd set on the desk upon arriving. I unfurled it, the elongated canvas cascading down and brushing the floor. On one side there were mountains and on the other side a waterfall, a pagoda nestled in between the two. A phoenix and peacock flew at the top, both of their colorful and long plumes flowing around them, their talons outstretched towards the moon that peaked above them all. "I thought I could hang it in your study so that you could see it and think of me," I explained.

The suspicion in his gaze melted, and his shoulders relaxed ever so slightly. He smiled, but it didn't reach his eyes. "I will look at it when I miss you, which is everyday."

Liar.

I kept the smile on my face.

He walked forward and took the painting from my hands. As he rolled it up he ordered, "Let's go. Your brothers and sisters have been pestering me to see you. They are waiting."

I nodded and walked around the desk, glancing to make sure my father was following. My eyes lingered for a moment on the wooden furniture before I turned my gaze back to the courtyard and exited the study. My father walked beside me, the painting in one hand and the other behind his back. Silence hung heavy between us while we made our way past the courtyard full of trees and flowers, past the small pond filled with lotus pads and fish that I had loved to watch as a child. The sun shone down upon the gardens with a gentle kiss. How beautiful our home was, unaware of the viper within it.

When we entered the main room of our family estate, my skin prickled with a sense of danger, as if I were a fawn in the presence of a tiger. My father veered to the left, disappearing around the corner, and with him, the looming sense of something sinister eased.

"You're here!" Iseul squealed and enveloped me in a hug. "You didn't tell us you were coming," she mumbled into my clothes.

Leaning down, I kissed the top of her head. "I wanted to surprise you all," I murmured softly, my stomach still not quite settled.

My eyes fixated on where my father had disappeared. Where was he going?

"Bora!" The collective shout of delight from my brothers broke my focus, and I turned to see Jinho wheeling Minho into the main hall, my arm still wrapped around Iseul.

"Orabeoni." I greeted with a smile, my worries momentarily displaced by the presence of my siblings.

We sat together, and I was able to forget about the letters hidden beneath my garments, the burning weight of the evidence to convict our father fading from my mind.

"How are you feeling?" Minho asked, gesturing to my right arm.

I looked down to my bicep, rotating my shoulder. "A little sore, but much better. I can't say I'd recommend getting shot with an arrow." I didn't allow myself to say by whom. They didn't need to know. Soon enough they would have to confront the extent of our father's crimes, but not now. For now, we could savor the remaining time as a whole family before it shattered.

"I can't believe the king didn't throw himself in front of the arrow to save you. That would have been so romantic," Iseul said wistfully, her fingers intertwined by her chin as a glaze glided over her eyes. She took after my love of stories, although she favored the romantic ones.

"You shouldn't talk about the king unless you plan on praising him," Minho warned in a gentle voice.

Jinho scoffed, "Oh please, it's not like she hasn't heard it from our father, and it's not like he isn't bad for other reasons."

I accidentally met Minho's eyes, which had been watching me like a fox, as he often did, observing reactions. Unable to bear the brunt of his gaze, I turned away. "The king is actually very kind. Father's words are not reality, only his perspective," I insisted, reaching to squeeze Iseul's leg.

"Don't tell me you're in love with that tyrannical trash," Jinho grumbled with a roll of his eyes. "He closed down two of our businesses last month."

"Hyungnim," Minho softly scolded Jinho.

Seojun hadn't told me about that, but I trusted that he had a good reason for doing so.

My words came out with a regal authority, my siblings' eyes widening as they leaned back. "Nevertheless, you will respect him, as my husband and your king."

Jinho gaped, Iseul already daydreaming about some romantic scenario as she giggled, and Minho just smiled.

"I'm happy he treats you well," Minho said, his eyes twinkling.

Iseul beamed and added, "It sounds so sweet. I want to marry someone who will make me feel like that."

"Like what? Like a love-blind fool?" Jinho huffed.

"Like a love so strong that I want to protect it with my mind and body," Iseul replied.

"Sounds like it is very one sided between the two of you," our eldest brother mumbled, leaning back on his palms.

I shook my head. "It's not like that. He would take a thousand arrows for me. He'd even drink poison for me," I argued, my lips curling as I recalled the memory. I stared down at my forefinger, my cheeks warming.

From the corner of my vision, I could see Minho elbow Jinho. "Be nice," he chided.

Jinho scowled, but all of us melted when Minho stared at him with his wide and innocent eyes, his lips puffed and pouting.

With a dramatic sigh, Jinho acquiesced, "Fine. I am so very happy for you two." I nodded in thanks, but then he added with a mischievous smirk, "And I promise not to challenge him to an archery contest, lest our poor sister take another arrow to her other arm."

Iseul started giggling, the spark lit a fire of laughter that swept through us all. The tension that was like a taut rope between my shoulders unraveled, cackles wracking my ribs. It was a precious moment. The calm before a storm.

Haeji entered, and the noise died down. "Excuse me, Mama, but it is time to return to the palace."

Sighing, I nodded and stood, giving each sibling a smile and said, "Take good care of yourselves and share my love with Eomeonim. I wish she wasn't gone to see our grandparents." I'd wanted to see once more—just in case.

A part of me wanted to say more, to warn them to beware of the serpent disguised as our father, but I chose to keep those words locked away. It was better for them that way. Ignorance was safer for them.

We turned and exited, the sound of Jinho and Iseul bickering sending us off. Had they come to recognize our father's lies? If they did, they never gave any indication of it. Jinho had even made negative comments about Seojun. One day, I would get to tell them about how wonderful he was, to correct their misconceptions.

"Bora," a voice called out softly.

I spun around where Minho was rolling his chair towards us, a rare frown dragging his lips and brows down.

"What is it, Orabeoni?"

He tugged his wheels to a stop and glanced around before replying in a quiet voice, "Something is happening between the father and the king, right?"

My eyes darted towards Haeji, who stiffened by my side. "What do you mean?" I asked, keeping my voice as steady and nonchalant as I could manage.

"I played omok with you more than anyone else. I know you, and I know our father."

He pulled up his sleeve, and I covered my mouth, gasping. A rainbow of bruises dotted his skin, some marks yellow and nearly healed, some dark purple like ink stains, while others were red and likely formed earlier today.

I fell to my knees and reached towards his arm, careful not to touch any of the injured areas. "Oh, Orabeoni..." my voice cracked, my vision beginning to blur from the tears.

"In the breath that I lost use of my legs, I lost my father, although I don't think I ever had his love to begin with. Love is not a fickle thing. It is dedication, a devotion that is of the mind and not the heart, that is not bound by the usefulness of the object of its affection," he explained as he patted my hand.

Biting my lip to keep from crying, I sniffled, urging the tears to stay put.

He continued, "Jinho has never told you or Iseul, but he actually owns a small fabric shop in the city. He doesn't care if the things father told us about the king are true or not, as he is more concerned with the tyrant in our own home. I think he doesn't care for either of them. Forgive him for how he thinks of the king."

"I understand." Enveloping his hand in mine, I squeezed his fingers.

"He has been saving up money to buy a small estate. It's on the outskirts of the city, quaint but big enough for him, mother, Iseul and I."

I threw my arms around him, Minho grunting as I swallowed him in an embrace. He had been ignored by our father, except for when he needed an outlet for his anger, apparently. But Minho had been observing, and now he knew I was going to do something.

How much had my brothers hid from me? How many times did they shield my sister and I from the man who was supposed to protect us?

"I am so sorry," I whimpered and released him.

He shook his head. "It is not your fault. Just know that we will not blame you if something happens. I trust you, and you trust the king. I know that only the guilty parties will be punished."

Minho waved goodbye and spun his chair around, leaving much unsaid but more than I had ever expected. As we left, I prayed, for I would not allow them to become pawns in my father's hand. We had to act quickly. Now that Jinho had passed his exams, our father would force him to enter one of the ministries of his choosing. He had sired servants, not children.

The marks on Minho were seared in my mind, and any final feelings of reluctance unraveled. The Dragon King would get no rabbit liver. It was time for Joseon to be free of its tyrant.

Chapter 31

Bora

After arriving back at the palace, I headed for the king's chambers, the papers in my waistband weighing heavy. My legs churned as I hastily made my way through the halls. How would he react? Once he had the proof of my father's treachery, would he execute him right away? Despite deserving such a fate, the thought still made my heart ache.

We reached the door of Seojun's room, a guard I had only met a few times standing outside.

"Jeonha," I called out.

In less than two breaths, the door opened, Seojun standing in the threshold. The bruising had almost completely healed, only a faint yellow tinging his skin. He pulled me inside and closed the door, not even allowing Haeji to enter. I thought he would ask if I found anything, but instead he yanked me into him, my face squishing into his chest.

"Thank the heavens you are alright," he said, letting out a long breath as he squeezed me tightly.

"Seojun, I'm sorry," I mumbled into his clothes. Would he shove me away when I showed him the letters?

He pulled back just enough to look at me, his hands still clinging to my sides. "Why are you apologizing? You came back to me unharmed, and that is the greatest gift."

Avoiding his eyes, I reached into my hidden pouch and pulled out the papers. Presenting the parchment to him, I stated, shoulders tense in anticipation of his rightful rage, "These are letters that prove my father's crimes."

I slowly lifted my face, prepared to see anger or grief or some mixture of the two. Instead, Seojun took the letters, his face calm as he flipped through each one. The silence was not what I was expecting.

"Seojun..." I stopped myself. It was best to let him talk when he wanted.

Once more, he reached out and pulled me into an embrace, the letters crinkling against my back. "Thank you. I can't imagine how hard it was for you," he said, his voice beginning to crack.

He buried his face into my hair, and I stroked his back as I felt something wet land on my head. But the man who mourned his father disappeared quickly, replaced by the king who was pursuing justice, whose responsibilities overrode his personal feelings. He wiped his face and stepped away, and I fought the urge to continue holding him.

"Haeji," he called out. The door slid open, and she entered. "Send for Inspector Kim," he ordered and resumed looking at the letters.

"If you don't mind, I'd like to return to my chambers. I don't think I want to be present for the looming discussion," I requested, rubbing my injured arm.

Seojun nodded, his voice serious. "Very well. I will come see you later." And with that, he turned and sat at his table, spreading the papers out across the wood.

Part of me was hurt because he did not seem to notice that I was upset, but I supposed that there would be many times in which I had to share my husband with Joseon, that he would have to prioritize his responsibilities as ruler over that of a husband. With a sigh, I left, Haeji following after me.

"I want to be alone for a while, Haeji," I said while we walked towards my palace.

"I cannot leave you unattended, Mama," she replied firmly.

"Then just stay outside my room for a little bit. I-I just need to collect myself," I rushed out, my emotions fraying.

After a few breaths, she agreed, "Very well, Mama. I will wait by the door."

My heart was being crushed into a thousand pieces as I prepared myself for the coming consequences my father would face. For the first time, I thought about my mother, how she related to all this. Was she aware of his schemes? Did she know of Minho's bruises? Before, I would have thought such things ludicrous, that such a sweet woman would be incapable of harboring ill intent. But I no longer trusted my ability to discern peoples' characters. My father, Jinyoung, Hanbin...

I could not recall my mother ever visiting my father in his study, and she had been against my marriage to the king. She and my father had never been affectionate in front of us, and I had always assumed it was due to propriety. Now, I figured it had more to do with the lack of love between the two. My father had none to give, of that I was certain. No matter how naïve I had been about the others, there was no way she was complicit.

What would she do after...after everything played out? Of course I could take care of her—Seojun would never let her want for anything—but did she have any dreams? I had wanted to start a restaurant. My mother loved to sew, unlike myself. Maybe she could join Jinho in his fabric business.

When we turned the corner, a palace maid nearly crashed into me, my thoughts blinding me to my surroundings. The petite woman fell to her knees, pressing her head to the floor.

"Forgive me, Mama!" she wailed, and her body trembled.

"No harm was done," I encouraged her. "You may go."

"Thank you, Mama," she gushed, quickly scrambling to her feet and scurried off down the empty hall.

Finally we reached my chambers, and for some reason that made my eyes water. But in the privacy of my rooms with no one else around, I could at least allow myself to cry, to feel angry at my father for causing all this, to mourn him and the relationship we would never have.

The tears would not stay put much longer, and without a word to Haeji, I opened the door and went inside, closing it behind me. A voice sounded from outside, but I ignored it. Whoever it was could wait. I made my way towards my bed, passing an incense burner.

This aroma...

A memory tickled the back of my mind. Why was it so familiar? I scanned the room, but it took no more than a few dangerous breaths for my eyes to return to the incense burner, small serpentine tendrils of gray coiling in the air.

Phoenix's Crown.

I clamped my hand over my mouth and rushed towards the bronze burner. Grabbing the container and its contents, I ran outside, chucking it as far away from me as I could. It collided with the ground with a clang, and I whipped my head around, searching for Haeji, Dongbin, or anyone I could recognize. The other maids could not be trusted.

Who had left it in my room? Who had closed all the windows? Who had made sure that no one else was around when I entered? I scolded myself for telling Haeji to leave me alone. Where had she gone? Did someone lure her away?

Panic overtook me, and throwing away all decorum, I sprinted towards Seojun's quarters. My chest heaved as my arms and legs pumped. The idea that someone—some assassin—could be waiting in the event that the incense failed spurred me to run faster. It was silent, too quiet for a palace. Where were the guards? I had been too consumed with my thoughts before to notice the lack of people near my quarters.

The birds chirping above cheered me on. *Go, go, go!*

My lungs burned, and my muscles cramped. Why was the palace so big? Were those footsteps behind me?

When I turned the corner and Seojun's chambers came into view, relief filled me at the sight of Minje standing outside keeping guard.

"Minje!" I hollered the best I could while catching my breath.

His eyes widened, and he sprinted towards me. "Mama! What is the matter?"

I skidded to a halt, my hands resting on my knees. The words that I wished to say couldn't budge as I fought to breathe. After a few agonizingly long breaths, I was able to speak, pausing every few words to pant.

"Something is wrong... There was poison... In my incense burner... No guards... No one at all," I huffed.

Minje's brows furrowed, concern coating his features. He gently grabbed my elbow and escorted me to Seojun's door.

"Jeonha, stay inside. There was an assassination attempt against—"

Minje's words were cut off as the door slammed to the side, the wood hissing as Seojun emerged. His eyes widened, panic straining his features. His gaze shifted to me, his expression softened, and relief visibly washed across his face.

"Bora," he rasped.

There was so much meaning in the way he said my name.

Relief. Rage. Regret.

It wasn't his fault. I was unharmed.

Forgetting Minje was present, I launched myself into him, his arms enveloping me like a city wall—safe and steady.

"Bora, I'm sorry," he whispered into my hair.

I shook my head the best I could while being tucked into his chest. "No, it is not your fault. I know whose it is," I mumbled, the last words coming out with bitterness.

I hated my father. I still loved him. I wanted him dead. The thought of his execution left me sad.

"I won't let them breathe another day," Seojun growled, his arms tightening.

"It was Phoenix's Crown," I stammered as I urged my body to stop shaking.

"I'm going to kill him, Bora."

"I know," was all I said in reply.

When my father had instructed me to poison the king, I had interceded, begging for his life. I would not do so again.

Minho, Seojun, Me. My father would not stop, would not have qualms about burning the country to the ground so long as he came out on top.

Twisting my head up to look at him, I whispered, "I–I want to stay with you."

The anger written on his face erased. "No more separate chambers?"

I nodded.

Seojun broke out into a grin as wide as a valley, his eyes glimmering like lantern light on the pond. His arms wrapped around me like wide wings, his warmth seeping into me.

"Don't misunderstand, I am still furious about what happened, but you have no idea how happy I am right now, Bora," he murmured into my hair.

I twisted my head to look up at him, returning his smile. "I think I know because I am happy too, Seojun. I feel safer with you."

So long as we were together, we could face any storm, any adversary.

His eyes widened. "Say my name again. Please," he pleaded, his voice coming out strained, like a parched man begging for water.

"S-Seojun," I stuttered shyly. He didn't need to make a big deal about it.

"Once more," he whispered.

"Seojun," I said with more ease.

He tucked his chin on my head, squeezing me into him until it was hard to breathe. But I didn't mind. I wanted to make him happy like this all the time.

My timing was terrible, and a couple months ago, I wouldn't have dared to ask, wouldn't have cared. "Seojun?" I asked, hesitation gripping my tongue.

"Hmm?"

"Are you going to take concubines?"

My heart hurt just at the thought of it. I knew kings were allowed to, and in fact it was customary to marry multiple women. There was not a single previous king in Joseon who had not taken on at least one concubine. There were stories of vicious infighting and poisonings, of women clawing for the favor of the king. I loved Seojun, I knew that much, but I had no desire to fight for his attention.

"There is room for no one else but you in my heart," Seojun said as sweet as honey.

"But there is room in the palace for more women," I grumbled, my lips drooping downward as I pictured Harem Hall that existed behind my palace.

Seojun stepped back, and his hands cupped my face, his eyes twinkling like stars. "Let me make myself clear," he said in a serious and low voice, his brows pinching together. "I will take no one else but you to my bed, will accept no one else being bound to me. You are my queen, you are my love, and you are the only woman to be mine."

My heart began to beast faster like a rushing river, a low thrumming in my ears as my blood pumped. My cheeks grew warm, my stomach filling with flapping wings, but the hand on my face refused to allow me to turn away.

He craned his neck forward, his lips soft as they met mine, sending tingles throughout my body. Without any thought, our limbs began to tangle around each other, and before I knew it, my skin felt the hot summer night, my garments pooled around me.

"Are you ready, Bora?" Seojun asked with a deep gravel to his voice.

So long as my father lived, there would always be a threat hanging over us. We could die at any time.

I leaned in and kissed his lips again and whispered, "Yes."

My mother had always told me intercourse was something to endure, but I could drown in him and still be thirsty. I eagerly pressed my mouth to his, fully prepared to fall deep into the water.

Chapter 32

Seojun

THE CHIEF STATE COUNCILOR needed to die. I thought it was better to not tell Bora of my plans, that I was protecting her by doing so, helping her not to worry about me, but I had been a prideful fool. My plan for the Summer Hunt was flawed from the start as I had misunderstood who the true target was. Bora was the one who was supposed to die, and her last minute movement, her attempt to save me, was what saved her. Or if I was being generous, he only intended to scare her. The poison in the incense burner was the final piece, the key that unlocked everything.

Councilor Min's objective was clear: he was going to kill his daughter, and then blame me, most likely using some planted evidence to help depose me. Nothing like a wife-killing-king to rile up the commoners.

He had failed the last time, but he would not fail again. He was getting more daring, more desperate. I had to catch him using his own trap all while keeping Bora safe. At least she was with me every night now, and the dagger that I kept under the blankets on my side of the bed was the only reason I could sleep.

I had come to know a lot about Bora, and one thing was that she kept a lot of her emotions to herself, not wishing to burden others. Guilt had gnawed at me the past couple days, as I had seen how sad she was the day she gave me the letters, but I had been too consumed with the investigation and allowed her to leave without asking how she was doing.

It would not be the last time I disappointed her, but at least I could make it up to her. I checked that everything was ready while I waited for her to return from her morning walk around the ponds.

There were two tables in front of me. One was covered in all her favorite dishes, including kimchi-jeon and a heaping stack of honey-drizzled hwa-jeon. An array of other sweet dishes, since she tended to favor those, were also there. On the second table sat a cloth-covered square. It had taken me over a month, but at last I'd finished it.

The sound of laughter like a sweet melody twirled in the air as Bora and her attendants came into view. Each woman had a smile on her face, and I couldn't help the small twinge of jealousy that sprouted. But that's who Bora was, a kind woman who brought joy to all those around her, a lantern casting its light generously, unconcerned if it might burn out.

Haeji helped Bora walk up the steps of the pavilion.

"Seojun," she greeted me with a smile, her cheeks rosy and her eyes shimmering.

My strength left me every time she spoke my name, and if I were not a king, I would be content to melt into her arms every moment of every day. I could not change my position, but I could give her brief moments of Seojun as a man and not King Seojun of Joseon.

She sat on the cushion.

"How was your walk?" I inquired, my finger inching towards her present.

"Too hot," she complained half-heartedly. From her sleeve, she withdrew a long, white feather. "It made me think of you," she explained, handing it to me.

It was smooth like silk, and it had cost her nothing. Yet it was the best present I had ever received because it meant I was on her mind, that even when we were apart, she would not forget me.

"Thank you." I gently set the feather on the table. "I have a gift for you," I said softly.

It was the first gift I had ever given her, and I hoped she liked it. Honestly, if she didn't, I would be crushed, although I would never tell her that because she would feel guilty. Bora pulled at the silk knot, and it unfurled like flower petals. It was a mahogany omok-board, but the pieces were what made it special. Normally, they were smooth circles, like polished white and black pebbles, but these were all carved to resemble peonies.

"Oh," she gasped, her hand covering her mouth before fluttering down to land on her chest. "It's beautiful," she whispered, her words like a soft breeze as she picked up a piece and inspected it.

"Things have been hard on both of us, but I hope you know that no matter what, I will always make time for you."

"Shall we play a match?" she suggested, already setting the bowls on the table.

"As you wish," I said, my lips curling upwards. "I won't go easy on you though," I teased, reaching for the white peonies.

Bora plucked a black flower from the bowl, placing it onto the board with a soft click. "Your confidence will make my win all the more satisfying," she retorted.

"Your tongue has gotten sharper," I remarked and placed my piece next to hers.

"A necessity of palace life," she quipped. "Speaking of which, I want you to teach me."

"Teach you what?" I blocked her row.

"How you think. How to navigate palace politics and all its dangers." She started a new row on another section of the board.

"You are unwilling to harm others for your own interests, willing to be injured rather than gain the advantage. Schemes do not become you." I ignored her new row and set a piece down to build my own.

"I was not before, and I still have no desire to be some great strategist. However, I need to be equipped for life as queen and need to be wise enough to recognize and evade traps and plots. Teach me how to defend myself in a place where enemies whisper sweet words and every shadow veils threats."

My fingers dug around in the bowl of stones. "Do you not trust me to protect you?" My words came out more accusatory than I intended.

"I trust you to try. But what happens when you are called away for some royal duty? What happens when we have children? They will need our combined efforts to survive these treacherous seas," she stated rather calmly as she plucked a peony from her bowl.

Children? I had not thought of them yet. The constant war I waged just to keep my power and to remove the corruption infecting the courts had not allowed for such imaginations.

I shifted and cleared my throat. "We will start immediately then."

Her head jerked up. "Really?"

"The easiest way to protect you is to teach you how to protect yourself. Tomorrow I have a meeting with a potential ally, and I'd like you to join me."

"Sounds like a plan," she agreed, giving a satisfactory nod. The peony stone clicked on the board. "Looks like a tie."

Indeed, black and white peonies speckled the board, only small sections of brown wood peeking through.

"Another match?" I suggested, a wry smile tugging my mouth.

Chapter 33

Bora

W HEN SEOJUN SUGGESTED ATTENDING the meeting with the ministers, I'd jumped at the chance. Now, my head was aching. I was drowning in a discussion far out of my depth with obscure innuendos and veiled threats—a dangerous dance with tongue blades. One by one, we'd already met with three, and we'd finally reached the last.

Minister Lee sat hunched over from age, a gray, wiry beard dangling like moss from his jaw, ravines lining his skin. "To what do I owe the honor of a private meeting with the king and queen?" he asked in a raspy voice.

"Have you ever been to see the bamboo forests of the southern regions, Minister Lee?" Seojun inquired, his elbow propped on the table.

"I have not, Jeonha. Though I have heard much about them," he replied with a tinge of curiosity.

Seojun's finger traced the top of his cup in lackadaisical circles. "Someone with your wealth and position certainly has the time to visit. I highly recommend them. Strong, fast growing, and easily able to conquer its surrounding area."

"Bamboo is often cut down and used," Minister Lee said, an air of warning to his words.

"Of course, since it is versatile in its usage. But it is never gone, and it always springs back no matter how many times it gets cut down."

Minister Lee tapped his forefinger against the table, his head tilted. "Perhaps...the king could send me a list of recommendations on where to visit."

"Certainly. And it is always better to visit late than never at all," Seojun replied, a smirk slithering along his lips.

This version of him scared me in the past, but now only admiration at his skills remained.

"I have been so preoccupied with serving Joseon and the king," Minister Lee responded, reaching for his rice wine.

"And I thank you for your service, as well as your continued striving for the nation and fealty to its ruler." Seojun lifted his wine bowl.

Minister Lee raised his drink and inclined his head. "To the prosperity of the country and its king."

The men drank until their bowls were empty, slamming them down with a triumphant smack.

I looked back and forth between the two men. Something had been agreed upon without ever being spoken aloud, and despite having been present for the entire conversation, I had no idea what it was. All I was certain of was that their discussion had nothing to do with bamboo.

I twisted to whisper in Seojun's ear, "What just happened?"

His breath tickled my ear as he turned to explain, "Minister Lee has promised to join my faction."

My mouth parted, and I nodded in understanding.

Seojun wielded fear and flattery as easily as his sword, always discerning which was better to use with an expertise that evaded me. A tinge of bitterness crawled through me. My father had intended for me to marry the king as soon as he realized he couldn't control him, but my father had also purposely kept me ignorant to the ways of court. I had no tools or tricks to navigate politics. He had prepared me to be a pawn, like one of the pieces of omok. He had never intended for me to be a player.

Later that night, as we lay wrapped in each other's arms, I became curious about the extent of my father's treachery, of how deep his greed went and how long it had festered to infect the kingdom so greatly.

Twisting my head up to see his face, I asked hesitantly, "Seojun...could you tell me more about my father's involvement during King Changwon's reign?"

At first there was no reply, but just when I thought he wasn't going to answer, he finally responded with a deep sigh, his words tinged with grief, "My father...was a kind man but a weak king. In his pursuit of pleasing everyone, he lost their respect. He assumed his honor would shield him from any conspiracies, but that is just idealism to the point of hubris. A leader can be friendly, but never a friend."

"That sounds...lonely," I mumbled into the silk of his sleeping garments.

"It is," he stated in a deep voice that held the pain of a thousand nights of solitude.

"But you have me now," I sang, careening up to kiss his cheek.

He kissed my forehead in return, then continued, "It wasn't a grand poisoning, but a slow and gradual one, physically weakening my father to the point where he relied more and more on his most high-ranking officials. He kept suggesting that I be included and handed more responsibility, but your father and his allies convinced the king that I was too young and not ready for such tasks. Unfortunately, my father listened to them..."

"Did no one oppose my f—them?" It felt strange to speak of my father as a villain in history. I still wished it was not so, but reality did not care for what I desired.

"As my father grew weaker and their influence stronger, there came a point in which they were able to kill the few that were willing to stand up to their rising tide," he stated sadly, as if he was still filled with sorrow at the thought of the brave men who dared to speak up—who were then executed for it.

"Is that why you are so familiar with poisons?" I asked quietly. It was a terrible thing to be so accustomed to, a terrible thing that life had inflicted upon Seojun where he *had* to learn.

"Yes. Did you know hedgehogs can resist poison? They could get bit by a snake and then eat it," he explained, a hint of amusement coating his voice.

"What a strange thing to know," I chimed with a chuckle.

"I was very studious when I was younger, far more used to books than blades, although I learned the latter out of necessity. Pacifists die young."

Well, that was dark. But I could not blame him for his cynicism, and Seojun had done his best not to degrade his morals despite having every cause to do so.

He interrupted my thoughts. "You know how your father's fingers are faintly dusted with black?"

I wasn't sure how this related to our conversation. "Now that I think about it, yes."

"I think it's charcoal. It is used to treat some poisons, and I'd guess is a common consumption of your father's, lest the snake be killed with his own venom."

I had always thought my father's black tinged fingertips were ink stains, but it appeared that there was another reason. Although I had no doubts of my father's vileness, I didn't desire to dwell on it right now.

"And what about the Queen Dowager? I heard she was kind and well-read, but that she passed about a decade ago from an illness," I said with some hesitancy, worried that I had touched upon a topic that Seojun was unwilling to discuss.

"She is...alive, actually," he mumbled slowly, his eyes watching my face for a reaction.

"W-what?" I spluttered, my mouth hanging open like one of the fish in my pond.

He scratched his neck. "I was able to deduce that my father was being poisoned, and when I brought my suspicions to him, he rebuked me. I was forced to kneel outside for a whole day. After that, I didn't trust in his ability to protect myself or my mother, so I concocted a plan. My mother had also harbored suspicion, but she had also met a stone wall when bringing it up to my father. She could see him weakening, knew him, and more importantly how he used to be, better than anyone else. She'd seen the rapid decline of his health, and due to the baby in her belly, she was quick to agree with my plan."

The kingdom had mourned for the queen when I was a child, and I could still remember the white ribbons and flowers all over the capital like snow in summer. But it turned out it was all a farce. There was even a prince or princess that never got to grow up in the palace. The previous king may have not been malicious, but his negligence and naivety was dangerous in a ruler. I reached a hand out and wrapped it around Seojun's.

"Do you think me cruel to have tricked my father?" he questioned, his eyes falling and chin tucking into his chest.

I could relate to having to deceive a father for the sake of others. With a squeeze of my hand, I replied, "No. I am sure it was very difficult for you to deceive your own father and king, but you saved your mother and little..."

"Sister," he said, a faint smile tugging his lips, and I could only imagine that he was picturing them.

"How often do you get to see them?"

"I haven't been able to see them for two years now. Your father and his faction have been watching me more diligently. It's fine if they discover my trips to see the children like we did before, but I cannot risk my mother and sister being found, not until I handle them first."

What a terrible thing to have to do. And it was all because of my father and men like him. "We will take down my father, and then the Queen Dowager and Princess can return," I declared and pulled his hand to my lips, pressing a kiss onto his knuckles.

Would the Queen Dowager approve of me?

"What's she like?" I inquired, picturing a beautiful woman with pink lips and regal posture.

"She would have made a better king than my father. She did not laugh often and could be strict, but she was never unfair. If only my father had heeded her words..." Seojun cleared his throat and shifted beside me. "When you do meet her, don't worry about her face. She wears a perpetual scowl, but she protects her loved ones fiercely."

"If our mothers ever meet, I think mine will faint," I joked, trying not to imagine our own meeting.

If she didn't like me, it would hurt, but Seojun loved me. That was all that mattered. From the sounds of it, so long as I loved her son and used my position to help the people, she would approve of me. It was nice though, thinking about the future. I went to sleep praying we would live to see it.

Chapter 34

Bora

I T FELT GOOD TO finally be a player. The time had come to initiate my own game; instead of waiting for my father, instead of focusing on foiling his plans, we had one of our own. I appreciated that Seojun included me in his meeting with the ministers, for it had taught me the skill of the unspoken, on how to convey a message without outright saying it. There would soon be an opportunity to show how much I had learned.

I chewed my lip and reclined behind the desk that Seojun had procured for me.

"Haeji," I called out to where she was sniffing a candle—always searching for potential threats after the previous attempt on my life.

She set the candle down and shuffled over, bowing. "Yes, Mama?"

"Could you compile a list of the wives of the ministers that are not in league with my father? Even if they are just neutral, I want them listed," I commanded with a confidence that sounded rather pleasant to my ears. It was the voice of a queen.

Haeji nodded. "Of course. Would you like any information I find pertinent accompanying the list as well?"

My shoulders sagged ever so slightly. I still had a lot to learn, but I was grateful that I had Haeji by my side to aid me. "Yes, that's probably important," I mumbled sheepishly, my cheeks warming.

She smiled, a rare sight, and said, "You are doing well, Mama. The king would be proud."

My posture straightened, my lips curling into a grin. "Thank you, Haeji."

Bowing as she left, Haeji paused at the door, pointing to two court-ladies. "Injeong, Mirae, keep the queen company while I am gone, and make sure to check any food she orders."

The two attendants nodded and entered, hands tucked in front of their abdomens. They were both at least a decade older than myself, with a maturity to their features, but despite their slim figures, they were most likely skilled warriors. I wouldn't have been surprised if every maid and eunuch around me was a secret soldier, but people only guarded what was precious to them. Seojun would be absolutely broken if something happened to me, and I felt the same towards him. I wanted to do my part in helping him.

The presence of the servants was comforting, especially now that even my own father was trying to kill me, let alone the normal attacks by those who wished for their own daughter to take my place as queen. At least I would never have a harem to deal with.

By the next evening, Haeji had already collected all the information I requested. "Here is the list of names, Mama," Haeji said and handed me a stack of parchment.

"Thank you," I replied, smiling as I took them from her hand, eager to begin reading about the women of Joseon's most influential men. One tool a woman could wield was her husband—to guide him in the right direction. At times a man may need to be restrained, and at others he may need a gentle push.

But Haeji lingered, her lips pursed.

"You may speak what's on your mind," I mused, surprised she hadn't already spoken of her own accord as she had in the past.

"If I may be so bold, I suggest you go over the list with the king. He may have suggestions on which women to invite," she offered.

I chewed my lip for a moment. I wanted to help Seojun, to show I was capable of handling things in court, but it was best to swallow my pride and do things the right way. I had much to learn, and I knew no better teacher than my husband. Every soldier had to work their way up the ranks.

With a huff, I stood, the parchment still in hand. "Alright, let's go see the king."

Wings fluttered in my stomach, my body light as anticipation and satisfaction in my plan filled me with an energy I had never experienced before. My legs carried me with the swiftness of a river towards the king's chambers—having agreed to spend the day in our separate chambers and nights in his.

"The queen is arriving," Dongbin called out, announcing our approach with a wink in my direction. "You look extra beautiful today, Haeji," he added, eyes sweeping over my court lady.

Haeji spared a glance his way, clearing her throat. "You look...not unwell."

"Especially well, now that I have seen you," he replied cheerfully.

Grinning, I entered the King's Quarters with a little hop, the papers flapping in my hand. Haeji entered after me, leaving behind the infatuated guard. Seojun leapt to his feet from where he sat behind his desk, rushing over to me, eyes tracing every limb and line.

"Are you alright? Poison? Arrows? Poison arrows?" he interrogated, the words spilling out like a broken string of pearls.

Shaking my head, I chuckled and explained, "I'm fine. I just wanted to consult you on a meeting I have planned with some wives."

He sighed, his shoulders relaxing and his lips curling up. "Well, that is easy." He pulled me gently by the arm towards his table, both of us sitting side by side on the rectangular cushion beneath us.

I placed the parchment on top of the dark wooden desk, and Seojun pinched the first paper and held it in front of our faces.

"Lady Jo Eunbi, age thirty-four, husband to the fourth son of Minister Han, who is an official in the Office of Records, and her husband is an official in the Ministry of Defense," his voice trailed off, his fingers tapping on the desk. "Actually, both of those are one of the few places where your father's hold is weakest. Members of the Office of Records are particularly difficult to manipulate and are usually just killed for their loyalty to preserving history. She is a good candidate," he determined with a nod.

"Haeji, why did you include the wife of a fourth son?" I asked, confused as to the reason she had included someone who most likely had no influence in his family affairs. I expected wives of the patriarchs or at least wives of first sons.

Haeji dipped her head and explained, "Mama, I have included the wives to not only firstborn sons but also the favored ones. Of course the hierarchy in Joseon is strict, but those who have their father's ears should not be discounted, no matter their rank or age."

I hadn't thought about that before. Jinho was the only child my father really ever talked to the older we got, the games of my younger days all but forgotten.

"Then this will be the 'yes' pile," I stated, placing the parchment of Lady Jo to the right. "And that will be the 'no' pile," I affirmed, my finger pointing to an open space on the left.

"Next is Lady Seo Hwajeong, age forty-one, married to the first son of Minister Oh who is in the Ministry of Taxation, and her husband is in the Ministry of Rites," I read aloud, holding up the paper.

"The Ministry of Rites and Taxation are two of the most corrupt, along with the Capital Bureau, with the majority of their members consisting of your father's faction. With the Rites overseeing the Kwago, it has made it hard to acquire real talent, most who pass doing so less on merit and more on nepotism. It forced any lower-class men to go to the military for social advancement, which means that the military is one of the few areas untouched by him. Of course there are a few spies to be expected no matter how hard we sift the chaff."

I reached over and placed the paper on the left. "So that's a no."

"Lady Hong Inhyeon, age fifty-nine, married to Minister Lee...we already know her husband is on our side, so we don't need to have her there, right?" I peered up to read his face.

"No, she should be there to lend aid to you and help discern the others," Seojun replied, his thumb rubbing against his forefinger.

Placing it to the right, Seojun picked up the next one.

"Lady Shin Munjeong, age twenty, wife of the second son of Minister Kim, her husband is in the Office of Special Advisors. Is he close in relation to Inspector Kim?" I wondered.

"Cousins, I believe. The Kims are very honorable, and they have been at risk of exile in the past for their blunt honesty to some more volatile kings."

"Definite yes," I said, nodding, and placed it in the pile with the others. "Lady Pak Sohyeon, age twenty-three, wife of the first grandson of Minister Yu of the Ministry of Personnel, her husband is a new general."

Seojun squinted his eyes, his fingers tapping on the desk to a steady rhythm like rain hitting a roof. "The Ministry of Personnel is about half and half with the factions, but the Yu family has been historically very loyal to the crown. I think it is worth inviting her," he decided with a nod, his lips pursed.

A sudden thought occurred to me. "Wait, shouldn't we also take into consideration the woman's side of the family? If their side is aligned with my father, wouldn't that exclude them?"

Seojun shrugged. "I am sure it influences them to some degree, but since a woman's fate is tied to the family she marries into, it is more likely than not that she will switch to her husband's side and their respective alliances."

"If they were offered in marriage in the first place, doesn't that imply that those two families are allied?" I questioned.

"Not necessarily, sometimes it is for advantage, like prestige and wealth, which in our case, being friends of the royal family is the highest prestige one can have if that is what motivates them. Some may have started as friends but turned into foes, and the enemy of my enemy is my friend. Some perhaps bet on one side for protection, so we just need to be the bigger predator to encourage them to stay under our shadow. Some families will be loyal to the throne as they believe it is heaven's will, and thus we need to do nothing to entice them. Motivations may differ, and it is up to you to determine what inspires each of the women you invite," he explained as I tried to remember all of the information and store it for later use.

I chewed my lip. *Find their motivation...*

Chapter 35

Bora

T HE SUMMER DAY WAS stifling, so I decided rather than my stuffy rooms, it would be best to sit outside in the open pavilion next to the pond. Extra tables were set up for each of the women I had invited. On each one was a yellow silk cloth, with cool wine, freshly cut fruit, baked pastries, and an array of nuts and seeds.

As I fanned myself, much to the displeasure of my maids who had offered to do it, I watched the entrance, my stomach refusing to settle until all the guests arrived, or didn't, if they were so bold as to refuse. Such a rejection would clarify which side they were on. Under the previous king, perhaps they would have all rejected, but Seojun's reputation demanded more respect—or fear.

At last, voices trickled over the walls, and soon enough, blue, pink, and yellow silks appeared around the corner like a moving meadow, hair from black as night to gray like ash bobbing while the women walked.

In tandem, the six ladies bowed. "Greetings, Mama."

Lifting my hand, I said with what at least I thought sounded like a regal tone, "Rise."

The six women rose, smiles plastered on their faces. Enemies could smile while they stabbed you. For a moment, I doubted myself. What if I misread them? What if I revealed information I wasn't supposed to? What if I had invited an assassin into the palace?

Haeji must have noticed my breathing beginning to quicken, for she leaned over and whispered, "Are you alright, Mama? Shall I get the king?"

I shook my head. "No." I cleared my throat. "I can do this."

Even though I had asked for Seojun's help previously, he could not always come to my rescue. I needed to do this alone and in my own way.

Lady Hong led the way, an arm intertwined with Lady Pak, graying hair feathered with lines of white adorning her head. After releasing the arm of the younger woman, she sat nearest to me on the right, her lavender hanbok pooling around her. Lady Jo sat on the first seat to the left, her round face soft and surrounding plump lips and kind looking eyes. On the middle seat on the right was Lady Pak, a petite and thin woman who sat with an elegance that befitted marrying into a family that had produced many queens of Joseon. Next, Lady Shin, who was the same age as myself, sat on the second to last seat on the left, her cheeks still holding fast to a plumpness of youth, reminding me of a peach.

Lady Song Sohee, whose younger sister had been assaulted at the instructions of my father to prevent her potential marriage to the king, sat at the last seat on the right—her rank not enough to overcome the age she had on Lady Pak and Lady Shin. She had not been included on the list, but Seojun had suggested it after explaining her situation. Her younger sister was one of many victims of my father and his fellow councilors. I could not restore her ruined reputation. Retribution, on the other hand, was something I could help provide.

The woman to take the final seat on the left was Madame Jang Cheorin, the wife of a rising merchant in the capital whose wealth was beginning to rival that of even the long-established noble families. Despite her age of thirty-three, she had no noble status and thus was seated at the lowest position.

With a wave of my fingers, I beckoned Haeji closer and whispered, "Let's invite the younger Lady Song to come to the palace as a lady's maid. She will be able to be looked after her whole life that way, and not at the mercy of whatever male relative becomes head of the family next."

Haeji smiled and nodded. "That is a wonderful idea, Mama."

I cleared my throat, pausing my fanning to speak clearly. "Thank you all for accepting my invitation," I said, doing my best imitation of Seojun's honey tone when he was trying to compliment one of the ministers.

Nothing like a little flattery to put people at ease. Or did that just make them suspicious? Maybe it just depended on the person.

I'd spent the previous week going over the list of names and relevant information of the nobles and officials' wives, excluding the ones Seojun and I had discounted. Taking a deep breath, I reminded myself that this was just omok. I had no hopes of mastering weaponry, but I could play games of strategy given enough time to learn. Now it was time to see how good of a student I was, time to play utilizing my own methods.

After handing my fan to Haeji, I leaned forward. "I will be honest with you all," I stated and placed my palms on the silk-covered table in front of me. "The reason I summoned you here is not for idle chat and snacks. I want your friendship, and if I cannot have that, I will accept loyalty."

From the youngest, their smiles faded, confused glances cast at each other. The older women kept their composure, their lips still curled in amiable crescents. Lady Jo reached for a pastry while Lady Song sipped from her tea. Madame Jang yielded nothing in her expression—the epitome of a skilled merchant.

Lady Hong broke the silence, her voice raspy but firm, "It is our honor to serve the king and queen. Please tell us what you require, Mama."

Seojun was skilled in subtleties and secret meanings, and it was surely what had allowed him, and his mother and younger sister, to survive. However, I was not a good liar, and there were different ways to kill a beast. You could set a trap and wait for it to fall into it, or you could charge towards it with your weapon bared. I felt more suited to the latter.

I crossed my arms atop one another, leaning further over the table and down towards the gathered women. "I am sure such intelligent women as yourselves are aware of the State Councilor and their faction."

The ladies gave nods of acknowledgement like a dipping swan's head, but Lady Song's hand trembled as she clutched her cup with such strength that I thought it might shatter the little ceramic.

While they had taken their seats, I'd decided how much I was willing to share with them, for although I could not tell a lie, there was a certain wisdom to omitting select information, such as the status of the Queen Dowager or that the previous king was killed by my father and his fellow councilors. In the event that one of the present women decided to run to the other side, it was best to keep some knowledge to myself.

"You are all from influential families, and I believe that you can assist myself and the king in improving Joseon. In order to do so, some things need to be cleaned out to make room for the new growth," I explained, hoping that my meaning was clear.

Lady Pak spoke up, her voice soft and hard to hear, "Mama, I would love to assist you, but we are only women, just mothers and wives and daughters. How are we to help?"

My lips curled upwards like the wings of a crane. "You undersell yourself, Lady Pak. As I am sure Lady Hong can attest to, you can never underestimate the power of a woman whispering into her man's ear. We can even look back into our own history to see evidence of queens ruling through their kings. If we go as far as Shilla, women even ruled on their own. Of course, I have no desire to do something like that, but I do wish to aid my husband, not only for our sake, but for all of Joseon."

"We are blessed to have such a wise mother of our nation in our Queen," Lady Hong murmured. "Being a woman in Joseon has its challenges, but we must make the best of it, using what we wield for the good of the kingdom."

The last part elicited a giggle from Lady Shin, who quickly covered her mouth and ducked her head. Lady Jo and Madame Jang both smiled at the youngest woman, sharing knowing glances between themselves.

Lady Hong continued, "It is the role of wives to help their husbands see wisdom and pursue a path of righteousness."

"Sometimes that requires a few sweet words and sweeter kisses," Lady Pak whispered to Lady Shin, receiving a glower and tsk from the elder seated at the top of their row.

"What exactly is the plan, Mama?" Lady Song asked, her voice full of bitterness that every woman present could understand, her younger sister one of many women whose lives had been ruined by the wickedness of a man.

"I cannot give specifics, but I do ask that when the time is right, your husbands and father-in-laws would speak up. The king promises their protection, and their courage will be rewarded and never forgotten."

"If I may be so bold, Mama," Madame Jang mused, her eyes scrunched as her fingers tapped against the table, reminding me of how Seojun looked while he was thinking.

With such a contemplative wife, it was no wonder Mister Kwon was able to own multiple businesses in the capital. Perhaps the source of their success had less to do with him and more to do with Madame Jang.

I nodded and she continued, "It could also be beneficial to send an agent, a spy of sorts, to gain information and make sure they are unaware of our own plans."

Turning my head to look at Haeji, I waited for her to whisper something, to give me some sort of hint as to what the king would want or if we already had such a person mixed into my father's faction. But she said nothing. I smiled. Seojun would want me to try for myself, to spread my wings and fly. This was my board.

"That sounds like a wonderful idea, Madame Jang. Thank you," I chimed, and she responded with a dip of her head and a smile. Addressing the others, I inquired, "Do you have any suggestions, ladies?"

And so the demise of many men was decided over tea and snacks. Who knew the scent of foiled plots and silenced schemes had the smell of honey, chamomile, and freshly sliced melon?

My eyes swept over the six women. They were all different ages and from different families with different occupations, yet they were willing to be loyal, knowing that with the size and power of the three councilors, that failure was possible. One misplacement of a piece on the board and the game would be lost. Their faith and fealty to the king showed that they were honorable, not blinded by the false stories of a tyrant king, nor was their honor bought with money. Joseon was slowly becoming more harsh towards its women, but even so, these ladies were willing to grab at the reins and steer the direction of our country.

There was no way of knowing if we would win, or even if we did, that the changes we implemented would be enforced by our descendants, but we had to try, no matter the personal cost.

Chapter 36

Seojun

FOUR WHITE PIECES IN a row. Despite not being the one to begin the game, I was going to finish it. *We* were going to finish it. I glanced up at Bora, her nose scrunched like a rabbit, a black peony pinched between her two fingers that hovered over the board. My gaze followed her hand as she placed her piece, cutting off one side. If I stared too long, I would lose my focus, her face far too distracting for strategizing.

"I win," I chimed, grinning, and placed the fifth white orb in the diagonal line I had painstakingly created. There was little room left on the board with how long our game had gone on.

But when I looked up, Bora's face was shadowed by sadness.

Reaching across the table, I grabbed her hand, my thumb rubbing along her knuckles. "I'm sorry. I hope I didn't hurt your feelings by gloating."

She peered up at me, her shoulders drooping as she replied in a low tone, "No, it's not about omok. The banquet is coming up. Soon we will set up our trap, and even when we win, it will still feel like I lost. My emotions swing between anger and sorrow—happy to take down the evil councilor leeching Joseon, but reluctant to extinguish the hope of gaining my father's affection."

I scooted on my knees over to her side, wrapping my arms around her. "Victory and mourning often accompany each other. I cannot spare him, Bora. He may be your father, and it may break your heart, but it would be a travesty of justice for all his other victims to allow him to live. I love you very much, but I also believe that one of the reasons you fell in love with me is for my honor. If I exile him, my honor goes with him. Forgive me, but I cannot grant him his life."

The cries of the slain and ruined kept me up many nights: my father, who died for trusting the wrong people, a multitude of government officials, who were assassinated for their honor, the younger Song daughter, whose future was stolen for daring to marry me, and young Gweonho, who was killed for overhearing a conversation. Too many had suffered at the hands of the councilors, and anything other than death would be a disgrace to justice.

Would she loathe me for it? I didn't think so, since that was not the woman I had come to know and love. But it could still hurt, even if it was the right thing to do.

"I know," she whispered in reply, sinking into my chest.

Suddenly, a deep voice boomed through the screen door. "Jeonha, we have found the maid who placed the poison in the queen's incense burner," Dongbin announced.

Bolting to my feet, I demanded, "Where is she?"

He slid open the door. "In the prison."

And that was all I needed to hear, my stride swift as I made my way to the dungeon. "I'll be back," I barked out, not bothering to look behind where I left Bora sitting.

"Wait," Bora called out, scrambling to her feet and shuffling forward. "Take me with you."

"The dungeons are no place for the queen," I argued.

"It didn't stop you before," she retorted, crossing her arms.

"I said no," I growled, my expression conveying the finality of the statement.

Her lips pursed, and she stormed past me, heading in the direction of her quarters. I didn't have time for this. Before the banquet in a few days, I needed to question the maid and squeeze all the information she possessed from her.

"Let's go," I grunted to the guards stationed outside, taking off towards the Royal Investigation Bureau's Office and the dungeon housed beneath.

There was a dark side of me that was tempted to torture the maid, even if she confessed to everything, I wanted to make her hurt, wanted her to wail, every scream a reminder of the pain she intended to inflict upon Bora, upon me, by attempting to take her from me. There had been very few times in my life I could remember feeling this way.

One of those was when I was eighteen, my father's health failing, his trust granted to the wrong people. A minister in the Office of Censors had brought his suspicions of wrongdoing by the State Chief Councilor, but instead of heeding his words, he trusted Councilor Min. The Censor official was found dead the next week. He had been the third minister to die under similar circumstances, yet still my father refused to remove the Chief State Councilor.

Joseon would suffer, and my mother would have been in danger even as queen—*especially* as queen. Her warnings would have eventually drawn the ire of the State Councilors, her life in jeopardy for her unwillingness to stay silent, to submit. In my frustration, I'd wanted to kill my own father. If Bora ever knew I had harbored such intent... She would claim me the monster she had originally thought me to be. I could not bear the fear that would form in her eyes, the disgust in the curl of her lip.

The thought of her disappointment tempered my rage enough that I would not hurt the maid. More than what was necessary, at least. It was Bora who was the target, so Bora could be the one to decide the punishment. I should have asked her before leaving...

I slowed my pace, calling out behind me to order one of the guards that accompanied us, "Fetch the queen."

"Yes, Jeonha," a guard responded before the fading sounds of his footsteps disappeared entirely.

As we continued walking, I asked, "Have you started interrogating her? Did she have any evidence on her? Where was she found?"

"We were waiting for you, Jeonha. She had more money on her than the palace salary provides, but other than that, there was nothing. She was found doing laundry. It appears that she thought she'd gotten away with it and was intending on staying for further use."

"How bold of her," I growled.

She would pay for her arrogance with her blood.

When we reached the towering entrance to the dungeon, Official Moon from the Office of Censors was already waiting, his satchel full of writing instruments saddled on his side. Inspector Kim stood next to him.

They bowed in greeting. "Jeonha."

I dipped my head in return. "We are waiting for the queen to arrive. Then we'll go in."

Crossing my arms, I stood and waited outside the entrance. The hot sun was doing nothing to help calm the burning anger inside me. If I entered without Bora, there was the possibility that I would renege on my plan to allow Bora to decide the woman's fate.

A little brown shrike landed above me on the wooden rafter.

Go away, little spy, I hissed in my head.

At last Bora arrived, and despite the severity of the situation, she took the time to reach into that pouch of hers and pull out some seeds. She tossed them on the dirt, and the shrike fluttered down, greedily consuming the food.

I stepped towards her, my hands gently gripping her elbows. "Bora, forgive me. I shouldn't have disregarded what you wanted. I just wanted to protect you."

"From what?" She peered up at me, hurt lingering in her eyes.

"From the uglier sides of me."

Her gaze softened, and she reached her hands up and cupped my cheeks. "I never want you to hide from me. I would rather confront problems together," she paused, her lips twitching, "including parts of your personality that need some work."

A smile cut away my shame. "You're a wonderful artist. I trust you to make me into something beautiful."

"We are married. It's our job to help each other become better people, to comfort and to cultivate."

Leaning into her touch, I replied, "I love you."

Her smile squished her eyes together. "I love you, too."

"Are you ready for this? Would you prefer to wait upstairs?" I asked, one hand holding her while the other gestured to the Royal Investigation Bureau office door that lay to our left.

She shook her head, straightening her shoulders. "I want to hear it all."

Dropping her hand, I nodded and pivoted on my heel, leading the way down the stairs into the hall of cells.

On each step, I imagined every corrupt official. *Ryu, Oh, Min, Shim, Kang...*

The goal was to clean them out entirely in one day, but just like mice, there were always a few rodents that got away and would need to be disposed of later. So long as the big fish were caught, the rest would be easier to deal with. With each removal, an official who actually earned their position could replace them, men who cared about Joseon, whose morals could not be exchanged for coin or promises of promotions.

The musty and metal stench of the dungeon was almost welcoming, so long as one was not a prisoner. To me, it was the scent of justice, where impurities were purged from the nation. Most of the cells were empty at the moment, but soon enough they would be filled.

A small squeak sounded from behind me, and I whipped around in time to catch a stumbling Bora. I had gotten so caught up in my thoughts that I had neglected her. Scolding myself, I kept a hold of her hand as we walked.

"Are you alright?" I asked.

"Fine. Just not the best memories here," she murmured, gripping my hand tighter as we reached the end of the hall.

Indeed, this was where her servant had died. I couldn't get myself to feel sorry for the woman, but seeing the sad expression on Bora's face made me feel as though I was wrong for what I did. Attempted murder *was* murder, at least in my eyes. Attempted assassination of the king could carry the consequence of entire generations of a family being executed. At least the maid had taken all the punishment with her in death.

Perhaps Bora was too softhearted for this. Nevertheless, she had chosen to be here, and she was free to leave if she was uncomfortable.

A groan of pain sounded from the petite woman tied to the post. Sweat trickled down her damp skin, although there was no visible injury to her body.

The woman's voice came out high-pitched when she begged, "Mama, help me, please."

Bora's eyes widened, and she jerked her head back and forth between the maid and me, her hands waving in the air. "Seojun, I didn't—"

I reached out and swallowed her hands in mine, my voice soft as I said, "I would never doubt you, Bora. This is just another trick of your father's."

She glared at the bound woman and replied coldly, "Please do not refer to him as such. From now on, he is only Chief State Councilor Min."

Lifting a hand to caress her cheek, I chimed, "And he won't even be that for much longer."

I studied her face. Had I gone too far?

But Bora showed no displeasure at my comment, leaning into my touch, her soft cheek nestling into my palm.

"Last chance to leave before things get ugly," I stated, glancing at where one of my Royal Investigators was sharpening a knife, the blade whining against the stone.

"I can handle this," she replied, her voice firm and features set in determination.

"Very well," I dropped my hand from her face and turned to face the maid and investigator. "Let's begin."

Official Moon scurried over to his desk and pulled out his paper and ink, already scribbling down everything that had occurred since we met at the top of the stairs. Inspector Kim stood next to Dongbin, both glaring at the woman tied to the post. Minje would be disappointed that he was missing out, but I'd given him another important mission to attend to.

The investigator approached the maid, his blade bared. "Who ordered you to kill the queen?"

The woman's body trembled, but she kept her lips sealed. But when the investigator placed the sharp side of the knife against her skin, the words began to spill.

"What? What is this?" the maid demanded, her pitch raising as she realized the nature of her situation. She shook her head back and forth and howled, "No, no, no! He promised me you were on our side."

I leaned forward, my head tilting. "Who told you that?"

The woman spat in my face before turning away. I stepped back, using my sleeve to wipe the saliva off, and a thundering smack rang through the air as the woman's head slammed against the post.

My mouth hung open as I gaped at Bora, her chest heaving and her palm red from the force of her hit.

"How dare you?" she seethed.

It was the first time I had ever seen her angry, truly enraged. What a sight to behold, when the gentle were pushed too far. However, I had no desire to see Bora break, to see her become what I tried so hard to keep at bay. I directed her hand towards my lips, pressing a kiss to her palm.

"I'm truly touched that you would sully your hands for me, but keep in mind what I said to you long ago."

Bora turned her face to me, her breathing becoming more steady, the rage melting from her eyes. "What?"

"That I can pardon many things, but not you getting hurt," I murmured gently, releasing her hand. "Which brings me to my point," I growled, my tone switching and sucking all the warmth from the air. I put on the cold mask that I had begrudgingly worn so many times before. This time I kept my face a safe distance from the maid when I sneered, "You will die, of that you can be certain. *How* you die is still undecided. I will give you the opportunity now to choose how you meet your end."

I held out my hand until I felt the hilt of Dongbin's sword rest in my palm, a play we had put on together often throughout the years. The woman's legs began to shake, her eyes darting between Bora, my face, and the blade in my grip.

"I'll tell you everything," she squeaked.

The secrets spilled from her sweat soaked lips, and the final foundations to our plans were solidified. In a few days, the banquet would bring an end to our game.

Chapter 37

Bora

THE PAST FEW DAYS had been full of last minute meetings with ministers, and I'd scrubbed my hands for an hour trying to get the ink stains out from all the letters I'd sent to the ladies from my previous gathering. Adjusting the norigae dangling from my dangui, I slowly inhaled and exhaled, doing my best to calm my nerves.

Haeji smoothed my hair, fixing the pin in my bun. "Everything will be alright, Mama."

I reached over my shoulder and squeezed her hand. "I know. After all we have done to prepare for tonight, I know we will come out victorious, but even though my mind knows that, my anxiety doesn't."

"You've changed so much, Mama," Haeji commented, a proud shimmer in her eyes.

"How so?" The only thing that changed was my naivety and my perception of those around me.

She stood and held out a hand, helping me up. "You're much more confident now. Even the way you talk now is different."

A smile blossomed on my lips. "Well, I had a lot of people help me grow." I added, voice full of mirth, "One might even compare me to fungus."

Haeji offered a rare laugh, and I joined her.

A voice called out through the door, interrupting our serene moment before the looming storm. "Haeji, it's time."

I recognized Dongbin's voice, and Haeji rushed to slide open the door. They shared a few words before parting, and although I couldn't hear what they said, the concern in Dongbin's eyes were clear as he brushed a finger against the court lady's hand. This time, Haeji didn't run away from his touch and even gave him a small smile.

Before leaving, Haeji turned around and bent her waist. "Forgive me for not being able to accompany you to the banquet, Mama."

I stepped forward, waving my hand in the air. "We all have our jobs to do. Be safe."

She rose, sparing one more glance at Dongbin and striding off towards the section of the palace that housed the kitchen. The guard's gaze followed her until she disappeared out of sight.

Turning back to me, he dipped his head. "It is time to go, Mama."

Inhaling, I tucked my hands under the long front of my dangui and stepped over the threshold and into the twilight. My group of court ladies and an extra set of guards followed me to the Throne Hall, each step thundering in my ears.

Tonight, the kingdom would come to know the depths of my father's and his fellow corrupt officials' crimes. A Min had started this, and it was only right that a Min would help finish it.

When we arrived at the Throne Hall, we paused. My gaze soaked in the beautiful sight.

Gold silk draped from the rafters, violet ribbons curled around the pillars, and a scarlet carpet snaked on the floor from the entrance to the dais. Gilded cups and white ceramic jars of wine sat on every low sitting wooden table, hanging lanterns illuminating the hall in a golden glow.

An arm slid around my waist, a warm body pressing against my side. I turned to look up at Seojun, his ikseongwan tall and his sharp eyes scanning the room. He reminded me of the tales of gumihos—nine-tailed foxes that could shift into humans—beautiful and cunning. He was always aware of his surroundings, his face a cold curtain veiling the calculations in his mind. Very few had the privilege of knowing the kind man beneath the king's façade.

I was grateful to be one of them.

"Everything will be fine," I said, smiling.

His hand pulled me closer, and he replied dryly, "I'm confident he will try something tonight, something that we may be unaware of."

Untangling myself from his arms, I stepped in front of him and placed my palms on his forearms. "I have confidence in *you*."

His eyes enveloped me in an embrace, love dripping from them like tears. "I can't bear to lose you, for you to even get hurt."

I cocked my head and smirked. "Let's finish this game—together."

He returned the smile, his eyes sparkling and squishing into crescents. "I am so thankful to have you as my queen, as my wife."

My skin tingled and warmed as if the sun was shining on me. "Well, let's go disappoint my father," I stated firmly, doing my best to ignore the pain in my heart.

Although my tone was light, my chest was tight. There was little joy in this, even if it was justice. I recalled the hungry children with little hope of social advancement, remembered the body of Jinyoung and the servant boy, imagined Minho's arms in my mind, and pictured the Summer Hunt except instead of me, it was Seojun who was pierced by the arrow. I held onto the feeling that those images elicited, held onto the righteous rage in order to reaffirm my resolve. The Chief State Councilor was a monster, a path he had chosen, a path that had only room for us or them.

Holding out his hand, Seojun smirked, his eyes dancing with danger. This was the tyrant the rumors regaled. I slipped my hand atop his, our skin sparking with a fire, the burning reaching my very bones, chasing away my nerves. We walked hand in hand down the aisle and climbed the steps to the golden throne. Sitting side by side, we waited for the show to begin.

One by one, the officials trickled in, donned in red robes with cranes delineating their high rank in a square on their chest and silk, black samos on their head. In the sea of courtiers, the Chief State Councilor appeared, his beard scraggly and graying at the ends. I noticed for the first time the wrinkles in his skin and the way he refused to allow age to hunch his shoulders. But also for the first time, the sight of him didn't elicit any feelings of familial fealty or affection.

He took his place closest to the throne, and I wondered what sinister schemes he had used to obtain that seat, how much blood paved the way to his power.

My gaze swept across the hall as I wondered where the threat would come from. Did the danger lie with the dancers, blades hidden beneath their silks and jewels? Or would there be a murderer amongst the maids, poison hiding in their palms? Would it be one of the guards, their loyalty gained by gold?

I glanced back at Seojun, his eyes equally cautious while he observed the hall. A pang of pity rang through me. This was how he had had to live his whole life, doubt and distrust his shield and sword. How terrible it must be to not know who to trust, for death to be dangling above one's head daily. My hand crawled over to his, and his palm opened to receive mine. We curled our hands around each other, and I inhaled. We would face whatever came our way together.

Flutes, drums, and zithers mixed into a majestic melody, the music whispering with the sweetness of honey. The maids brought in the dishes and laid them on all the tables: gan-jang tteok, fermented vegetables, smoked fish, rice, squash soup, boiled pork, and lastly, kimchi-jeon.

For a moment, the looming threat was pushed aside by the plates in front of me, my eyes devouring the delicacies and my stomach expressing its eagerness to eat with a loud growl that was thankfully drowned out by the music. The savory scents wafted into my nostrils, and my mouth began to salivate. If the Chief State Councilor was going to kill my husband and I, at least I would get to go out with a satisfied stomach.

I reached out with my chopsticks towards some fermented radish, but Seojun darted his hand out to stop me. Doing my best to hide my surprise, I glanced at him from the corner of my eyes, and he slipped a silver needle out from his sleeve and inconspicuously dipped it into the food. There were many poi-sons in the world, but some of them were not detectable even with the silver needle. I looked at the thin sliver of metal, holding my breath as I waited for it to change colors, but even after a minute, it remained the same. I sighed in relief and plucked a piece of radish and plopped it in my mouth.

The crunch echoed in my ears and drowned out the music for a few seconds before the burst of red pepper, vinegar, and garlic coated my tongue. A small moan escaped my lips, eliciting a chuckle from Seojun.

He leaned closer and whispered, "Only you, on the verge of potential death or injury, could so thoroughly enjoy food."

I gazed back at him, my brow cocked. "What? The past several months with you have taught me that I should enjoy every meal as if it's my last, since I never know when someone will shoot me with an arrow or kidnap me."

His smile was dazzling, and I chewed on my lip as we stared at each other. He was more delicious than any of the dishes displayed in front of us.

"Well, then," he said in a sultry voice, reaching over and picking a slice of pork and bringing it to my mouth, "you should eat as much as you desire. Whatever you want, you shall have."

I opened my lips, and he released the piece of pork into my mouth. I smiled as I chewed, grateful to have a man who loved me and was not concerned about how much I ate or how I looked. Of course, I had my own confidence, but it was certainly nice to have someone else who shared it with me.

His hand approached my face, and his finger brushed a grain of rice from my chin, his thumb caressing my skin, his eyes sparkling brighter than the lanterns in the hall. He leaned forward and pressed his lips, warm bend soft, against my forehead. The gathered ministers grumbled in displeasure at the obvious indifference and neglect of etiquette, but Seojun had never cared about such conduct.

When he pulled away, he whispered with a conspiratorial smirk, "Let's begin the game."

I nodded and set down my chopsticks, turning my attention to the banquet attendees. The Chief State Councilor was deep in discussion with the Right and Left State Councilor, and seeing them—the three men who were supposed to be honorable above all others and unafraid to keep a malevolent king in check—boiled my blood. They were as cruel and corrupt as one could imagine. Over the past few weeks, Haeji and Seojun had informed me of the multitude of crimes each had committed on top of the ones I already was aware of.

The Ryus, who had come over often for dinners and married with the Min clan over many generations, were notorious swindlers who purposely withheld food to fill their personal storages while also raising the prices of the products they sold in their many stores. The Shims would leak false Kwago exam questions, selling them for an expensive fee only for the client to find out on the day of the test that they were provided with the wrong information. Of course, the noble families the Shims were allied with got those questions for free. Cheating was wrong, but it was still a disgusting way to take advantage of the commoners. The Ohs embezzled public funds for infrastructure or aid, claiming that during transport bandits stole the money or supplies. The Kangs used a multitude of illegal methods to run a monopoly on real estate in the capital, and thus got to control the pricing—which was unjustly high.

Although my heart would hurt, I was not afraid to face the reality of their vileness, nor would my familial fealty be greater than my integrity. No amount of blood shared between us could make up for the blood they had spilled: my blood, my husband's, and the people of Joseon's. Their hands were covered in it.

From beside me, Seojun shifted and placed his hands on widespread knees. He cleared his throat, and the music came to an abrupt end like a thread being cut in half. The dancers bowed and slunk to the sides of the hall, and the ministers' whispers died down.

"Thank you, my faithful officials, for attending tonight's festivities. I wished to show my gratitude for the exemplary work of Joseon's finest and brightest men."

Grunts of agreement and low chuckles echoed in the hall as everyone grabbed their gilded rice-wine filled cups. My eyes were fixated on the Chief State Councilor, wary of every move and facial expression, waiting for some glance, nod, or wave of his fingers to give something away, the signal that would be the catalyst of whatever scheme he had under his sleeve.

He suddenly stood, and I flinched, my heart beating as rapidly as a panicked bird. He flicked his long sleeve out of the way and brought his cup up in front of him and faced us.

"A toast to our great king and all his contributions to Joseon. Under his reign, the people have been blessed," my father bellowed, voice tinged with a confident authority that rang like a gong.

His words were as hollow as a vase though, and I knew he would be grinding his teeth with every word of praise. The ministers were either ignorant or indifferent though, and everyone cheered, even if it was insincere. I brought the drink to my lips and sipped the wine.

It took only a few seconds for my eyelids to grow heavy and my head to grow light. My vision blurred, and I swayed in my seat.

I felt Seojun's arms wrap around me, and his voice strained with panic as he yelled, "Bora! Someone fetch the royal physician!"

Chapter 38

Seojun

B ORA'S BODY WEIGHED HEAVY and limp in my arms, her head resting against my shoulder like a sack of rice. As the servants rushed towards the dais and guards lined the bottom to create a wall, I glared down at Bora's father, a sliver of shame still digging into me like a splinter, but he had schemed his way into this situation. Justice was just as important as mercy, and the victims of the Chief State Councilor would have their retribution.

It was unfortunate he'd chosen this. I would have been such a good son-in-law.

Councilor Min met my gaze, a fiery rebellion in his eyes, the corners of his lips slithering upwards. My hands trembled with rage, that small remnant of reluctance melting away from the audacity of a father willing to harm his own child for his own ends.

My voice came out cold and low, devouring the warmth from the air. "Guards, lock down the palace. No one may leave until the culprit who poisoned the queen is found."

The guards saluted and a handful left to relay the instructions to the rest of the palace soldiers. I turned back towards Bora, her closed eyes reminiscent of slumber. The physician burst into the hall, sweat already forming along his brow as he scurried to the dais with hasty steps and pursed lips. The wall of guards parted to allow him through, and he kneeled before Bora and I, his hands scrambling to grab her wrist and feel her pulse.

The physician gulped, refusing to meet my eyes, and he spoke, his voice quivering, "The queen...is dead."

Gasps and murmurs washed over those present, but only Bora's father lacked a look of shock and horror. My chest and hands tightened, but before I could speak, the Councilor beat me to it. None of the other ministers would have been able to see the calculated change in his expression, his eyes watering and mouth turning down as he collapsed to his knees, one hand clutching at his heart while the other reached towards the throne.

"My daughter! My precious daughter," he wailed, his chest heaving and his voice shaking.

My lips curled in disgust of their own accord, and I fought the desire to spit at his display. How dare he claim that he cared for her when this was of his own doing? He had caused all this, and I would not let him walk out of this palace unless it was in chains.

"Jeonha! Why must you take my daughter from this life? Was it not enough to have taken her from my house?" he cried out, the men of his faction gathering around him to offer sympathetic pats to his shoulder.

I noticed Right State Councilor Ryu was first amongst them. I had not forgotten the iniquities of his nephew, who had been exiled, and my blood boiled even hotter.

"Are you accusing me of poisoning the queen?" I questioned through gritted teeth, my tone as sharp as a blade.

Councilor Min thumped his chest like a drum, but his cheeks remained dry despite the watery look to his eyes. "All the court is aware of your disdain for me, but you should have taken it out on me and not my daughter."

His fellow councilors wailed with him, "Jeonha, what have you done? Such immorality is an affront to the heavens!"

"How can you prove that *I* did it?" I snapped.

"Who else has a reason to? You already exiled Minister Ryu's son. You must be trying to target us all one by one until we submit to you and allow you to bring the wrath of the heavens upon our nation!" Councilor Min hollered, waving his hands in the air.

What a grand show, and I had to admit it was a smart method to get the other officials to fear me—and betray me.

Councilor Ryu spun around, addressing the other officials, some of whom looked weary of me, others outright rolling their eyes at the claims of the councilors. "The king unlawfully took my nephew from me, and he will do it to your sons too! If he can even kill the queen, what is stopping him from slaughtering us?"

A slow and echoing clap.

After laying Bora down so that her head was nestled in the armrest of the throne and allowing the physician to attend to her, I stood and applauded their show, my hands clapping together in a thundering amusement.

"Bring out the maid," I commanded, and two guards dragged the petite woman from the prison into the throne hall, her eyes averted from the councilors and head hung in shame. I took great satisfaction in the look of surprise that flashed across the Chief State Councilor's face.

"Recognize her?" I asked wryly.

"Falsified evidence will not appease the court officials," he retorted.

But I caught the falter in his confidence, the way his hand closed into a fist.

The first piece in row.

"Forgive me, Jeonha, but I have the record of a servant from the Min family purchasing poison at one of Mister Kwon's shops," Minister Lee held up a receipt and a drawing depicting the image of the customer. "I received it from the owner myself," he added, smugly grunting in anticipation of protest.

Second piece.

Bora had informed me that a Kwon Minsoo owned most of the apothecaries in the capital, a place where for the right price poisons could be bought. Although the Chief State Councilor was capable of growing, mixing, and keeping such poisons, it was too big of a risk in the case that his estate was searched. He had operated on the promises of power and prosperity, trusting a hefty pouch to handle matters discreetly. Of course, the tools he used were often disposed of, which had made it so difficult to find enough evidence to prove his guilt in the records and minds of the people.

"It was a prescription by a physician. If the concoction is poisonous, then he must have made a mistake," the Councilor argued in a low voice.

I glanced to make sure all the Royal Guards was present.

A cornered animal was the most dangerous.

The younger Minister Han, whose wife I had seen in the company of the queen, rose and shuffled into the center of the aisle, bowing as he bellowed, "Councilor Min had approached me to join his faction and partake in a plot against the king. Forgive me, Jeonha, for only coming forward now, but I knew I needed to gain his trust to be able to better assist you. I will gladly go to the Royal Investigation Bureau's office to divulge all the information I have gathered."

Third piece.

Minister Song, who had not joined the Mins despite their vile plot against his younger daughter—which would have intimidated a lesser man—stepped forward as well.

His voice held the wrath of a furious father, and he pointed an accusatory finger towards Chief State Councilor Min. His words rang through the air like an angry gong as he said, "I have the confession of the man who was sent to violate my daughter to prevent a marriage to the king!" He withdrew a paper from his sleeve, the words illegible from the distance, yet the red thumbprint that belonged to the criminal was a clear crimson circle.

Fourth piece.

Inspector Kim lurched forward and bowed, his voice strained as it echoed in the hall. "Jeonha, please arrest the Chief State Councilor and his accomplices. Let the Royal Investigation Bureau and Ministry of Justice look into this matter with all due diligence."

A few more ministers left their tables to join the bowing man, each repeating his sentiment.

I turned and cocked a brow at Minister Yu, his head lifting enough for us to meet each other's eyes. He gave a short nod, and I stood, my robes fluttering behind me as if the winds of heaven had blown through to grant their blessing.

"The Chief State Councilor has not only attempted to assassinate the queen, but also successfully murdered the previous king, my father, Yi Changwon. Arrest him and his fellow traitors," I bellowed, and the Royal Guards came pouring out, their feathered gats bouncing while they ran.

The Chief State Councilor's eyes widened as round as a plate, a spark of fear flashing in his eyes. "You have no real proof. This is all fake. If you purge honest ministers just so you can replace us with your own men and do whatever you want, the wrath of the people and heavens will reign down upon you and all of Joseon!"

A voice interrupted, words dripping with disgust. "That would only occur if you were an honest man."

I looked back down at where Bora was slowly sitting upright, pulling the letters she had stolen from her father's study from her sleeve.

Five in a row.

Game over.

"Here is the evidence of the Min, Ryu, Oh, Kang and Shim families colluding to kill King Changwon," she announced and waved the papers in the air.

The Chief State Councilor, along with all the present officials, gaped at the sight of the healthy queen. He clambered to his feet, raising a trembling arm to point at Bora.

"You're alive." Not a question, just an accusatory statement.

No father was ever this disappointed to see his child alive and well.

He should have employed people with tighter lips.

The maid who'd attempted to poison Bora had revealed all that she knew, including the eunuchs, court ladies and guards that had been bribed or planted by the councilors. We could not arrest them, as that would have alerted the enemy. Instead, other precautionary measures were taken. One of the servants who'd poured Bora's drink was included in the list of traitors, but before the poisoned wine even entered the hall, Haeji had switched it.

Bora stood, her shoulders straight and chin raised. "Yes. Despite your best efforts, I am perfectly fine. And if you'd paid any attention to me at all, you'd have known that just a small amount of alcohol makes me drowsy."

"You–You—" He lurched forward, the barrier of guards catching him before he could even reach the first step of the dais.

"Don't worry. This will be the last time I disappoint you," she said, and although she intended for it to come out cold, her voice broke at the end, the pain evident as she looked away.

"Arrest them all," I ordered and wrapped an arm around my wife, and the guards surrounded the group of officials.

"You have to help me, Bora!" he barked when two men grabbed hold of his arms.

"I am bound to uphold the law," she replied.

"Where is your family loyalty? I am your *father*," he seethed, spit spewing from his mouth.

"I am your *queen*."

"That's not the kind daughter I raised," the Chief State Councilor growled, his fangs bared as he scrambled to hold onto control of her.

"First of all, you did not raise me, my mother did. You simply housed me. Second, being kind does not mean being feeble nor covering up crimes just because you're of my blood. It would be very *unkind* of me to allow you to wreak havoc and amass wealth and power for yourself at the expense of others. It would be very *unkind* of me to allow you to avoid the consequences of your actions. It would be very *unkind* of me to refuse you the opportunity to repent. Kindness requires courage and pursuing justice, not keeling over just for you to give me a smile and compliment. Kindness is not quiet," Bora retorted, her voice a mixture of brokenness and bravery.

I could tell how much those words pained her, how much she wished this wasn't so. Nevertheless, my chest swelled with pride at how far she had come. It took all of my self control not to kiss her. She was such a beautiful and wise woman, a jewel born to a serpent.

As for that snake, he had made his choices, and he would bear the consequences of them.

"Take the three councilors Min, Ryu, and Oh, as well as ministers Shim and Kang to the dungeons to be interrogated and detained. The fathers and their sons," I bellowed.

It was common for more than one man from the same family to become a minister, even up to three generations serving the court at the same time. If the sons were ignorant of their father's scheming or vice versa, then they would be freed, although stripped of their positions. If any of the women were found to have colluded with them, then they would join them in execution.

Taming my grin to the best of my ability, I watched the traitors be hauled off. As soon as they and their shouts of protest were gone, I nodded at each minister who had spoken up before turning back to Bora.

Despite our victory, she looked deflated as she collapsed onto the throne.

I sat next to her, and ignoring the fact there were still others in the hall, I wrapped my arms around her and whispered, "I am so proud of you. I know it was hard, but you did so well." My lips pressed against her temple.

I heard sniffles as she buried her face into my chest.

The half of my heart that Bora occupied hurt because she was hurting, but the other half took great satisfaction in watching the Min patriarch unravel. In life, success was often accompanied by sorrow. One side always had to lose.

Chapter 39

Bora

THE DAY OF MY father's death was beautiful. The summer had relented of its stifling heat, and clouds offered a reprieve from the sun while birds fluttered to and fro, sweet songs chiming in the air. The front courtyard of the palace was full of spectators, a tension present as all held their breaths. This was a day of mourning for a few but a day of triumph for most.

From atop the steps, Seojun and I stood above the crowd, Haeji holding an umbrella over me despite the clouds' shade. Amongst the sea of people, I spotted my family, since all the nobles were required to be here. Jinho stood behind Minho, his hand curled tightly on his wheeled chair. Iseul clung to my mother. Did they hate me? Was Iseul old enough to understand? Had our brothers explained it to her? And my mother...

Was she broken-hearted or relieved?

"It's time," Seojun murmured softly, his fingers brushing against the back of my hand.

Nodding was my only reply. I couldn't speak, afraid that I would burst into tears in front of everyone. Was I a terrible person for being sad about my father's death? After everything he had done, I still could not gloat over our victory, although I did not regret it.

"These men and women are all convicted—their crimes known by the Office of Inspector-General and Records—and their punishment is death. After two weeks of careful investigation, these people have been determined as treachers. Those not complicit will be spared, those who were not involved directly but were aware have been exiled to the north. Joseon will be no haven for the unjust."

Inspector Kim stood at the bottom of the steps along with fellow inspectors from his office and members of the Royal Investigation Bureau. His face was blank, the others around him giving satisfactory nods at the announcement of the criminals' punishments. This moment had been years in the making, the combined efforts and sacrifice of many allowing justice to be served.

Seojun inclined his head, and rows upon rows of bound men and women were forced to their knees, their clothing nothing but burlap baji and jeogori. Some were commoners: merchants, maids, and mercenaries. Many were nobles, their families well established since before the dynasty began. At the front was my father, along with the men who I had called samchon, their visits frequent and full of fondness. They'd smiled, patted my head, and given me sweets as a child. Hanbin's father had brought me and Iseul flowers whenever he came over. Now he was about to die, his son exiled. I did my best to ignore the sadness, reminding myself why they deserved this.

"May this mark a new era of prosperity," Seojun bellowed over the crowd.

With a wave of his hand, the cacophony of swords being unsheathed hissed in my ears. A nod from the king, and bloodied blades protruded through chests as groans and screams of pain rang out. There were wet spots under some of the bodies. I urged myself not to look away, not to look weak in front of everyone. This was the palace. This was life as queen.

Seojun turned his back on the corpses and went inside, his face calm and his shoulders straight. Was he unaffected by what we had just witnessed?

I followed him inside and quietly spoke to Haeji, "Bring my family to my palace."

"As you wish, Mama." Haeji bowed and sped off to catch my mother and siblings before they left.

Spinning around, Seojun looked hurt, his brows furrowed as he frowned. "You're not coming back to my chambers?"

I wrung my hands together. "Later. I want to see my family first—what remains of it."

He took a step towards me, gently placing his hands on my shoulders, "I'll be waiting for you when you're finished." His lips brushed my forehead before he stepped away, heading to the right towards his quarters as I went to the left towards mine.

When I was alone at last—well, I was never truly alone, the rest of my attendants trailing after me—my emotions welled to the surface.

No crying yet, I begged myself.

I bit my lip as hard as I dared and forced myself to walk, focusing on the pain to keep from thinking about everything else. I was almost there, and I nearly ran the last few steps, throwing open my door and slamming it shut behind me before anyone had the chance to enter.

Worried voices cried from outside, "Mama, please let us in!"

"I just need a few moments alone," I croaked.

Thankfully, they acquiesced, their protests fading, and I stumbled towards my bed, collapsing to my knees and laying my head against the blankets. Soon the fabric beneath my face was wet, my sobs muffled by my sleeve.

My father was dead.

Gone.

If I went to our mansion, he would not be there. If I attended court, the Chief State Councilor position would be empty. Min Seungho was no more. His name would be associated with some of the worst crimes in history.

King Killer. Corrupt Councilor.

None of the commoners would mourn him and would in fact celebrate his death. Seojun would not shed a tear for him. Would Minho?

A knock on the door sounded, and Haeji's voice filtered through, "Mama, your family is here."

I climbed to my knees and wiped at my eyes and nose.

"Enter," I called out, my voice cracking.

Haeji slid the door open, and Jinho maneuvered Minho over the threshold, the chair creaking in protest. Their faces gave no indication that they grieved our father. Iseul clung to our mother as they entered together, wet lines streaking down her face which matched the swollen, red eyes of our mother. Haeji closed the door behind them to grant us privacy.

We sat in a circle, a heavy weight pressing down on us, a dark shadow hovering over us despite being the middle of the day. My chest tightened, a lump in my throat refusing to budge.

No one spoke; no one moved.

It took me a moment to realize that they were waiting for me. Despite being the second youngest in the room, I outranked them all.

I cleared my throat, my fingers wringing together tightly under the fabric of my dangui. "I am sorry I didn't warn you all. If I had, you could have at least prepared emo—"

"Don't feel bad, Bora. You did us all a favor," Jinho grumbled.

So much for being concerned about etiquette.

Our mother glared and scolded, "Don't be so callous."

"I have a long way to go before I even come close to *him*," he retorted coldly.

Had Minho not told me about Jinho's secret shop the last time I'd seen them, I would have been taken aback by his harsh outburst. I wondered what Jinho had seen and experienced growing up.

"Eomeonim, I don't want to discount your feelings, but he is—was—a cruel person, both in the home and in court. The man you loved was the same others hated, and for good reason," Minho said softly, leaning from his chair to pat out mother's shoulder.

My eyes were drawn to his arm, the bruises obscured by the sleeve of his po, and when I looked up and met his gaze, I cocked a brow.

Had he told them?

He gave a subtle shake of his head, and I pursed my lips before dipping my head. It was his story to tell—or not tell at all if that was his choice.

Our mother said nothing, her face becoming older as she let her head fall to her chest. Had she become so accustomed to defending him that even in death, even in the face of his crimes, she could not speak ill of him? Minho bore bruises on his body, and as I watched my mother, I wondered what marks she bore unbeknownst to us all.

After a few moments of silence, she allowed herself to finally speak freely. "Your father was always ambitious, but it wasn't until after we had Jinho that I saw the dark extent of his greed," she mumbled, stroking Iseul's hair. "With each child, his goals grew bigger, his heart colder."

There was a deep pain in her eyes, a mixture of missing something that died long ago and a relief that whatever nightmare she lived was over.

"Oh, Eomeonim," I sobbed, launching myself towards her and enveloping her in my arms, Iseul squeaking as she was squashed between us.

"I don't know what you went through, Eomeonim," Jinho began, his voice softer than before, "but I will take care of you now. You just focus on raising Iseul."

"Hey! I'm thirteen," Iseul protested, attempting to wriggle free.

We all laughed at the youngest member of our family. One day she would actually be grown up, but until then, we would all take good care of her.

I wasn't sure how long we went on that way—crying and comforting each other. How did one mourn a monster? Guilt still clung to me for feeling sad about his death, as if by grieving a criminal, I was one. There would be no official mourning period, of that I was certain. To don the white clothes and hold a funeral for a treasonous man that was executed by the king would call for the same sentence upon our heads. Our tears would only occur behind closed doors.

Forgiveness would help, but it would be a choice we would have to make throughout our lives in order to keep the bitterness and hatred at bay. He had killed people, stolen loved ones from their families, and he had killed the love between us and him in the process. He was even prepared to murder me, along with my husband. Power was his mistress, and he had forfeited us for it. Loathing and mourning knotted itself together in my heart, and it would take time to unravel it all.

After my family left to go back to the Min Mansion, which Seojun hadn't confiscated for the sake of the innocent members of the clan, I'd walked with solemn steps to Seojun's room. As I reached the door, I inhaled, forcing a smile on my face.

"How are you doing?" he asked right when I entered.

"Did you see the trees have pears on them now? I wonder when they'll be ripe," I mused and walked past him, staring out the window.

"Bora—"

"And one of the lady's maids voiced an interest in painting, so I thought I might gift her some supplies."

"Bora..."

"Something I have been considering lately is learning basic healing techniques. As you are well aware—"

"Bora," Seojun interjected firmly, his hands gentle as they gripped my shoulders, forcing me to face him. "Why won't you answer me?"

"Because," I rasped, "if I try to talk about it, I will cry."

"I told you, you don't have to pretend in front of me," he murmured, palm cupping my cheek and thumb running across my skin.

Seojun guided me to the bed, and we sat across from each other atop soft blankets, my fingers fumbling together.

One uncomfortable conversation after another, and yet, once I had spoken to my family, I'd felt better. Having someone with whom I could share my deepest worries and darkest thoughts was a true blessing. If we had talked with anyone else, they would have cursed us for caring about the Chief State Councilor's death. Would Seojun be willing to listen if I cried and said I missed him? Would he be disgusted at another thought that I had not even dared speak aloud in front of Jinho?

I missed a man that didn't exist, and I was glad that the man that did was gone.

"I know what he did isn't worth shedding tears over, but...can I still be sad?" I choked out at last.

Seojun nodded and opened his mouth to speak, but before he could even get a single word out, I broke out into sobs. He rushed to wrap his arms around me, and I buried my face into his chest. The warmth and pressure of his body was a small comfort as I wept for what I promised myself was the last time over the man I once called father.

His breath washed over my head as he murmured into my hair, "You can always be yourself with me, Bora. Give me your best and your worst, and I will hold you through them both."

Forcing slow and long breaths into my nose, I lulled my weeping to sleep and cleared my throat. "I want to be the same for you. Outside, you are a king," I leaned back and placed my palm over my heart, "but in here you are my husband. When we are alone, I hope you will share your burdens and victories with me. I want all of you."

In his eyes, I could see his mind working while he thought hard about something that, as time passed, I wanted to know more and more.

"Bora..." he began hesitantly, his eyes carefully studying my reaction. "What would you think...if I said I killed my father?" He rushed to finish before I had time to even think, "I didn't murder him literally. Just once in my mind... He was killing the kingdom after all, letting it rot, allowing the corruption to fester and undoing all the great works of the previous kings. I thought, for a few moments, that maybe things would be better–easier–if he was gone and I was able to take the throne." His eyes were fixated on me, his face desperate as he held his breath, waiting for how I would respond to his confession.

"I think..." I started slowly, "that I cannot condemn some-one when I am no better. You think too highly of me, Seojun. Before I knew you, in my arrogance and naivety, I would have judged you, but not now. I have changed—how I think about things has changed." I grabbed both of his hands in mine and continued, "And I share the sentiment. When I saw the marks on Minho's arms, I wanted to see my father suffer the same. I wanted him dead."

"But not when he wanted to kill me?" he asked in a poor attempt to alleviate the tension, the hurt in his voice evident despite the lilt to his words.

I couldn't look at him when I answered, "I—I wanted him to be punished then, too. But even then I did not feel the hatred, the desire for revenge, the desire to inflict pain to ease my own. And when I think about how he stole a king from the country and a father from you..." The tears threatened to return, and I dropped one of his hands and thumped my chest, begging them to stay put. "I'm sorry," I croaked.

Hands cupped my face, and through watery vision, I looked into Seojun's eyes.

"I love you. You have nothing to be sorry about. You went your whole life trusting your father, believing that I was the bad one, but you had the courage to confront not only your father, but yourself. You are the bravest and most beautiful woman in all of Joseon."

"Not the whole world?" I asked in a half-hearted joke.

"Even if there was someone in the world who could compare, I wouldn't notice because I'd be too busy staring at you. How could a candle compete with the sun?"

That elicited a feeble chuckle from me. I laid down, and Seojun followed suit, his touch never leaving me for even a breath. He took out my dragon pin so I'd be more comfortable, my hair unwinding.

As we held each other, I murmured softly, "My father did one good thing for me."

"And what is that?" he asked, fingers playing with my hair.

"The best thing my father ever did for me was bind me to you."

Chapter 40

Seojun

Bora's hand hovered for a brief breath before she dabbed her brush against the thick paper, a pool of peonies already formed. I admired her skills, the way she held the brush with a soft but confident grip, the tip dancing across the paper in expert strokes. Careful to keep my footsteps quiet, I crept up behind her. It would be nice to have a portrait of her to hang in our chambers. Maybe one in every room in the palace. She probably wouldn't like that idea...

Maybe a personal miniature one I could carry with me?

"It's dangerous for a beautiful woman to—"

Bora yelped at the sudden touch of my hands on her waist, and she spun around, her brush assaulting my face with its pink-coated bristles. Paint felt a lot like blood dripping on skin.

"Oh, Seojun," Bora gasped, her hand flying to her mouth. She turned back, setting her brush down and grabbing a cloth. With soft touches, she wiped my face. "I'm sorry. Why didn't you say anything? My heart practically leapt from my chest."

"Because seeing you flustered is so adorable. However, if you dislike it, I promise not to do it again," I said a tad more seriously.

She smiled and shook her head. "It's fine."

Pressing a kiss to her forehead, I announced proudly, "It's finally finished."

"Really? Can we go see it?" Bora asked, getting to her knees.

"As you wish, my beautiful queen."

Presenting my hand to her as I got to my feet, Bora took it, her other hand braced on her stomach as she stood.

The entire ride, Bora kept her hand on her abdomen. She had also kept touching it earlier when we were at the palace. Was she ill? Her expression did not appear pained though, and her normal smile graced her lips. However, she often hid her discomfort behind a pleasant expression. When we got back to the palace, I'd call for a physician just in case.

"I can't believe we have already been married a year," Bora exclaimed, a bright grin dusting her lips like starlight. "The days go by too quickly with you."

"And I can never get enough of them," I chimed, reaching out to give her hand a squeeze.

Despite palanquins being the customary mode of transportation, they only allowed for a single rider, so in order to be with Bora, I opted for the carriage. Maybe it would become a tradition for Joseon.

The carriage jolted to a stop, and I scurried out, turning to hold back the curtain and presenting my hand for her.

"Are you feeling alright?" I asked, my voice revealing my concern, since even though all the traitors were executed, poison was still on my mind.

As her feet hit the ground, she looked up at me with sparkling eyes, her free hand resting against her stomach once again. "Looks like Lady Hong will finally stop badgering me about an heir," she stated.

Did the time stop? My breathing did.

"Seojun..." Bora began, her smile faltering. "Are you not ha—"

She didn't get the chance to finish her question, my lips crushing into hers and my arms wrapping around her torso. When I pulled away, I didn't know if I should laugh or cry or climb to the top of the nearest building and shout to the entire world that I was going to be a father.

I settled for stroking her hair, my other fingers squeezing hers. "Words cannot express how happy I am."

Her face brightened while the red that bloomed during the kiss slowly faded. "I'm sorry I only told you now, but I didn't think I'd be allowed outside the palace if everyone knew. I wanted one more excursion before I got ordered to stay inside."

I gave a low chuckle. "I won't do that to you. Yet." I brought her hand to my lips and pressed them against her knuckles. "I'll make sure you have every food you are craving, and after meetings, I'll come to rub your feet."

She frowned. "My feet are ticklish."

"I'll rub your head then."

"Deal."

My eyes lingered on her face as we slowly turned towards the freshly finished building. The library was a sprawling two-story structure with multiple rooms, including a public study hall where a scholar from the Royal Academy would offer free tutoring to commoners. We approached the covered, wrapping porch, and a boy emerged from the square entrance, his clothes fresh and without soil.

Minhyeok had sprouted like a bamboo shoot, his height nearly overtaking mine since I had last seen him when we had gone to the village to reveal our identities as well as plan for the public library. If he wasn't so inclined to studying, his stature would have made him a great soldier, but I doubted Bora would be pleased if he joined the military.

Smiling, he rushed down the steps, bowing and greeting us, "Jeonha, Mama."

"You've gotten so big over winter," Bora exclaimed and placed her hands on his shoulders.

Minhyeok's posture straightened, his grin growing wider. "I am preparing for the Kwago now. Scholar Yeon says I am the brightest of his pupils, and even though I started late, I will soon overtake many of his other students."

I reached out and patted his shoulder. "I expected no less."

"I am so proud of you," Bora added with pride as if he was her own child she had borne.

"One day, I'll become a minister, too," Minhyeok promised.

"Before you are too occupied with matters of the state, I should play as many games with you as possible," Bora quipped.

Minhyeok glanced back to the entrance of the library, his feet shifting. "I should get back to—"

"Don't tell me that studying is more important than playing a game with Imo Soyeon?" she interjected in faux offense.

Scratching the back of his head, Minhyeok mumbled, "I suppose a few matches wouldn't hurt."

Bora slipped her arm around his, dragging the boy towards a nearby tree. Releasing him, she picked up a stick and began drawing in the dirt. "I've improved since our last match. Don't take it too hard when I beat you," she teased.

"I have learned a lot since then, Ma—"

The look she gave him cut the formal title from his lips.

"Imo," he rushed to say, receiving a nod of satisfaction from Bora.

I shook my head with a smile and walked over to them. "I can't believe you have traded me for another man, Soyeon."

"If you are jealous now, what will we do when our child is born?"

Minhyeok's mouth dropped open, his eyes darting between us.

Throwing my arm around his shoulders, I whispered, "Good luck. It's two against one."

"I may not always win, but I never lose," Bora threw out, a smirk tugging her lips as she drew a circle in the dirt.

Chapter 41

Bora

IT HAD BEEN OVER ten years since the Queen Dowager had stepped foot in the capital, and although I expected a large banquet and decorations taking over the palace, everything was quite mundane. Seojun had made an announcement that the Queen Dowager and Princess were alive and well and would return after the snow melted from the northern mountains in which they had been hiding—the deceased treachers never would have guessed the former queen would hide in the land of exiles. Rivers were swollen from the snowmelt, but it had finally been deemed safe for them to make the journey home.

A home that they had been denied for decades due to the dubious actions of the late State Councilors.

Although none of it was of my doing, guilt still pricked me like a stubborn splinter. Seojun had stated over and over how I shouldn't feel shame, but it was easy to hear and harder to feel.

One thing he said had comforted me though. "The actions of Councilor Min may have caused this, but so did my own father's choices. And it was because of your courage and kindness that they get to come home."

Today was that day. At any moment they would arrive, and my stomach was knotted like a norigae. I went through the list in mind, double-checking that everything had been properly prepared. Their rooms were cleaned and ready, the palace cooks were made aware of their food preferences—courtesy of some of the older servants who had served the Queen Dowager and Late King—and maids and allowances had been allocated for the Queen Dowager and Princess.

There was one more thing to confirm. "Okjeong, would you mind fetching me the gift I prepared for the Queen Dowager?"

The younger daughter of the Song family had adjusted well to her new position, albeit there were always a few maids whispering malicious words. Luckily, Haeji was quick to dispatch some justice on behalf of the young Song woman. There would be no backstabbing or slandering in my palace. This life was hard enough, and there was no reason to make it harder by malignant gossip.

"Here it is, Mama," Okjeong replied, smiling and handing me the curled parchment, her expression brighter with each passing week.

I sprawled the painting out over the table, my eyes dissecting each stroke as I chewed my lip. Would she like it? Were the blossoms too dark pink? Did the way the river wound look natural? What if she preferred animals to landscapes?

"What do we have here?" a voice drawled next to my head, a warm breath tickling my ear.

Twisting my neck to look at Seojun's face, I replied, "A gift for the Queen Dowager. Do you think she will like it?"

His body pressed into my back as his hands covered mine on the table, warmth seeping into me and settling my nerves. "She will love it."

Thundering footsteps echoed down the hall until Haeji came to an abrupt halt in the open doorway.

"They're here!" she announced through labored breaths.

I was unsure if it was the baby or anxiety that was causing the turmoil in my stomach. Taking a deep breath, I ungracefully clambered to my feet, Seojun helping me up with an outstretched hand. Why did my back hurt so much today? It was the worst timing imaginable.

He must've noticed my nerves, and he whispered in my ear, "Don't worry, she will love you."

"How can you be sure?" I whimpered.

"Because I do." He pressed a kiss to my forehead.

With a squeeze of my hand, we exited our chambers and made our way to the main palace. The same birds that cheered me on when I had first arrived to the palace were present now, their spring chorus giving me courage. We came to a stop at the top of the stairs, looking down on those gathered. From court officials to the lowest ranking maid, everyone had come to greet them.

The Chief Eunuch called out, "Queen Dowager Yun Jindeok and Princess Yi Jinseong enter the palace."

I held my breath, waiting for them to appear at the secondary gate that lay between the throne hall and the main gate. Seojun pressed his shoulder against mine, the only acceptable way for us to touch in this emotional moment. I spared a glance at him, his jaw clenched and eyes already shimmering with water.

At last, two women emerged from the entrance, their maids and guards stopping just inside the walls to allow them to proceed alone. Their entrance was humble, their hanboks simple. It was not the grand procession of royals, and my chest tightened as I imagined what hardships they had suffered over the years. It must have been so cold in the far north, so lonely. I missed my mother and siblings, and we lived in the same city. I couldn't imagine living so far apart, unable to meet for almost three years, unable to visit home in over a decade.

The gathered officials and servants fell to the ground in a deep bow as they passed, some even sobbing while they cried out, "Mama, Mama! Welcome back."

As the two of them approached, I was able to make out their features. The Queen Dowager had raven hair and thin eyes, her frame reminiscent of a tree in the way her long limbs stemmed from her. Wrinkles lined her skin but the angles of her face were still sharp enough to cut with one look. Her brows pinched at the center, her lips favoring a frown. Did her features rest in a perpetual scowl? I glanced at Seojun again. The same cold beauty resided in both of them. Perhaps after getting to know her, I would find her soft like her son.

Or maybe she would loath me—the daughter of one of the men who killed her husband and forced her from her home.

The princess stood shorter than the Queen Dowager but shared the sharp face of her mother and brother. Her cheek bones protruded like wings, her chin tapered like a crane's beak. Unlike her mother, she wore a smile, her eyes wide as she gazed at the enormous palace. Once again, my heart ached. She would've grown up here, all the sights familiar, if not for the councilors.

It's not your fault. I could almost hear Seojun's words in my head.

Princess Jinseong would be about the same age as Iseul, and perhaps later I could introduce them to each other. I glanced at Haeji. It was nice to have friends, people to laugh with and share worries with.

When they reached the bottom of the stairs, the Queen Dowager paused, and I could not tell if it was because of the way the sun hit her eyes, but I swore I saw tears. She slowly shut her eyelids as she took the first step.

I glanced at Seojun, reaching out towards his hand. It was closed in a fist, and I wormed my way into his palm, wrapping my fingers around his despite the presence of all the people below. Comforting my husband was more important than palace etiquette. He would not cry in front of them, but I knew he was filled with both sorrow and joy in this moment, regrets and excitement mixing in his mind.

They reached the top steps, and Seojun dropped to his knees, clutching the chima of the Queen Dowager.

At that moment, he was not a king—just a boy who missed his mother.

"Eomeonim," he choked out. "Welcome home."

The Queen Dowager yanked him by the arms, dragging him to his feet. "That is not how a king behaves," she chided, her brows furrowing.

"Apologies, Mama," Seojun said, coughing to clear his throat.

That was not what I was expecting.

Seojun dipped his head, and his mother headed inside, the princess quiet as she followed.

But then the next unexpected thing happened.

As soon as we were out of view of the servants and officials—except for the guards and maids that trailed us everywhere we went—the Queen Dowager spun around and wrapped her arms around her son. Seojun shoved his cheek against the side of her head, and the two of them stood, locked in their embrace, communicating everything that couldn't be said in the nearly three years since they had last seen each other.

The princess waited awkwardly beside me, her eyes looking everywhere except me.

I leaned over and murmured, "My name is Bora."

She finally met my eyes. They were the same midnight ones that Seojun had.

"I know. Orabeoni wrote letters talking about you," she replied in a soft voice, the opposite of her mother's stone-hard tone.

Seojun spoke with both, the king using a cold voice that dripped with authority while my husband whispered sweet words when we were alone. And apparently he spoke of me even in letters to his mother and sister.

I felt all the tightness in my chest and shoulders loosen, the tumbling in my stomach ceasing. Seojun would always protect me, always love me—and I him. The smile that bloomed on my face made my cheeks ache, but my heart didn't. My hand fell to my abdomen. He would be such a great father, the one that neither of us got.

The Queen Dowager released her grip on her son, and the two broke apart, turning to the princess. Princess Jinseong did not squeal with delight as Iseul would have done, instead she simply took a few steps towards her brother and hugged him without a sound. Her head barely reached his chest. I couldn't imagine being away from my siblings for so long. As they held each other, and with my nerves nearly gone, I approached the Queen Dowager.

"Mama, I am sorry for all the hardship you all went through. On behalf of the Min—"

"The king pardoned your clan, and the guilty members have all been executed or exiled," she interrupted, giving me a sharp stare through cold eyes. "Some may say it was unwise. Leaves too much room for revenge."

I opened my mouth to defend his decision and the rest of my family, but she held up a hand, silencing my rebuttal.

Her gaze thawed. "But I trust his judgment. And he trusts you."

Glancing at Seojun, who was already observing our interaction with a grin, he gave a small nod, and I let out a breath. It was the closest I was going to get to her verbal approval.

Time had flown by, faster than the fluttering shrikes and magpies around us. The Summer Hunt was already upon us, and I was eager to replace the previous memories with new ones. With my protruding belly, I was in no state to ride, and I had bribed the royal physician with a few ornate pins and tea I had received from a Ming emissary to tell Seojun I was fine to attend the Hunt so long as I was seated. Seojun reluctantly agreed after I promised that I would not leave the tent the entire time.

From inside the shade of the canopy, I watched Seojun and Jinho mount their horses.

"Don't exile me when I get more kills, Jeonha," Jinho chimed with a wry grin.

"Don't expect me to take it easy on you just because you're my brother-in-law," Seojun retorted, a mischievous twinkle in his eyes.

"At this rate, I'd be able to beat you both!" Minho hollered from his chair beside me.

Our mother shook her head and covered her face with her hands. My brothers' improper quips would bring her more embarrassment than my twisting hair ever could. Seojun just smiled at their teasing, and the Queen Dowager's lips even turned up at the corners.

Something tickled my ears, and I twisted to find Iseul and Princess Jinseong standing behind me, proudly grinning at the flower crown they'd finished weaving.

"Much better than an arrow to the arm," I said with a chuckle.

"Take good care of the queen, or I'll have all of your heads," Seojun called out, eliciting laughs from all those around. "And if any assassins show up, let Minje take the arrow this time," he added, winking at me.

"It's good to know that after all my years of dedicated service, you find me dispensable, Jeonha," Minje grumbled from his position guarding the tent.

"I'm glad you realized it," Seojun teased.

I leaned in my seat to whisper, "You're invaluable to me, Minje."

The guard smiled, crossing his arms and straightening his posture.

Maybe when Dongbin and Haeji returned from their honeymoon, Seojun would worry less about me. Without our faithful guard and court lady, Seojun had been stuck to me like tree sap. Although I was happy for them, I wished they'd return quickly. At least for today, Seojun would be off with my brother, Minje and my family watching over me in his stead.

"Oh, stop worrying. You're a king, not a hen," the Queen Dowager scolded, but not harsh enough to take her seriously. "We won't let anything happen to our Bora."

I smiled at the word 'our.'

"My soon-to-be niece or nephew will be just fine while you two are off hunting," Minho called, a jovial expression illuminating his face.

"Maybe I'll be getting a niece or nephew soon, too," I snickered. "I saw you making starry eyes at that palace healer."

Minho slumped in his chair. "Daeun is just a friend."

"Oh, Orabeoni has a girl he likes!" Iseul squealed.

I muffled a laugh, my eyes turning to Seojun who gazed at us, a grin curling his lip and squishing his eyes.

The horn blew, and the Summer Hunt began.

Bonus Scene

Seojun

A STAR HAD FALLEN to the earth, luminescent under the lantern light, eyes shimmering and smile shining. I forgot to breathe, my legs forgetting how to move, my mind a blank field of snow. Bora was beautiful. Time seemed to slow, everything around me a giant blur as my gaze was glued to the woman in front of me. Were there other people here? I couldn't tell. When she turned, her dusk eyes meeting mine, my heart skipped a beat, my mouth going dry. I was suddenly very, very thirsty.

A lack of words was never a problem for me before, but my tongue seemed to be fettered when she approached. Her smile was always brilliant, able to outshine the sun. I could look at her every single day and not be satisfied.

After that meal with Hanbin, I finally realized my feelings for her, and I was going to let her know how I felt. Butterflies fluttered in my stomach, a strange sensation that I couldn't recall ever experiencing before. I'd been worried and even afraid for my life before, but never anything like this. It was like being intoxicated despite not having even a sip of wine. Would wine help calm my nerves or make them worse?

But there was no wine here, only the woman whom I had been forced to marry, and was now so very glad that I did. Did all the people in the streets not see her? How could they walk by without stopping to gaze upon her. The way her full face reflected the light with a soft glow, my fingers twitching with the urge to touch her cheeks. Her plump lips resembled a glistening cherry that was begging to be tasted.

Get a hold of yourself, I scolded.

She came to a stop before me. "Jeonha," she murmured, bending her waist in a bow.

Her voice was as luxurious and enticing as a zither, and I wished for her to speak more so that the song would never cease.

How had I resisted her for so long? From the moment I saw her, I thought she was beautiful but dangerous, like a poisonous flower. But something had changed since then. A thread had ensnared me, drawing me to her. A small bit of fear remained lodged in my mind though. What if everything up until this point had been an act? What if I was falling into a trap? I was a king and could not jeopardize my kingdom for the sake of love.

Love.

I loved Bora.

My mouth opened to say those very words, but even kings could be cowards.

Instead I asked, "What would you like to eat first?"

Fool, I cursed myself.

But her face lit up at the mention of food, and as she gave her answer, her excited expression chased away all my self-deprecation.

"To the hwa-jeon stand then," I stated.

As we waded past the variety of vendors, weaving through the crowd that pressed in on us from every side, our arms brushed against each other. I held my breath each time, hoping that our touch would last, but each time we broke away as the people gave way to our entourage. All too soon we arrived at the hwa-jeon stand, the chance for any more contact gone.

For now.

Bora took the flower-covered cakes from my hand and shoved one halfway into her mouth and passed out the others to Haeji and our guards. I pressed my lips together to keep from laughing. She was adorable. Instead of leaning over and stealing the other half of her cake with my mouth like I wanted to, I turned back to the stall owner to order more. If Bora wanted every cake he had, I'd have bought them for her, but knowing her, she would want to try some of the other treats.

After several more stands, we found ourselves by the stream, little lotus lanterns dotting the water. We crouched to send off our lanterns, and I whispered a prayer in my head, *Don't let me be wrong about her...*

Slowly standing to our feet, Bora stared at her flower as it drifted downstream, but my gaze was pinned to her. Courage had never been difficult for me to conjure, yet this time I found myself in want of it. What if she didn't feel the same way? What if she was her father's spy? What if I brought my kingdom to ruin all because of my yearning for the daughter of my biggest adversary? Why was this so hard?

Bora turned around just when I opened my mouth to speak. There was a tiny crumb of cake next to her lips. Without thinking, my arm lifted, and my fingers braced her chin. Her eyelids began to flutter. She let her lids close, her breath paused. Was she expecting a kiss?

The words I wished to say didn't come out right. "You look hungry, Bora."

Her eyes flung open, and she gasped. She stammered, which made her all the more endearing, "I'm not. We have eaten a lot…"

My voice came out in a deep growl, a strange desire overtaking me, "I wasn't referring to food."

Her face flushed as if a red flower was blooming under her skin.

Now. I needed to say it clearly.

"Bora, I need to tell you something. The reason I was so irked by Hanbin was—"

The pouch of food she had been holding in one of her hands dropped to the ground, her palm whipping up to cover her mouth.

"I'm sorry, but there is something I need to do," she rushed out and spun around, taking off into the streets.

My hand reached for her but grasped only air, my fingers dangling from a precipice while the moment slipped away, her aroma lingering as she left me behind. The crowd swallowed her up before I even registered what happened.

"Follow her, Haeji," I barked, already moving in the direction she disappeared into.

The court lady was smaller, and hopefully she would be able to navigate the swarmed streets to find Bora. It wasn't safe for her to be alone. Something bad could happen. Maybe I was being overly paranoid, but life in the palace taught me that danger lurked in the mundane. Serpents could hide in an innocent patch of flowers.

Nothing was allowed to happen to my queen.

To my wife.

Glossary

Abeonim: title for addressing one's father

Eomeonim: title for addressing one's mother

Gama: small box-like litter used to transport noblewomen

Gat: a wide brimmed hat (the material and adornments delineated the wearer's status)

Hyungnim: a man addressing an older brother or older man

Imo: Aunt (used with older women whom you're close to)

Jeonha: title for addressing the king

Mama: title for addressing the queen and queen dowager

Orabeoni: a woman addressing an older brother or older close male friend

Samchon: Uncle (used with older men whom you're close to)

Samo: official's head piece

HANBOK (한복)

Ikseongwan
익선관
Gonryongpo
곤룡포
Dangui 당의
(only worn
by royal woman)
Jeonbok 전복
Dopo
도포
Baji
바지
Jeogori 저고리
Chima 치마
Norigae
노리개

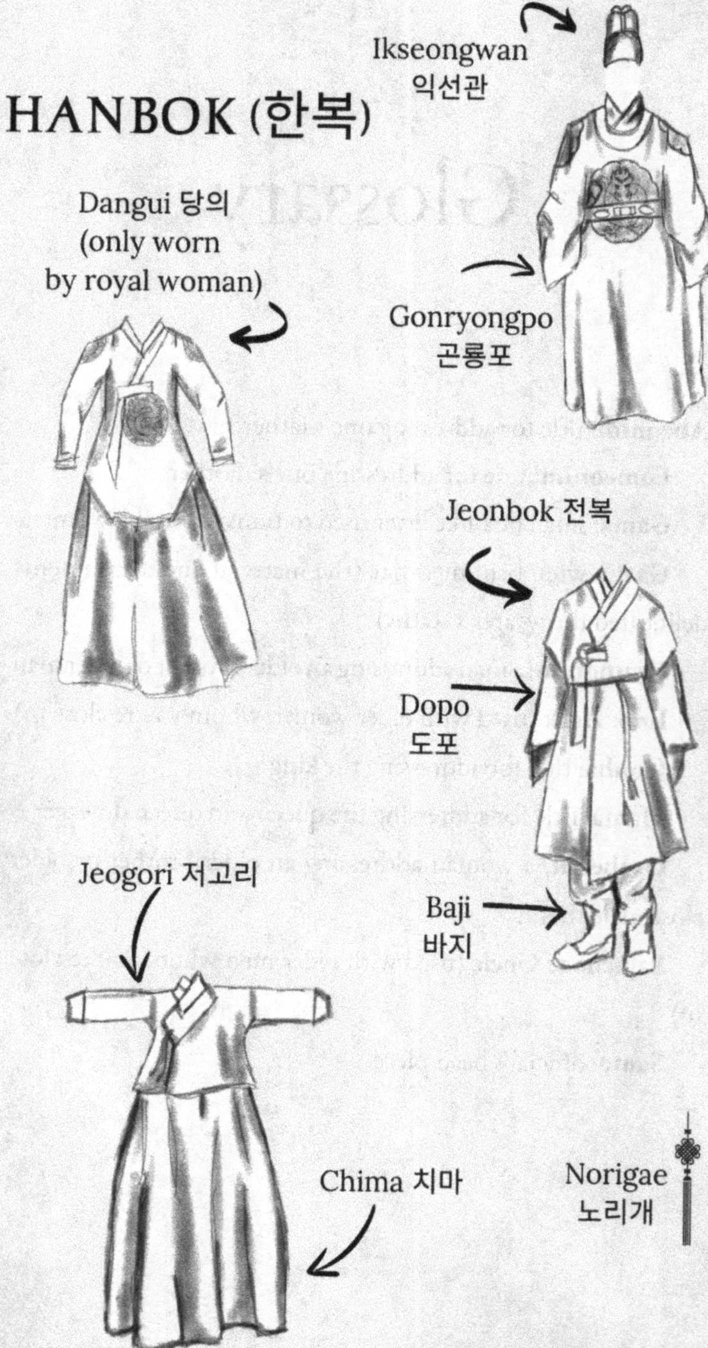

Korean Food 한식

Flower Rice Cake
(Hwajeon) 화전

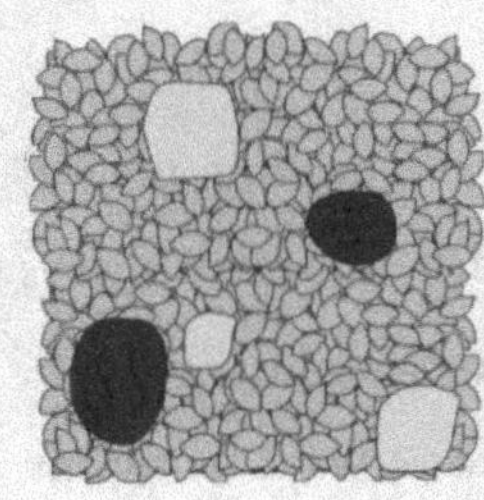

Sweet Rice Cake w/ Fruits & Nuts
(Yaksik) 약식

Korean Honey Cookie
(Yakgwa) 약과

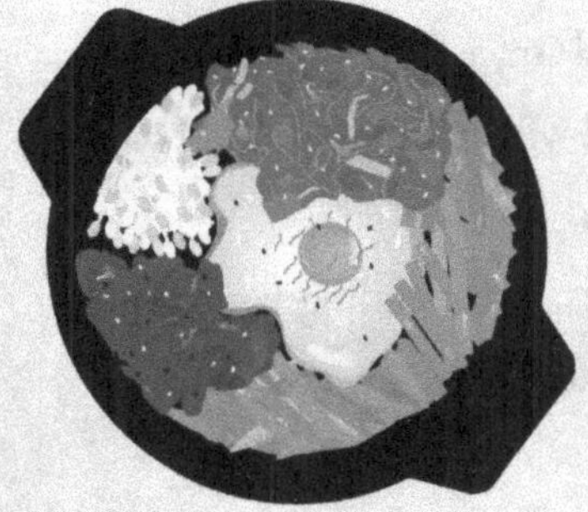

Korean Rice Bowl
(Bibimbap) 비빔밥

Acknowledgements

I cannot believe this is my third novel (on top of one novella and one kindle vella story). I am so grateful.

Firstly, thank you to my parents for never making me feel like a burden despite being nearly bedridden. You both always support me in all my endeavors, and I am so blessed to have you.

Thank you to my husband, Minje, for always being my cheerleader and rubbing my shoulders and knees when my fibro flares up. I couldn't do this without you. I hate crying in front of people, but I don't mind crying in front of you. Thanks for forehead bbo-bbos (kiss in Korean) and for holding me when I'm sad.

Thank you to Ellie (author of Paper Castles—a new adult dystopian novel) for basically being my editor. Thank you to Jordy for beta reading this book.

Thank you to Desiree, Ashley and Grace for being such huge supporters. One day (Lord willing) I will make it big, and I will always send you all the book goodies.

Thank you, my beautiful readers, for spending your time and money on this book. I appreciate all the reviews (reviews seriously help authors so much) and the dms talking about whichever part of the book you're on. I hope that my fellow mid to big girls will feel seen, feel loved, and feel beautiful reading about our big babe Bora. She is strong and sensitive and has tummy rolls and plushy arms, and Seojun LOVES her. You are lovely no matter your shape and size. God made each and every one of us, and I am a big supporter of respecting and being thankful for our bodies (because honestly I don't love mine). My husband has really helped me accept my rolls and even find them cute (unless I am on my period and then I feel like I'm an ugly troll). A good man will make you feel gorgeous and treasure your body and heart.

Lastly and most importantly, thank you Jesus. I hope I'm making you proud. Thank you for giving me the skills to edit, make covers, draw character art, and format (but if you wanted my books to take off so I can afford to hire people, I'd love that hehe).

If you have read to the end of all this, here is your golden heart sticker <3 (you have to imagine the gold part).

And once more, just for good measure, **thank you.**

Books by Bex

Throne of Anguish Duology
Throne of Anguish
Crown of Sorrows

Daughters of the Sun

Kindle Vella Story
The River Sings for You

www.ingramcontent.com/pod-product-compliance
Lightning Source LLC
Chambersburg PA
CBHW011845300726

48970CB00009B/2664